SHADOWS OF REGRET

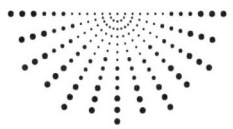

ROSS GREENWOOD

If your life was ruined, would you seek redemption or take revenge?

SHADOWS OF REGRET

Copyright © Ross Greenwood 2019

All rights reserved

No part of this book may be reproduced in any form by photocopying or any electronic or mechanical means, including information storage or retrieval systems, without permission in writing from both the copyright owner and the publisher of the book.

All characters are fictional.

Any similarity to any actual person is purely coincidental.

The right of Ross Greenwood to be identified as the author of this work has been asserted by him in accordance with the Copyright, Designs and Patents Act 1988 and any subsequent amendments thereto.

Revenge is the ultimate pleasure. But you still don't win.
Radic.

But do you feel remorse, for that is the higher calling?
Thorn.

Life rains on us all
Irina

1
JANUARY 2010 - AGE 34

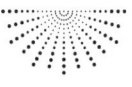

PRISON

It's quiet at six a.m. for a place like this. The madness of yesterday is over, and the chaos of a new day is yet to begin. I can hear people opening the house block door and the clang of the wing gates as they shut. I recognise they are women due to the lighter step of their work boots. Even so, their strides are purposeful. The bolt locking my cell scrapes back, I hope for the last time, and light floods in.

'It's time, Katie.'

I stop pacing. I've spent years waiting for today, and now I wish it were tomorrow. One officer checks my demeanour, decides two escorts aren't required, and leaves. I step out of what's been my home for many years and look back. My shadow stretches into the room, and I wish I could leave it behind.

It belongs with me though, and its presence will always be felt. The people I've lost, the evil deed that sent me here, and the unbearable pain that followed are waiting to be re-discovered. Regret has no place within these walls, but I'm leaving now and we will depart together. The young girl who came here is long gone. A new Katie will emerge, one with hopes of a normal life.

I shove my belongings — a bag and a box are all I own in the world — onto the landing. Prison Officer Alison Wilde offers an open palm, and a raised eyebrow, but my hands need busying to prevent them from trembling. I'll carry them myself.

'I'm ready, Alison.' My words crack as I speak.

'Have you got your ID card?'

I bob my head because I lack confidence in my voice.

After taking a deep breath to compose myself, I follow her along the line of closed cell doors. Their inhabitants are listening and they chant my name. Many of them are little more than children. To some, I've been the mother they never had, and now another who leaves them behind.

The wing gate banging into place silences them. I can handle anything, I remind myself as tears build. I won't cry today.

We pass officers on the way to start their shifts and a few of them nod and say good luck. One even comes over and shakes my hand. He always was formal. It's a small gesture but a meaningful one. My new trainers squeak on the polished floor as we approach reception. It takes a long time to save up for a pair when you get paid £1 per shift. I wanted something new for a fresh beginning though, and they are worth every drawn-out hour I spent working for them.

At the doors to reception, Alison holds the last one open and smiles.

'Good luck, Katie. You're familiar with the way from here.'

I appreciate the comment and she's right. I know it better than she does. Alison has only been at HMP Peterborough for six months. I transferred in when it first opened five years ago. She isn't much older than the girls who cheered when I left the wing. Her full make-up looks unnatural here. As if she is too shiny for somewhere so dull.

The officers held a collection for me as I'd been here so long and bought me a box of cosmetics. It remains unused with my things as I rarely wear any. However, that kind thought is important and so is Alison's light tone. They are slim layers of gloss for my fragile self-esteem.

I still can't trust myself to speak and, despite her tender years, she understands. She gives me a brief hug and sends me on my way. Prison will always be a place of surprises.

The staff member processing releases has been here from the beginning. He is one of many ex-forces I've met on both sides of the bars, but Prison Officer Grant lost something during his spell in the military. Perhaps, he never possessed humanity. Over the years, in various establishments, I've been molested and spat on, ridiculed and pawed, but he is the only person who succeeds in making me feel truly worthless.

Grant doesn't waste his precious oxygen by talking; instead he beckons me over using a slow finger. With a clatter, he empties all my belongings onto the desk. They look pathetic and are a shocking reminder of how far I will need to travel in life. Some say the sentence is the easy part, and the hard work only begins when you leave.

He ticks my things off against the property card. There's a pause and a grin.

'Most of this stuff isn't on your list.'

He smirks and uses his pencil to lift a pair of frayed, grey knickers off the pile. They aren't bloomers but embarrassing, nonetheless. Leaning back, he holds them aloft as though toxic. My strained nerves snap.

'You prick. Did you think I'd still have the same underwear after sixteen years?'

I bark the insult, but a hot flush burns my face as I remember that I did indeed have that item near the start. To my credit, they were whiter then.

'If it's not named on here, it stays in the prison.'

'Everything I'm wearing is unlikely to be on there apart from my footwear which I signed for a few weeks ago. Shall I take my clothes off and leave naked?'

A squint of an eye indicates what he thinks of that idea. I could slam my fist into his chin and he'd never know what hit him. That said, I plan to avoid violence, so it would be a poor start to my new life.

I swore not to hurt anyone again when I was put away. But jails the world over don't allow that. I began my sentence at Holloway: a hard place overflowing with despair and anger. I learned shows of strength were necessary, and that inevitably meant hurting someone else because it was them or me. Over time, different people needed new lessons. It was a circle of pain.

The overriding emotion here at Peterborough is sadness, but there's also hope. That's a vast improvement on living amongst fear. I won't allow Grant to upset me this morning, so I will be defiant if nothing else. 'You believe you're better than me, but today I win.'

'How so?' He sweats despite the early chill, and for the first time I wonder if the bravado he shows hides his own worries. Why have I never considered that he may have a cheating wife or sick child at home? Perhaps he's always stressed or exhausted. Maybe he is as scared as we are.

A senior officer walks past.

'Let her have it, Grant.'

Grant scrunches my carefully ironed clothes into a ball and wedges them in the large, plastic prison bag. He hurls the rest of my knick-knacks into the box. The last item, my one and only photo of my parents in a cheap wooden frame, he holds for a second too long. Before I can react, his chubby fingers have squeezed and cracked the thin glass.

'Oops.' Cold eyes yearn for a reaction.

He won't get to me, not today. 'I win because I'm leaving. There's no end to your sentence in this hole. Pointless, desperate, cold and pitiful is how prison is best defined, and it also describes you.'

I snatch my possessions off the desk so he can't damage anything else and smile at his angry scowl.

'You'll be back.'

'If I get recalled, I'll kill you when I return.'

I know it's childish, but his shocked face is worth it.

The senior officer directs me to the holding cell. They used to search us all the time; arriving, transfers, hospital appointments, and so on, but things change. They can't do internals anymore, or even look in our bras without good reason, so they might as well not bother at all. Nevertheless, the man is all business, and his face is stone.

'Need anything?'

'How many of us are there, guv?'

'Only you and Rada leaving this morning.' He pronounces it in the same way as you would the car — Lada.

He locks me in, which seems a strange thing to do on my last day. I'm hardly an escape risk. The holding cell is a big, bright room with large Perspex windows so there's no hiding. Many brutal fights occur in here, although they're usually between those whose journeys in this place are just beginning.

The other lucky soul on this icy morning shrinks in the far corner, as if she'd rather not be noticed. I'm aware of her, have chatted to her, but can't say I know her. She's been in the system for years. I've only heard her called Radar. I thought it was a nickname because she says nothing but hears everything, not that anybody worries about bad pronunciation here. She's foreign but I couldn't tell you which country she's from.

I recall her story and it's distressing. She must be in pain. For her to last as long as she has is a triumph over adversity. It's something I don't think I could have done. There are no secrets in jail. Everyone knew of her crime, and she was treated accordingly but I suspect the harshest criticism came from within.

People handle long sentences in their own way. Her method was to shut down. She became a person on life-support. One with a minimal amount of function to get her through a horrible experience. I worked in the segregation unit as an orderly for six months, and I was resident there upon her arrival. They placed her on suicide watch, but I never caught a sound from her cell. In fact, I've barely heard her talk since then, and I was on her wing for two years.

Before, I didn't care. My own cross was heavy. Thinking about it now, I would guess her to be one of the many young girls shunted through fifteen countries in three days. Raped at every port and addicted upon arrival. Their lives are tough to contemplate. Some break away from what isn't even living, few escape those memories. I know that better than most.

Again, why am I considering others? Am I waking from a long dream? I'm a human being that's slept for over a decade and a half. Rada's eyes follow me as I approach the breakfast cereal and bowls in the corner. The things stay untouched. There's no way I could eat anything either. It will take more than coffee, cornflakes and daylight to release fear's grip from my throat.

They can't discharge until nine, so we have hours to burn. If you have too much of something, it becomes worthless. That's what time means to people like us. I was relatively uneducated when I arrived here, as are most, but I wasn't stupid. I asked others in the same predicament how they coped at the beginning. Drugs seemed to be the answer. If you can survive a year, even if you spend it out of your mind, then you can deal with another. And then one more. Until the end.

That's what I did. Although I waited until I'd discovered how to get them without burying myself in debt and favours. For those initial few weeks, I wracked my brain for answers. I never slept. If I ate, I don't recall doing so.

I made a friend in the early days who was obsessed with other people's first memories. She believed hers was being loved and lying in a warm cot staring up at a branch bending with juicy apples. Too many cider adverts under the influence, I suspected.

She was crazy as hell. Every few weeks, she would cover herself in her own shit and fight with the staff, but it got me thinking.

I wrote a list of the events in my life that had led me to a hopeless future. I began as far back as I could remember, and when I stopped there were a dozen that defined me. They are the twelve memories of a broken heart. They are my shadows of regret.

Some people slide down to the depths of despair, descending under the weight of a thousand wrong choices. They live a gradual horror, getting used to every new, spirit-crushing day. Each one being a little worse than the last.

For others, such as me, luck played a part. A trap door opened under my life and I plunged below. I remember nothing before that defining moment. It's as though that incident became my ground zero and creation. I've had good experiences since then, but most were bad. My first recollection was a distressing thing to recall but, as my memories go, perhaps not the worst. For a child though, it was the end of the world.

2
THE FIRST MEMORY - AGE FIVE

I deemed it necessary to line them up in pairs, the big dollies at the front with ones of equal height and so on. I must have got it from how children walk when they went on a school trip. A little girl, whose name I have long forgotten, helped me. We beamed at each other when they were ready. I grabbed my favourite dolly of them all and prepared to lead the way. Reception class had drifted by in a pleasant haze, but it came to a juddering halt on that distressing day.

Our teacher was a gruff old woman. She petrified me, but I felt safe with her, if that makes any sense. She wasn't one for emotion, so I knew something terrible had happened when she appeared at my side with tears pouring down her face.

'Katie, can you come with me, please?'

I stood and smiled hesitantly. My friend began to cry next to me which made me more confused. The teacher placed her arm over my shoulder and guided me out of the classroom.

'Do I need my coat?'

'We have all your things, dear.'

'I still have dolly.'

Kind eyes implored me to hang on to her. We entered a large

office which contained the headmistress and a youthful woman in smart clothing. They both had blotchy faces.

'Sit there, please.'

I did, and waited for something to happen. My left leg jiggled, and I stifled a laugh. The younger lady's shoulders shook. She rose, sat next to me and took my hand. Hers cocooned mine in warmth. I can feel them when I recall that time. Why was I the only one not crying?

'My name is Bethany, Katie. I'm a social worker. There's been an awful accident. We're waiting for your uncle to arrive. Try not to worry, we'll look after you. It will all be okay.'

'Uncle Jack is coming here?' It had to be him because I only had one uncle.

'That's right.'

'I like him, but he smells funny.'

At that moment, he arrived with a policewoman. Bethany vacated her seat so my uncle could take it. He put his arm around me and kissed the top of my head as he often did. He still smelled odd. I looked up into his eyes and saw him struggle with a poor smile. Then, he glanced at the policewoman and nodded.

What she said was complicated for a five-year-old, but I understood. There had been a fire. A fast-moving, ferocious one that consumed our house, its contents, and the inhabitants before anyone could be saved. I was all alone in the world, except for Uncle Jack and Auntie Gwyn.

It would not be okay at all.

3
HOLDING CELL

Rada surprises me by appearing in front of me. It's so unexpected that I jump a little in my seat. I've been so away with the past that her movements went unnoticed. I don't let people creep up on me. Radar, or Rada, as I guess I should call her now, maintains eye contact, and I see her pale green eyes for the first time.

'You leave today?'

'Yes.'

'Me, too. I am pleased. This is bad hotel.'

I uncross my legs and smile. Comments like that have kept me sane in here. It's easy to change someone's day if you try. 'You're telling me. My room was freezing, and the towels were very hard.'

'The menu was poor also, but hotels like this back in Ukraine much worse. Sometimes no food.'

'Were the other guests as badly behaved?'

'Yes, rude people. Extremely noisy. Steal fork out of your mouth while eating.'

This time we both laugh. It's a necessary release. I keep the conversation going. 'I liked the gym.'

It was the only place that made sense. You could train your body, improve it, and you never finished. There was always a new target. Obviously, girls messed around, but most treated it the same. There was an atmosphere of kinship. You could have conversations without negative implications. It was where I learned to become human again.

She sits beside me. 'Are you also scared?'

'Yes.' I've never admitted that to anyone, but we are alone.

'I am the same.'

We sit in peace for many minutes. There's no clock and neither of us have a watch. She tenses before forcing herself to talk. 'I want to tell you something. I need to explain properly what happened to one person here. Then, someone at least won't imagine the worst.'

A conversation like this isn't needed today, so I attempt a joke. 'I think they prefer you to confess on the way in.'

Rada doesn't reply.

'Why me?'

'Because you have been here longer than I have. And something dreadful must have happened to you too.'

'Go on then. Explain away.'

She takes an enormous breath. 'I killed my daughter.'

'I know.'

She doesn't break stride. It's as if she's reciting a well-practised speech. 'I arrive in your country after terrible experiences, and have many more afterwards. I end up pregnant, and it gives me strength to escape. They put me in a hostel for broken women but forget to fix me. I return to heroin even though I take methadone. I keep my methadone in an unsafe bottle. My daughter drink it and it stopped her heart.'

Time stalls between us.

Rada's haunted, tearful grimace shows her mind has returned to the moment she found the body.

My hand raises to reach hers, but you're careful who you touch here, and I place it back on my lap. There are few appropriate words. I don't have any of them. All I have is honesty. She shudders and I let her whimpers subside before I reply. 'I know. I think everyone did.'

'Then why were you not rude like the others?'

'Because it was an accident.'

'How can something so evil be a mistake?'

'There are worse things. Believe me.'

She rises and sits back in the corner but continues to talk. 'You saved my life.'

'Really, how?'

'They had me cornered in the laundry room. One had a homemade knife. Someone knocked on the door many times and worried them. They left because of it. I followed and saw it was you.'

'Perhaps I was the lookout.'

She grins and wipes away the last tear. 'I do not think so.' The smile stays on her face. 'You have a place to go now?'

'Yes, they don't let prisoners like me just leave.'

'Peterborough?'

'Cambridge.'

'Is it close? Will you come back here?'

'Cambridge is an hour away. I grew up in Peterborough, but I doubt I'll return. I only want to think about today, or the future overwhelms me.'

Those feelings are hers too, and she returns to my side. Her hand was in her coat all this time. Does she have a weapon? She slowly removes it.

'Here, take this. If you need to, find me. Then you can tell me the real reason why you were here.' She hands me a small folded note which I accept, feel how worn it is, but don't read.

'Why?' I ask.

'Your shadow is heavier than mine. I have a sense we'll see each other again. I hope so. Sometimes, you smiled as you walked past, and I would keep those smiles with me. I'd like to help if I can.'

I can't remember being that person. Perhaps I wandered around with an inane grin on my face all the time. I open the piece of paper. The message says: Polish Porsche Garage, Fengate.

'Are you going to be a mechanic?'

She giggles and I catch a glimpse of an innocent child long missing.

'I hope not. No, a friend runs the business. He'll support me.' She takes my wrist and closes my fingers around the note. 'Keep it. I will remember. I looked at that writing for four years. It gave me a reason to continue. We both still have lives to live.'

This time she stays next to me. I rest the paper on my leg, then place it in my pocket for safekeeping, and finally hold her hand. It seems natural and we sit quietly.

My thoughts focus on her words. Do I have a life left? It felt like mine was over before it began. When they sentenced me, I understood so little of the world. I hadn't been in a taxi or on a plane. In fact, I had barely been out of the county, never mind the country. Back then though, I wasn't aware people remembered their first sip of champagne, and I didn't know love. Well, not the kind I've since seen in films or listened to on the radio. I think I want those experiences, even for a while, or maybe just once.

A female officer opens the door and shouts, 'Radar.'

Rada stands and grins.

'It is good that we sit here. It's lucky before a long trip.'

'I'm only catching the train to Cambridge.'

'Perhaps in this case it's a spiritual journey.'

'You're actually very talkative now you are about to leave.'

'Don't give in, Katie. Best of luck.'

I watch her disappear and send her off with a small prayer. On my own, I'm lonelier and more afraid. My hand checks the paper she gave me is still there. The same officer returns.

'Time's up, so let's get going before we change our minds.'

Her joke adds to my worries. That thought had crowded my dreams.

I carry my things to the final desk and sign for my discharge grant — £46 — and the £85 I've saved. It seems a lot, all folded up in an envelope. Television has taught me it isn't. They pass me a warrant to exchange for a ticket at the railway station. The reception gates bang shut behind me and I'm marched to the visitors' entrance from where we depart. I encourage my trembling heart to stay strong and pray my legs don't fail.

I step through more doors and see the exit.

A last officer bars my way. She is from resettlement and wants the best for those who leave. 'Do you know the directions to where you're going, Katie? Are you okay?'

'The railway station, please. I'd just like to get out of here.'

'There's a taxi outside.'

I'm confused. 'It's fine, I'll walk.'

Now she smiles. 'We pay for the taxi, sweetie. Go to the station, hand them your warrant and catch the next service to Cambridge. The house is only a few hundred metres from there. Here's my number. Ring me for anything. Anything, Katie.'

I force a grin after she puts the small card in my box, but there's too much noise in my head. My life resumes now because it has been suspended. I step towards an uncertain future.

4
DISCHARGED

I'm not sure what to expect when I stride from the jail — a drama or a thunderclap — but nothing happens. It's cold and miserable, and that's appropriate. The sun went down on my life long ago. Of course, there's no family to meet me. To my surprise, I think of Tommy and wonder where he is. Looking around at the stark buildings, I consider my earlier words to Grant and decide I was wrong. If I got sent back, I'd kill myself.

I realise I don't know where the car park is. The officer is still peering through the glass at me. She pushes open the door, points and shouts.

'The taxi is that way. A-2-B. He knows what he's doing.'

A sea of vehicles greets me and one flashes its lights. I was expecting a black cab. The drizzle picks up as I approach the saloon. This rain is different. As though each splash on my forehead washes away a piece of the prisoner I became.

A short old man with a bald head gets out of his car and puts his newspaper above him.

'Come on, luv. Stick your stuff in the boot quick, or I'll catch my death.'

Honed instincts tell me to keep my things beside me in the car.

I realise straightaway that I need to start again. Maybe in this world if you put something down, someone won't steal it. He grins at me — it's a look of relaxed pleasure. He chooses to be happy, and I must do the same. I sense no malice or agenda.

Prison taught me almost everything I know. I passed my English and Maths exams before I arrived there but improved my grades over the years. I chanted Spanish in my cell and learned computing in the technology room. There were business studies classes, programming, and creative writing. I started many and persevered despite them making little sense. My head struggled with the concept of the wider world. That's not surprising if you've been in jail since you were eighteen.

What do youngsters know of how everything works? Have they divorced, been made redundant, cared for sick children or relatives, fought for school places, coped with a serious illness, or buried their parents? Generally, of course not. I attended a rough comprehensive where the main motivation of the teachers was to make sure everyone arrived and departed in the same condition. There were few field trips and no work experience placements.

As for comprehending budgeting and advertising? Those things aren't needed when pool balls enter pillow cases and sharpened broom handles appear from beneath beds. I can smell bullshit from three wings away and spot liars in seconds. I experienced little of joy and commitment and less of innocence, patience and understanding.

'Sit in the front if you want.'

I believed I'd have to walk to the station, and an unexpected rising tide of excitement lifts my cheeks. Conscious of false dawns, I double-check.

'This is a free ride?'

He gets in and chuckles. 'Free to you. I hope the prison will pay me for my efforts. Is it your first day out for a while?'

'Yes. Well, in a car. I had a few trips in the meat wagons.'

He reverses out of his space and drives away. I can't stop

myself turning around in my seat to watch the gate house through the back window recede into the distance. My spirit soars of its own accord.

The driver laughs again. 'I've been doing this for years. I love observing youngsters' faces when they get out. They're often the same. Excited and hopeful.'

'Is thirty-four still young?'

'It is. Hell, fifty-four is young to me.'

I notice the car's interior for the first time. The instrument panel looks strange yet familiar. Cars weren't like this when I was little, and they were noisier. However, the media kept me up to date. It's a weightless sensation to understand the world second-hand. As we progress, the roads are full of similar flashy vehicles. My spirit descends, and my nerves return.

'You been in for much of a stretch?'

'Sixteen years, a bit more.'

It's an impulse response because inside a long sentence is kudos. Outside, the driver stiffens beside me. He'll know you don't get bird like that for white-collar crimes and he's uncomfortable. He glances down at my hands and looks away from the prison tattoos. We continue in silence.

I've been to railway stations before but never on my own. It's busy, really busy. My lips purse at the streams of people.

He pulls into a bay marked for taxis and gets out. I take a deep breath, and another. Normal folk do this every day, it isn't a big deal.

By the time I'm standing next to him, he has my box on the floor and the bag in his hand.

'I guess this must be pretty daunting for you.'

'A little.'

'You want me to come in, help exchange the warrant for your ticket, and point out where to wait for your train?'

Fighting back tears, I simply nod. I love the resilience of old people. Don't they care what others think? Perhaps experience has taught them the worst you imagine is unlikely to occur, so it's best to just get on with it. I grab my box and shuffle after him. It's crazy. The sensation is identical to the long walk down the young offenders' wing when I first arrived all those years ago. I kept close to the man showing me the way that day, too.

I look nobody in the face. Focus on his back. He tells me rush hour is nearly over, and we go straight to the front at a desk. The teenage assistant passes my ticket to the taxi driver but she can't resist a sneaky glance at me. We both shift our eyes away when they meet.

'Watch that screen. There's your train. The 10:18. Get on that one and you won't have to change. Platform four, over the concourse. Relax, you have plenty of time. Don't be afraid to ask someone if you're not sure. Got it?'

It's too much information. I know he's going to leave when I reply, so I say nothing...

He considers giving me a hug. His feet shuffle, but instead he places the bag he carries next to my trainers. 'Good luck.'

Getting through the barriers is a disaster as my coat gets caught when I lift over my box, but someone releases it with a cautious smile. Head down, I make it to my platform and stand apart from the others. My breathing slows. I could do with a cigarette but gave my tobacco away to the needy I left behind. There's twenty-five minutes to my train, but I daren't leave to buy more.

The platform opposite fills up fast with busy unfamiliar people. Where did all these suited types come from and to where do they rush? There are ladies who must be models in towering heels and skin-tight trousers. Clothes are different now. Hairstyles, too. Even amongst all this madness, I stick out. There are few females with loose jeans, and less without make-up. No one wears a zip-up tracksuit top like mine.

A sleek train whisks them away to London and my platform fills. I'm left alone as if there's an exclusion zone around me. Can they see what I've done? It probably doesn't register that my clothes shout prison, but they are aware I'm different. An unkempt man with a scruffy dog stands near me. Our eyes meet and he winks. We are the same, him and me. To everyone else, we are invisible.

My pulse quickens as the large clock ticks down. They announce the Cambridge service and in it glides. The reflection of a nervous, pasty woman with mid-length mousey hair flickers past. I board last and am relieved to find the carriage is only half-full. I sit on my own in a window seat and allow my scowl to lift — mission accomplished. Out of jail for less than an hour and I've negotiated a taxi ride and a train journey.

It's easy to focus on the negatives, so I resolve to change. Distant memories surface, and I recall there were happier times after the devastating day I lost my parents. I sink into my seat and remember a little girl at Christmas.

5
THE SECOND MEMORY - AGE SEVEN

When I moved, plastic crinkled. I didn't want to get out of bed and look as I had no idea of the time. Gwyn and Jack reckoned if you saw Father Christmas when he was delivering presents, he'd feed you to his reindeer. Someone had explained what drunk meant, so I suspected they were joking. Fate had made me cautious, though, and he might have been telling the truth.

The darkness faded, so I knew it must be morning. I held my breath as I slipped from the sheets, and eased on the light switch. Blinking, I scanned the bottom of the bed, but there was only another white pillow there.

Stifling a snigger, I noticed my name written on it in messy pen: To Katie, love Santa. I stroked it. Every touch of my hand caused the pillow to crackle. I saw bright colours underneath thin cotton and then I laughed as I thought of who I was being quiet for.

I tipped the contents out and marvelled at them. The selection box triggered nostalgia but of exactly when was out of my reach. It's strange, but I couldn't remember the next Christmas after I was left alone, or the following birthday. Although knowing who I lived with, they may have just forgotten.

After a few minutes of placing everything side-by-side, I admired my stash. There were toys and games and more sweets. I was tempted to eat them, but if they were all I was going to get, I would savour them.

I'd ended up calling my aunt and uncle by their first names. I barely knew Gwyn anyway, and Jack said uncle made him sound old. Jack had been different recently, like he'd emerged from a fog. He blackmailed me with 'Santa's watching' every chance he got. I owned the cleanest teeth in England.

When I stepped from my room, his echoing snores engulfed me. I poked my head around his door and he lay clothed and spread-eagled on the bed. As always, I considered going in, but it was as if a loud voice prevented me, saying he's not your father.

I trotted down the stairs and heard Gwyn's rattling gasps as I edged into the lounge. She had slumped down in her usual chair with the oxygen mask around her chin. The Christmas tree lights glittered in the cold smoky air. And there were presents. Lots of them, and a special one.

Trust Jack to have wrapped every single part of a bicycle. It must have taken him ages. I almost dared not touch it in case it vanished.

I stifled a sob as my brain created an image of my brother, Billy, helping me to sort the gifts into piles. I pictured him as a small boy with messy hair, but he was only a baby when he died in his basket alongside my parents. I'm unsure why my mind dragged those images in as he'd disappeared from my thoughts. Maybe recognising his loss as well would have been the final blow that defeated me.

I battled with the gas fire, having to ignite it three times to get it to stay lit, and allowed myself a smile, and some peace perhaps. My pyjamas began to burn my skin, so I left the warmth and built individual piles with the presents. Mine towered over theirs. Perhaps it was a good day to recall Billy's cheeky face. For the first time since I arrived, I felt like I belonged.

I sat in the glow of the fire for hours. Gwyn woke and had a cigarette. Her coughing seemed to increase afterwards, so I wasn't sure why she persisted with that habit. She had emphysema. I read it on the leaflets she brought back from the hospital. At least they'd stopped smoking those funny-smelling cigarettes as they gave me a headache.

Jack said Gwyn's health stopped them having children. I thought that was for the best as, since I started living with them, she did little except smoke, watch television and drink fizzy pop. They got together at school nearly thirty years ago but oddly had different surnames.

Jack was my dad's elder brother. He told me my dad called him 'Idle Jack', and they only ever saw each other at Christmas and birthdays. Mum didn't like him much, said he was a bad influence. That's weird, because he was such good fun, almost like a clown. Sometimes happy, occasionally grumpy, but never scary.

Jack came downstairs as the doorbell rang. He swaggered past me.

'Maybe it's Santa Claus, bringing the rest of the presents.'

He'd changed, from being the kind of huge six-foot-tall tramp that ate a pound of sausages at a time and played computer games all night, into a man who went to work each day. He was slimmer, cleaner, smarter and happier. Turns out he was a talented electrician. Having said that, he seemed greyer of late, like he was exhausted. He took my hand, and we opened the door together.

'Hey, Bethany, we weren't expecting you today.'

'I was driving by, had some presents, and wanted to drop them off.'

It was my social worker. She had been brilliant. To start with, she'd worried that it would be more me looking after them. I somehow felt she was responsible for my uncle's transformation, too.

'Here you are, Katie. I heard you like dollies.'

I thanked her and gave her a curtsey which made her laugh.

'You can go off and open that one. Show Gwyn.'

They always tried to get rid of me. I vacated the room but left the door ajar and listened.

'You didn't have to come around.'

'I wanted to. You're doing great.'

'It doesn't feel like it. There aren't enough hours in the day to do a job, run this place, look after those two. I'm knackered by eight most nights.'

'That little girl is a credit to you. You know what the alternative is.'

'She'll never go to a children's home while I have anything to do with it.'

'I've just been at one. The kids are safe, and there's love in those places nowadays. It isn't the seventies, but it is clunky. They aren't nurtured. I suppose there isn't the time. It's sad. We know children in care are more likely to end up homeless and in prison. You supporting her through this trauma is priceless. You're a good man.'

'I'm a bad man. Come here. Thanks for the gifts.'

She sounded upset and made a lot of strange noises. I remembered my other presents and returned to Gwyn. She was struggling back from the toilet with her stick. Despite her poor health, she remained content most of the time. Yet, on this day, of all days, she was sad.

'Let's open some, Gwyn.'

'Let me have a rest, pet. What do you think that big'un is?'

I looked at the bike knowingly. 'I'm sure it's a hippo.'

'That's right. It is. A pink hippo. If you ride it to school, try not to squash anyone.'

'Can I open it now?'

'Of course.'

It felt like unwrapping an orange, so thoroughly had Jack

covered it. Each piece was a joy to remove. I uncovered a red unisex cycle. The one I'd pointed at in a book a while back. Afterwards, I left it leaning against the sofa, and took my new dolly to Gwyn's lap where I sat with a contented smile.

6
CAMBRIDGE

The train pulls into Cambridge station and I'm the last to get off. I follow the crowd out of the exit and hate the hustle as they barge and tut. Who should I ask for directions? Everyone looks so stressed. Life has moved on and no one told me. People rush, staring at small computers and mobile phones, as though they are waiting for instructions, or orders. I step away from it all and put my things down next to a man with a sign asking for spare change for food.

'Just got out?' he asks.

'How did you know?'

'The box and the bag. That's what I leave prison with. Your face is the real giveaway, though. This world makes you run, not walk. It's quite a shock after being inside.'

A woman with a pushchair throws some coins into his bowl with a wink and tells him to get a Happy Meal. Her daughter sticks her tongue out and giggles. She leans out of the buggy to look at me as they disappear into the station.

'Not everyone's crazy. Where are you heading?'

'Brookfield Avenue.'

'The probation hostel?'

'Well, they called it *an approved premises.*'

Yet again, he frowns as he considers what I may have done.

'It's down there. Follow that road, and after a while take the fourth on your right. Got any change?'

'That lady just gave you the equivalent of six hours' wages in the prison sewing room. Perhaps you should give me some money.'

The emotion leaves his face like a sink draining. He stares at the coins he's received today and pulls his baseball cap over his eyes.

I smile. Now, this behaviour is familiar. I'm tempted to kick his bowl as I walk by, but it's only a fleeting thought.

I follow his directions and, although my things are heavy and unwieldy, I can't help feeling excited. Everything looks vivid. Vehicles, houses, people, even the pavement's unevenness is distracting. I turn into Brookfield Avenue and I'm surprised that the street is normal, nice in fact. I arrive at a suburban detached house and presume there's been a mistake. The curtain twitches and I know there hasn't.

'Welcome, Katie. My name's Sally.' A big lady smiles warmly at me from the open door. 'Come in, I've got the kettle on.'

I edge into my new home.

She ushers me into a bright kitchen and points at a seat. I wasn't expecting this normality. The tea she puts in front of me is too milky, but I spoon three sugars in and wait.

'Katie. This is an independent approved premises. I don't know what they told you, so I'll start from the beginning. If you have questions, please interrupt.' I blink, so she continues. 'Places like this are a half-way house between prison and home. Their purpose is to help rehabilitate and resettle some of our most serious offenders, and to make sure we protect the public in the offenders' early months in the community.

'The public are not generally aware of the locations, but the neighbours are. We accept some of the highest risk individuals when they are released from prison, so you have a responsibility to ensure no one has reason to resent us being in their neighbourhoods.

'Here, you will receive a structured re-entry back into normal life. You've been allocated a probation officer who'll be here at three this afternoon. I understand you haven't decided where to live yet. Tim Thorn is from this area. He will manage your reintegration. You need to maintain an honest and professional relationship with him.

'I am your key worker here, and I will offer support and advice during your residency. I may be able to help with jobs, benefits and housing. You'll probably be here for three months; certainly no longer than six months. I'll help to involve you in purposeful activities and programmes including education, training and employment; accommodation; drugs and alcohol rehabilitation; life skills; practical skills; and thinking skills.

'Reintegration and resettlement are our primary goals. This establishment accommodates up to four females. There is one other woman here already, and in a month we are expecting two more. We have decorators in over the next few weeks and an overhaul of the heating, so there may be some disruption.

'You can lock yourself in your room but we also have a key. We don't expect to have to use it. The front door is bolted at all times and is the only way in or out. There will always be two members of staff present. You'll meet the rest of the team soon. There is a communal fridge and we encourage you ladies to eat together, but it's your call. You have a lot of decisions; we'll help you make the right ones. Any questions?'

'Around a million.'

She laughs in a manner that says she's heard it all before but still enjoys it.

'Your probation officer will state your restrictions. No alcohol is allowed here and obviously no drugs. If your offence is linked to alcohol, you'll be prohibited from having any at all and will be tested to confirm you are obeying the rules. There is a curfew at eleven o'clock, and you will need to sign in at pre-determined points throughout the day. At the start, that may be as many as five times daily. You'll be given more and more rope, so to speak, as the months go by, until we believe you are ready to leave.

'There can be troubled individuals here, so treat each other with respect. Violence is not tolerated and will result in an immediate recall to prison. Let me show you to your room.'

I follow her up creaky stairs to a landing with four doors.

'That's the bathroom for you and the other two on this floor to share when they arrive. The room upstairs has a girl called Tammy in it. She has her own shower.'

More stairs go up to a small dark landing, which I assume is the attic. I hear light footsteps patter across the ceiling and what might be laughter. I'm glad I'm not up there.

'This is your room.'

It's bare and clean. An open window lets in freezing air. I wonder who slept in that thin bed before me. A single wardrobe leans in the corner near a wooden table and a rickety chair. There's nothing else except a hard-wearing carpet.

'Don't worry, you'll soon make it your own.'

'What did Tammy do?'

'We don't gossip about people's crimes here. However, Tammy spent time inside for arson. In this case, for obvious reasons, it's pertinent that you are aware.'

'Do you know what I did?'

'Yes, they told me what you were convicted of. I'll discuss that with you and anything else later. I'll be downstairs when you are ready for a chat. Relax, have a shower, sleep, do what you like, you're free.'

The door closes behind her and I feel very alone. Despite

sometimes reading a dictionary during endless long hours inside, I'm not entirely sure what pertinent means. It seems I'm to be monitored more closely than in prison. My eyes stray to the sounds above me. I consider if I've left one prison to come to another.

7
IMPRISONED STILL

I lie on the bed without sleeping and stare out the window; it's strange to look through one with no bars. There is an entire world beyond, but I choose to stay in my room. As dark thoughts bubble, I plod downstairs and find Sally doing a crossword.

'Come in, sit down. Do you want a drink, maybe some juice?'

'Sure. I'm hungry, too. Is there a shop nearby?'

'We have the basics here. There's a mini-supermarket around the corner on the right. I'll cook you some beans first if you like.'

She plonks a tumbler of orange on the table and I take a sip. It's chilled and tastes amazing. There are no fridges in prison cells, so I'm used to it lukewarm. The glass clunks against my teeth and I recall the blue rubber beakers I left behind.

As my lunch arrives, a long-forgotten memory surfaces of beans on toast being slid in front of me by someone busy. The cutlery is heavy, not plastic, and scrapes on the porcelain. I eat slowly, savouring the sensations.

Sally smiles. She knows.

Afterwards, I sit and watch television in the lounge. There are a crazy number of channels. They disorientate me as, judging by the wide range of clothes and hairstyles, they could be current shows or from years ago. I hop through them until the doorbell sounds.

'Tim's arrived. You can chat in here.'

'Hi, Katie. Tim Thorn, probation.' He takes a chair opposite and appraises me.

I do the same. He's good-looking, mid-thirties with a full head of black hair. His clothes look expensive although they could just be new.

He grins and something long dormant stirs inside me.

He talks about my licence. I have to see him every three days to start with. He'll come here next time, but after that I must sign in at his office in town. There are many guidelines, more than inside. I can drink but any drunkenness would be frowned upon. I expect him to tell me breaking wind would result in my return to custody. Most of the girls I met inside wouldn't last an hour. I have only one question.

'What happens if I get recalled?'

'If you break any of the rules or the law, the police will arrest you. Depending on the time of the day, they may take you to the police station, or they'll just drive you back to prison. You received a life sentence, Katie. You'll always be vulnerable to this happening.

'If you return to prison, you must sit before another parole board to get out again. Even failing to keep your appointments with me will lead to six months locked up. Over a year is likely for missing an appointment without a good reason, many years for serious breaches. I hold a lot of power over you, Katie. Remember that. Do as I say, and there won't be any problems.'

I hate the way he says that. I fear the look in his eyes. When he's gone, I feel trapped and ask Sally if it's okay to go out. She laughs and tells me requesting permission isn't necessary anymore. I fail to smile as my mind raises dreadful suspicions.

The walk to the small supermarket lifts my spirits. I expect people to stare at me, but of course they don't. Food crams the shelves as I pace up and down the aisles. The astronomical prices start my heart pounding. Two pounds for a tiny individual slice of cheesecake. I'd have to buff the wing for a day to earn that. It won't leave my thoughts, and I keep circling back. I need to have it.

The shopkeeper gives me nervous glances. I'm not surprised. I pick the little box up and wave at him. This is going to be my first purchase. I disregard the cigarette prices behind him. The girls inside always complained about them. There are few things I can control, so that habit will remain in my cell. I hand over the money to a relieved man. Back at the house, Sally lets me in with a questioning expression.

'All okay?'

'Yes, good.'

The dilemma hits me in the kitchen as I select a suitable spoon. Inside, I'd rarely share a treat like this. After staring at it for a few seconds, I find a surprisingly sharp knife, cut it in half, and leave one piece on a plate for Sally. I shout through to her in the office that it's there and run up the stairs. There's still no sign of the arsonist, Tammy, from above.

The cake, to my amazement, tastes better than I expected, leaving me wide-eyed and lip-smacking. I wonder if I've eaten cheesecake before today. It is lucky I left half downstairs, or I'd have been sick.

I empty my box and bag out and put my things away. The insignificant trip to the shop was mentally exhausting, and the nerves of the past few days catch up with me. The narrow mattress is way too soft, like lying on a jelly. The duvet cover smells clean and fresh, but I struggle to settle. I remind myself that it's just a different pillow to lay my head on. I'm used to that. There have been so many, and there'll be more.

The last place I could call a proper home was with Jack and Gwyn. I became happy and secure there. They created an environment where I could be a child, but that was a long, long time ago.

8
THE THIRD MEMORY - AGE EIGHT

The church was dark and the faces bleak; they matched my future.

'We meet here today to honour and pay tribute to the life of Jack Blake, and to express our love and admiration for him. Also, to try to bring comfort to those of his family and friends who are here and have been deeply hurt by his sudden death.'

Mourners were scattered around the crematorium chapel pews. Only Bethany, the social worker, sat beside me on the front bench, though. Gwyn shrank in her wheelchair next to me. Bethany was devastated which felt strange as she only knew him through work. She sobbed enough for everyone.

A stunned Gwyn stared forward. It was devastating news for her, too. Worse in fact. My future had the possibility of hope, hers only pain. A strangled cough or cry from her, I can't recall which, broke down my walls and, hand-in-hand, we shed our worried tears together.

The house was empty without Jack. Before, his large presence lingered even when he wasn't there. We had a week to cope while they conducted the autopsy. Heart failure caused his death. An electrician fell off the scaffolding but a dead man hit the concrete below.

It was soon clear we wouldn't be able to manage. I was too young and clueless to be the woman of the house. Gwyn too poorly and frail. Even though I'd grown up having to look after myself, it became obvious how much Jack had done. With him gone, the washing machine belched water over the floor and we struggled to control the central heating.

Everyone left quickly after the service. Bethany drove us to our house in silence and pushed Gwyn into the lounge.

'Let's take a walk, Katie.'

We shuffled along the path in the warm sunshine. Bethany cried again. A deserted playground beckoned, so we sat next to each other on a swing.

'We've found a place for you in a children's home in Peterborough. I didn't want you to go into emergency foster care. Sadly, it's plain to see that you can't stay with Gwyn.'

'Is that the care system?'

'I suppose so. Why?'

'I remember you telling Jack that children struggled if they had been moved around the care system more frequently.'

Bethany collapsed in tears, and I wondered why she did the job. Turns out she'd been thinking the same thing.

'I'm afraid the home is thirty miles away so you will be out of my area. Besides, I've decided to leave the service. You'll be my last client and my favourite.'

'Can't I come live with you?'

Her shuddering gulps indicated that wouldn't be possible. I feared as much. She couldn't say that which I suspected was true. I must be an unlucky person as bad things happened to the ones I loved.

'What's heart failure?'

She recovered to explain. 'I believe when you're born, your heart has a set number of beats. I think your uncle just used his up.'

The next morning, I packed my belongings. I gathered my

clothes, my unused bike, and the only picture I had of my parents. Bethany failed to arrive. When a lady with a name I couldn't remember drove me to the home, I realised I didn't have a photo of my aunt or uncle. Gwyn had hugged me goodbye and promised to visit but she never did. They told me she died some time later. I didn't get to attend that funeral.

Bethany told the lady she'd write, but I saw no letters. I heard from her replacement that she took a job at an insurance company and moved to Cardiff. I was alone again, but experience had hardened me. Do not get too close to anyone as you can't rely on them and they soon disappear. What flaws lurked inside me? I wasn't angry about events that were out of my control. That would engulf me nearly twenty years later.

9
FEBRUARY

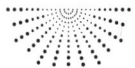

APPROVED PREMISES - CAMBRIDGE

I've spent many hours staring at the television but not seeing it. I remember watching a film while I was inside. There was a sad part where an old felon killed himself because he had been incarcerated for so long, it institutionalised him. I didn't understand it then, but I do now. I crave the routine. Prison regime left you little time for daydreaming. With nothing to do, I stare at the clock and think I would be working right now, or in the gym.

It was the hours in your cell that were tough. Then your memories found you. I could spend the entire night stuck at the moment before dreamless sleep, subconsciously replaying the facts over and over and yearning without hope for a different outcome.

I've only seen the girl upstairs a couple of times and she barely acknowledged me. Familiar smells of illegal substances filter through the ceiling. Sally seems content to let her be. She said that it was nigh on impossible to house anyone with an arson conviction as they were such a danger to others. At the incredulous look on my face she explained that Tammy had been assessed and her risk was low. That wasn't reassuring, but it made sense. She had to live somewhere. Otherwise she would be homeless, uncared for, and slip into old habits. And there'd be more fires.

The night worker told me Tammy's peccadillo was putting lit envelopes through people's letter boxes. We didn't have one as the building was always staffed, so we should be okay. I thought the craziness of prison would finish after I left, but real life is worse in some ways.

I have to sign in at regular times so even if I want to venture out, I'm not able to go far. After another month, they will lower the frequency so I can do more. In the meantime, this is it. I must push myself to do things, yet every time I step through the front door, I feel vulnerable.

England is out there. I could sightsee or watch a film but instead, I slump on the sofa. Sally reassures me it's normal after so long in prison and to take each day as it comes. The inactivity makes sleep impossible here, too. Today, I'm going for a run. It's hard to get my head round the fact I can go anywhere if I return by lunchtime.

The best thing so far about being free is the shower. You didn't hang around in prison bathrooms. Although as my sentence progressed they introduced lockable cubicles. But the doors were still low so staff, or anyone else, could look over them. Here, I'm safe. I've spent money on toiletries as a treat, and fifteen minutes under a blasting stream of hot water makes me feel human and alive.

I even take a shower before my run to wake me up. When I'm finished, I find Tammy chatting to a bloke in white paint-splattered overalls outside the door. Tammy has a towel in her hand and, despite the wild hair, looks normal. There's even eye contact and I hear the first clear words from her mouth.

'My bathroom's being painted, so Sally said to use yours. I almost gave up as you were in there so long.' She casts a sneaky look at the workman. 'She must have been especially dirty.'

I step out of her way, unsure what to say to that. I sidle by as my embarrassed face registers her meaning, and she delivers an unwelcome compliment.

'Nice tits.'

The man and I both stare down at my chest which a damp T-shirt struggles to hide, and I sprint away to my room.

You could say I have been blessed or cursed on the boob front. They were, after all, the cause of my downfall. Never having had a proper relationship, I struggled to understand the fascination. It didn't take long for people to notice in the prison — staff and inmates.

After the mind-blowing implications of the sentence had receded, I'm ashamed to say I used that fact to get what I wanted. A strange young officer would bring me in virtually anything if I let him squeeze them for a minute or two. That was it; I didn't even have to undress. Other officers would insist on that, and I sunk to a blowjob once. I had no idea what I was doing and suspect I wasn't very good at it because he never came back for more.

In fact, he was wary of me afterwards. Perhaps he was more ashamed than I was. Maybe he felt guilty at taking advantage of me, even though you could argue I was getting something off him. Twenty cigarettes in that case. Prisoners can only afford rolling tobacco, so an actual fag was a real treat. I kept them as they were fantastic currency.

Inside, people exchanged cigarettes for drugs or cash even though you weren't allowed either. Buyers would ring their friends and get them to transfer money to a bank account of your choosing. The powerful would offer beatings for less than a pack of smokes.

Later, I realised that the officer's lack of control shocked him. He was married and if I'd reported him to the authorities, they would've prosecuted him for misconduct in a public office. Dismissal and prison would have been his reward for a few minutes of pleasure. Definitely not worth it with my poor technique.

I put my tightest bra on under a baggy top. My best leggings — with only one hole — go above my new trainers, and I wave at Sally as I leave the premises. The air is sharp and welcome. Being cold never bothered me after I went away. It rarely kills you, and in the scheme of things it seems unimportant to moan about.

I jog in a straight direction. Getting lost would stress me. I know the name of my road, so can ask for directions but would rather not. And then I increase my pace. As the miles tick by, I experience a sense of contentment I can't describe. Other joggers nod at me as we meet. I admire their purpose-made outfits and resolve to change mine.

Gears shift inside me as I reconnect with the world. Everything is clear; cars, people, even leaves and blades of grass are defined. By the time I return and burst through the door, I sport a sloppy, foolish expression. The painter I met this morning greets me on the stairs. He steps aside. His smile is coy.

'Sorry, about earlier. I didn't mean to, well, you know.'

Up close, he has nice white teeth and a twinkling grin. I glance at his fingers and see a gold band. History has taught me not all men respect their vows, so I'm wary.

'No problem.'

His eyes search for confirmation that he hasn't overstepped the mark.

'You aren't going to finish your painting loitering around here.'

His laugh is pleasant and easy, and I surprise myself realising mine is too. As he canters down the stairs, something else shifts in me. I have much to learn. It's good to think some of it will be fun.

10
THE GIRLS ARRIVE

After another heavenly shower, I head to the kitchen for breakfast. My probation worker, Tim Thorn, is leaving. He gives me a cold smile and says he'll see me next week. I've been to his office twice where he is all business. Only here at the house there is something off with him. It's only a shadow, but it is there and I'll need to be careful.

There are two women in the kitchen with Sally. They must be the prison releases she said would arrive. After introductions, I casually glance at them and, even though I know their types, they couldn't be more different.

Maleeha has the same shocked expression on her face that I wore. She must have served serious time. By her looks, I guess she originates from Pakistan or India. There were few like that in the prison system. Maybe their supportive culture is a factor, or they hide their crimes in their communities. The odd heroin addict slips through, but they've often been rejected at some point. They struggle in jail with stigma and shame.

Her race and demeanour mean I can have a guess at what she did, but I'll let her tell me. The other lady, Nancy, has the pockmarked skin of a committed user. Due to the lack of teeth, her face is sunken, which makes her age difficult to judge, but I'd say they were both in their mid-thirties like me. Sally leaves us to get acquainted.

Nancy assumes her stereo type. Inside, there are many more like her. They are loud and brash, rude and uneducated. Most suffer hard lives. They hide themselves behind an arrogant, cocksure, jokey demeanour as they've found it the best way to stop themselves being hurt or taken advantage of.

'What are you two here for?' she asks.

You've got to give her credit. It's a great first getting-to-know-you question.

Maleeha ponders this and decides she doesn't want to start her day with a fabrication, so she admits to what I suspected. 'Manslaughter.'

I lie and use the same reason.

'My days! I'm stuck here with you two murdering bastards, and with old Firestarter upstairs, it'll be a struggle to get life insurance in this house.'

She grins at me and I have to smile. I wait for her to continue as I know she will.

'I got six months for nicking Lego. Can you believe it? The judge told me he was sick of seeing me and sent me down for longer so I could get clean. Probation promised to help me when I was released. So here I am.'

This time I can't resist. 'Why did you steal Lego? Was it for your children?'

'I had kids and lost them years ago. Careless, really.' A cloud passes over her face and gets pushed away. 'The Lego was just there, near the shop exit. You get how it is. What did they expect? I picked it up and legged it. Unluckily for me, a gym freak was on security, and that was it.'

Maleeha and I aren't surprised by any of those statements. We were the first time we heard stories like that. It's depressing to believe people think that way, but they do. Nancy continues.

'I was in one of these places before. You need to keep signing in. What a massive ball-ache! I'm not allowed any booze either as part of my licence conditions. How shit is that?' She glances at Maleeha. 'I bet you don't drink?'

'Why do you say that?'

'Your type never does.'

'My type?'

'Yeah, you know. Pakis.'

Maleeha shakes her head. 'It may surprise you to hear I was born in Leeds. My parents are from Sheffield. My husband and his parents grew up in Peterborough.'

'So, what? You still look like one. Talking of which, don't you lot go back to your families? Where's your husband?'

'I killed him.'

I stifle a laugh at Nancy's wide eyes even though she recovers fast. Good for you, Maleeha. You'll need that punch to get through the next stage of your life. She has brown skin, but her accent is broad Yorkshire. Her English is a lot better than Nancy's. She speaks slowly.

'I read an article suggesting that it doesn't say alcohol is haram — forbidden — in the Quran like it does with pork, only that it's not advised. Admittedly that would probably infuriate the majority. Someone got 80 lashes recently for drinking in Saudi Arabia. Let's hope that isn't in your conditions.

'And, our families, as you so sweetly put it, disown us after we do something terrible. The community rejected me for bringing shame to them. I was in prison for eight years and not one person came to visit, and I have two brothers. My children were kept away, but I had no choice in committing that crime.'

'There's always a choice,' said Nancy.

'He was beating me and my sons. He was so abusive.'

A lifetime of knocks prevented Nancy getting an education, but she is street sharp.

'You would see it like that. You could look at it different. When you took his life, you erased their father. Then, when you went to jail for eight years, you also robbed them of a mother. Before your actions they had two parents, now they have none.'

Maleeha collapses into her seat and weeps. I'm shocked to the core by Nancy's brutal perception. I locked my emotions away when I first went inside and they are yet to reappear. Others, like Maleeha, keep them on display.

Nancy recovers quickly. 'Come here. Give us a hug. Don't mind me. I say it how it is.'

She smothers Maleeha in a strong cuddle and rocks her back and forth as if she's trying to shake money from her. Remarkably, it works and Maleeha's sobs quieten.

'You've had no contact with your kids in all that time? Knowing they were living with your family? Wow. Can't have been easy. You'll be able to visit them now, won't you?' asks Nancy.

Maleeha breaks down again. I pick up the mantle.

'They tend to be prudent with letting you see vulnerable children if you've stabbed their father to death.'

Nancy considers my words and nods. 'True dat.'

The slightest whiff of marijuana drifts in with the draught made from someone opening the front door. Nancy's eyes imperceptibly widen. She picks up her plastic prison bag and says she's off to her room.

'Catch you ladies later. I'll cook council house curry. You'll love it.'

I decide that I like her, despite her ignorant views. The curry sounds dangerous. Unsure what to do, I make Maleeha and me a cuppa. Then I sit next to her and wait until the tears stop. It's a long five minutes before she gathers her composure.

'I'm sorry. You don't want to see that. I don't know how I can move on. They were my world. He beat the kids so badly that I feared he would kill one of them. Their parents are gone but at least they're safe.'

People's lives are so complicated. You would think a child's safest place is by her mother but that's not always possible. I remember Rada's gesture from the day I left prison, and slide my fingers across the table. I take her hands in mine, and she squeezes back. It's comforting for both of us.

'She's right in a way,' Maleeha says. 'Her attitude was common in jail. Few females in our community are behind bars, and I was completely unprepared for it. I'd never been exposed to drugs, the constant scrutiny, or being questioned by staff. Before, I was a private, tolerant person. The anger and perpetual arguing wore me down.

'There was little support for Muslim women inside, and I was disowned outside. Although, I can't blame them because I did a wicked thing. Other Pakistanis in the system told me they were rejected and criticised when they tried to return to their home town. They had to start from scratch and, without help, they fell into lives of theft and prostitution. What am I going to do?'

My path is as uncertain, so I have little advice. I decide to try. 'We're in the same place, me and you. How about we look out for each other? We can't be alone if we support each other.'

Her grip tightens to confirm acceptance. I'm drawn to Maleeha, too, but I fear for her. She is a troubled, lonely soul. Moving on will be difficult. Perhaps impossible.

11
MARCH

MAKING FRIENDS

Having the two girls in the house has been a tremendous help. It's nice to be with others who understand what you're going through. Sally lifted some restrictions and extended all our curfews to eleven p.m. We've been to the cinema and Maleeha and I ventured to the swimming pool. I could barely remember how to swim, it had been so long. Judging by the splashing around of my friend, she'd barely learned. Nancy declined, cryptically saying people like her drown in water.

Nancy told me she attempted to buy weed off Firestarter as she still insists on calling her, but the girl slammed the door in her face. We've discussed getting a flat together after our time is up here. I asked Sally about it, who smiled and said it was something to consider. It was a sad knowing smile that only I picked up on. I know when I'm being humoured, but I deemed it unnecessary at this stage to push for reasons.

A girls' evening for my thirty-fifth birthday was Nancy's idea. I've never had a night out *on the town* as she called it. Maleeha hadn't either as her group of friends weren't into that sort of thing. I had a nasty feeling that it was going to be a big let-down as the build-up consumed us. With nothing else to focus on, we planned it to the nth degree.

Maleeha said she'd do our make-up. Before her crime, she wore it all the time. Muslims like her show little flesh, so they wear nice clothes and keep their nails and hair looking beautiful. She stated she didn't have much left and couldn't afford more but would share what she had. Nancy said not to worry about that as she had loads.

None of us owned anything suitable to wear either. To my surprise we used charity shops. It's crazy what people give to them and you can pick up for a few quid, especially in a place like Cambridge. Nancy knew all this. A life with no money means you learn all the tricks. We bought a dress each, and shoes. I couldn't cope with the high heels Nancy pointed out. At five feet eight, she declared it wasn't that important for me if I chose some flats.

We had a rehearsal and got changed together in my room. Nobody had qualms over seeing others' naked bodies after being around hundreds of women. They both commented on my figure. Maleeha's body was slim but untoned. Nancy looked like a plucked chicken covered in smudged blue ink. It made me look at the similar tattoos on my hands and the one on my bicep. I tried to remember my mental state when I let a stranger put them on me, but it was too long ago.

Maleeha put nail varnish on us. She took her time and it was a pleasant experience. That said, I stared at our hands throughout. They seemed so normal, yet they had committed appalling deeds. Were they capable of more?

When they went back to their own rooms, I stared at my body in the mirror. Having become an avid reader when sleep failed to materialise, I studied healthy eating and exercise. I looked in good shape for a number of reasons. There was no sun damage because tanning in the prison yards was an infrequent treat. I swapped desserts for vegetables and salad, but there were usually leftovers.

I should think the last time Nancy went near a lettuce was when she was stealing from people's gardens.

Prison doesn't have to age you. After my first year, I avoided drugs. There were no late booze-filled nights to slacken my face. And no children to wear me out. All the prisons I was in had gyms. My only vice was enjoying a few cigarettes at night. After bang up, I'd sit with a coffee in silence and smoke one as a reward for getting through another day.

Finally, I learned to fight. Some girls in jail, as you'd expect, were violent. They were used to scrapping. I felt unmatched, having avoided conflict even in various children's homes. Many women added ten years to their looks through missing teeth lost in fights. I asked those who knew how to defend themselves to teach me. I picked up bits here and there, but it was more the confidence it gave me that would cause others to back down.

Of course, as the saying goes, you can't win 'em all. An eighteen stone Latvian named Gripa once bounced me off every wall in my cell and broke two of my fingers. She would have killed me if someone hadn't called the guards.

12
TWO DAYS LATER

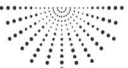

ACCEPTANCE

Saturday night arrives and we totter downstairs at six p.m. The painter feigns a heart attack when we sashay by. I turn and smile at him as I go down the stairs and I'm pleased his gaze lingers on me. The open-mouthed expression declares attraction. That's nice as I usually see lust and a desire for control.

When I walk my dress rises up, and it's already short. We stare in the mirror under the stark kitchen strip light, and I think the girls must have been out of practice as my face paint looks more Comanche than Clinique. Our outfits are completed by ridiculous winter coats. It's too cold without them because none of us has much insulation.

Sally says she will take a picture, so we haul off our jackets. I watch in awe as she uses her mobile phone and shows us the photo straight after. I'm amazed by the leap in technology. Maleeha is shocked by how we look.

'Are we going to a whorehouse?' she asks.

'Why's that?' says Nancy as though it's an option.

'It's the only place we'll fit in dressed like this.'

This gets me giggling and soon we're all at it. When we've settled down, Sally reminds us to focus on our behaviour. She says it's important that we're able to have fun but still be in control. She tells us not to drink alcohol and to stay clear of trouble. Most importantly, she pleads, look after each other.

The painter remains astonished in the hall when we stride past stinking of perfume. Nancy had a range to choose from. I'd had small plastic bottles of cheap stuff over the years — obviously we weren't allowed glass — but nothing that smelled like this. I must resemble an undercover cop with my nose attached to my wrist. When we get outside, Maleeha whistles.

'He has the hots for you!'

'He's married.'

'I think he forgets that when you waltz around in a towel after one of your many endless showers.'

'Maybe he's married with kids, but his wife doesn't understand him,' Nancy adds. 'They haven't made love for years, and he has never met anyone like you before.'

'That's right, He'll definitely leave them because he lurves you.'

Maleeha's face drops at her own joke. The following silence enables me to consider if I'm ready for sex. It's been a long time. I had female affairs at the beginning of my sentence. The butch daddies aggressively pursued me, but they held no interest.

Gay for the stay is definitely a thing. Straight women start relationships with women for the comfort. There wasn't that much physical contact with the partners I took. I couldn't share a cell due to my crime. You might grab the odd furtive shower or fumble in the laundry room. The environment meant that it usually ended in tears. Bitch fights were common, and you would find your girlfriend had been ghosted to another wing or even to another prison.

That was one reason I needed to defend myself. The management didn't encourage inmate relationships, but there was nothing they could do to stop them. They would ignore it as long as there was no aggravation, but women scorned can be evil creatures.

Every now and again you would meet inmates with skills. A corrupt solicitor, perhaps, who could advise on appeals, or someone happy to teach you a foreign language to while away the time. I found Mai.

I met her in my third year. She was a Vietnamese cannabis farmer with a six-year tariff. Obviously, she wasn't. People traffickers smuggled Mai into the country and then presented her with an impossible bill. Her options were nail bar, prostitution, or sitting in a semi on a council estate and growing dope in all the rooms except the one she inhabited. She chose the latter as it cleared the debt faster. When the police raided the house, she was the person they found.

I decided I needed to learn some form of defence and spotted Mai practising moves in her cell with a girl from the Philippines. They moved in poetic unison.

Mai was a peaceful lady, in her twenties, who knew a Vietnamese martial art, Vovinam, which combined many forms. She was tiny but packed a stinging punch. I remember her attempting to teach me flow. 'When you kick, use all your body. Strike through your hips. It is how you push a vacuum cleaner.' She was right. She taught me it all. My technique was donkey-like compared to her crane, but I made great progress.

Shortly after we met, an illegal immigrant from Barbados attempted to throttle me with a mop. Mai dropped her in seconds. All that over me walking on a wet floor. Regardless, I took note, and we became friends.

I called in a favour from an officer. I'd given him information about an inmate who had promised to hang herself. They caught her in time, so he owed me. When wing cleaning jobs came up, the two martial artists were first in line. They worked as though they were scouring their own homes. Most unusual for prisoners. After they were sentenced, they got promoted to a big double cell. No one complained. Especially the other wing workers as their work load had decreased dramatically.

We would enter their larger room and practice tai chi and Vovinam. The latter used special combinations of other arts, taking into account the Vietnamese small stature. It focused on speed. Mai was only a dot of a thing, but she was so quick it was beautiful to watch.

I got nowhere near her level but it gave me self-assurance. She'd urge me still to be sensible; there are weight bands in fighting for a reason. Someone who's twice as heavy as you is unlikely to lose. The exercise helped tone my body and emptied my mind. Mai promised peace could be attained through acceptance but that particular state eluded me.

We became lovers for a year until they deported her. She was the only lover I didn't instantly forget. That was the last serious relationship I had inside. I was devastated when she left. She thanked me with a warm smile and told me to celebrate how lucky we were to find each other. That wasn't so easily done when I still had over ten years to serve.

After she'd gone, I felt I had more control. If I was stressed, I would slowly do the exercises and be marginally more relaxed. Prowling my cell was still a common occurrence.

I push those distant thoughts away and consider my new friends. Tonight will not be a relaxing time.

13
CLUBBING

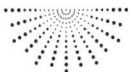

When we reach the town centre, we hold hands in a line on the pavement and separate only to let others walk past. It feels good to be part of something. I'm nervous as hell, though. I've no idea what to expect, but I feel silly saying so.

'Are we going to a bar or the pub?' I ask despite not knowing the difference.

'It's a cross between the two,' Nancy answers. She's jittery, and I recognise the signs match those of someone about to get a fix. 'The chain is called Wetherspoons. I like it and it's perfect for tonight, mostly because of the cheapness as we don't have much cash.'

I imagined a swanky venue full of men in evening wear sipping whisky, and glamorous women enjoying cocktails. It's quite a shock when we arrive and find it very different. It's loud and packed. Maleeha keeps my hand in a vice-like grip while Nancy charges to the bar like it's one minute before closing as opposed to seven p.m.

It takes us a while to catch up to her. Many of the people we brush against have been here for a long time. The chatter, stares, laughs and cheers overwhelm my senses. I'm glad of my bulky coat. The place has a smell that I haven't encountered. I make a note to ask Nancy although the slight pull from the carpet on my soles distracts me.

Nancy passes over ten-pounds and collects her change. She turns with a grin, holding three big glasses of a yellowy substance between her small bony fingers. I have a flashback to random drug testing in the prison.

'Come on, let's find a seat.' Her smile is wild and white. Maleeha and I are more shocked by that sight than all the other strange ones. It's heaving and the only place to rest our drinks is a high table near three young lads. They eye Nancy warily as she plonks our glasses down.

'Bottoms up, ladies.'

'What is it?' asks Maleeha.

'Old Rosie. It's like apple juice.'

We all drink together. My right eye waters as I swallow, Maleeha spits hers back in the glass, and Nancy drains hers in one.

'My juice has gone bad,' says Maleeha, causing us to laugh. 'Does it have alcohol in it?'

'Of course. No apple juice is worth two quid a pint.'

'Okay. I'll try but I don't really like the taste of alcohol.'

The mass of bodies has made the room warm, and I remove my coat. Nancy is always cold and I sense Maleeha also thinks hers is a shield against this place. I pull my dress down but note girls with shorter skirts than mine. Some look like they've just come from cheerleading, while others could be lawyers. Intermingled between them are scruffy types of all ages and a lot of old men glugging soapy-looking drinks.

Nancy scans the crowd with a practised eye. Ten minutes later, she's twitchy and eyeing her finished drink. She starts on Maleeha's who looks pleased. Nancy must have forgotten the spit in it. I persevere with mine and find it gets easier. Maleeha asks me what I'm thinking as I scowl.

'What's on your mind?'

'What's that funny smell in here?' Nancy takes centre stage. 'Who knows? Could be the toilets, but most likely it's the carpets. You can imagine the vomit, blood and booze that's spilt on it over a week. No Shake'n'Vac's up to that task.' She's finished Maleeha's drink now. I eye the carpet like it could absorb me any second, and then down my cider with a gasp.

'Why are we drinking so fast? Do we have to go somewhere?' I ask.

'We're time restricted. We want to have a boogie at a club and guzzle plenty of drinks, but we don't want to pay nightclub prices. It's cheap here, so we stay until nine and get pre-loaded.'

'Sally told us not to drink alcohol,' Maleeha recalls.

Nancy grins. 'Sally said to be careful. She meant don't come home pissed. Right, I'll buy another now we've drunk up.'

'Can I have a glass of water, please?' asks Maleeha to Nancy's disappearing back.

'Here, you ladies can have these.' The guys next to us offer their high stools. It's so unexpected, the one near me receives a beaming smile in return as I gratefully peel my shoes off the floor. The lads can't be more than twenty-years-old. Nancy returns at that point with a suspicious stare. Soon, however, we're all chatting. They're students, reasonably good-looking and polite. They are also giggly.

Maleeha complains to Nancy that her drink is warm. Nancy explains that the barman must not have run the tap long enough. Maleeha's look of disgust has me chuckling out of control. I feel great, confident even. The lads buy us a round of drinks. Maleeha fakes a swoon as she's passed a chilled bottle of sparkling mineral water. I'm not sure what mine is. It tastes sweet and fiery. I forget there's alcohol inside, and it's gone in minutes.

Too soon, Nancy declares leaving time. She explains where we're going. The boys say they have to study tomorrow. The most confident one, who has shuffled himself to my side for the last few minutes, holds my hand and looks me in the eye.

'It was a pleasure to meet you, Katie.'

He dips his head to kiss my hand and pauses. Again, my prison tattoos register in a depressing way. To his credit, he completes the manoeuvre, but his enthusiasm visibly chills. I glance at Nancy who observes on unsteady feet. The scene amuses her no end, and she barks out a laugh. Her top set of false teeth fires from her mouth and clatters along the surface of the table. Now, that is funny.

We burst out of the pub leaving the men with an image they'll never forget. Nancy guides us through the streets and to a back alley.

'Here, everyone, have one of these mints and we need to take our coats off so we'll get in for nothing.'

She ushers us around a corner to a big brown door. A wide man blocks the entrance. As we walk up to him, he raises an eyebrow.

'Workers around the rear.'

I picture pole dancers. Maleeha must do too, and whispers too loudly.

'I said we looked like hookers.'

Nancy moves swiftly to plan B. 'How rude.' Her aggression surprises him.

'We only just opened. I thought you worked behind the bar or in the coat room.'

'I want to speak to the manager. Unless you let us in for free. You can't go around calling women prostitutes.'

He isn't sure whether to be worried or angry. Nancy presses home her advantage.

'Look, we've got to leave soon. Catch the last train. We just wanted to have an hour dancing. The blokes who get in early love to see birds doing their thing. That'll keep them happy and not fighting until it gets busy.' She leers at him. 'We turn into pumpkins at midnight.'

He ushers us in. I hear him tell the ticket girl he'll explain later. We go down steps and through another set of doors. The music blares louder as we approach. We barge through more doors and there we are. It's like a huge school disco hall. The song vibrates through my soles.

Even Maleeha looks excited. 'Come on, Katie.' She drags me onto the shiny wooden dance floor, and we begin to step around. I shuffle my feet even though there's only about ten other people scattered around the sides. When Nancy joins in, I relax. She frowns at the music and walks up to the DJ stand. A minute later, a song from Dirty Dancing roars out of the speakers. I watched the film so many times in jail I could sing them all.

A blast of smoke envelops us and I leave Katie the prisoner behind. As the others disappear in the grey clouds, years drop away like leaves and finally, I am me.

14
PUMPKIN TIME

It feels like the same song is playing when Maleeha gasps in my ear and tells me we need to go. The place is filling up and I hate to leave. We find Nancy slumped on a sofa looking tired. She has our coats on her lap and may even have been asleep. We haul her up with little effort. She's such a big personality, it's a surprise she's so light.

The foyer heaves with new arrivals. Everyone's in high spirits. We catch sight of ourselves in the mirror and flinch. We look like we've been through a car wash. Nancy is bedraggled. She pulls her hair back into a ponytail, shrugs, and leads the way out.

As we depart, I glance at the women queuing to leave their coats and bags. I've never seen so many tattoos. They are everywhere. People wear them with pride. Arms have full sleeves, backs are adorned, and necks are decorated. Wow! is all I can think. The only people who had tattoos when I first went away were sailors, other prisoners, and David Beckham.

Imagine the quality of work from a prison tattooist. Spelling mistakes were a common theme. One poor mare had *home sweat home* on her shoulder blade in the ubiquitous off-blue shade. The designs here, though, are colourful and beautiful. A lady turns around displaying a peacock on her bare back. She winks at my open face, clearly used to admiration. Her make-up is flawless.

In fact, most girls are immaculately dressed and shimmer like film stars to my inexperienced eye. I feel like a cleaner leaving before the celebrities arrive. Eyeshadow dehumanises the pretty faces we pass and I find myself wondering who these people really are? What do they actually look like?

The queue to enter the nightclub stretches along the building. We walk alongside them as we make our way home.

A tall, ginger youth appraises me as though he's a farmer at a cattle market. A small, black man further down the line whispers, 'Nice coat,' to his mate. They both glance away and laugh.

Maleeha and I exchange glances. The fresh air perks Nancy up and she starts to sing *The Fairy Tale of New York* despite the time of year. We join in and stagger home. Around the corner from the premises, Nancy's self-preservation kicks in, and she gets her mints out again.

'No alcohol passed our lips, remember?'

We nod in unison, take deep breaths and enter with fifteen minutes to spare. The staff member on tonight is an old guy who's seen it all before. He lets us in, looks at his watch and smiles. He's thankful for the lack of aggravation and paperwork that our late returning would have caused.

Nancy barges into her room and slams the door. We hear her bed squeak, a thump as she falls off it, and a chuckle as it amuses her. Then silence. Maleeha takes my hand and pulls me through her door.

'Did you have fun tonight, Katie?'

'Yeah. I loved the dancing, although the pub was mad. Good though, but I felt overawed most of the night, as if I was operating on a slower speed than everyone else.'

'I know what you mean. The world's got loud and frantic. What's with the mobile phone thing? Everyone's glued to them. It's weird. It wasn't just that. Did you feel like you didn't belong?'

'It was strange, but I think that was just because it was all so new. We dressed differently, and we definitely did not have on enough mascara.'

'I'm not used to those places, Katie, and I don't want to be. I enjoyed the dance floor, too. Yet, there was an aggressive tinge to everything that didn't exist in our community get-togethers. It's made me homesick.'

I sit on the bed next to her and pull her close. I expect trembling shoulders and loud sobs when she remembers her family, but she remains quiet and stiff. Deep down, I understand that the difference is worrying.

15
GONE

I stay in bed all morning. After some rolling around, I get up around two p.m. and slip into my running gear. A hangover covers me like a wet blanket but after thirty minutes of grind, it dissolves. I flag at the hour mark and return to the house. There's a police car leaving as I jog up. Tim Thorn, who does all of our probation work, watches me in the same way as the ginger man outside the nightclub did.

'A word please, Katie.'

'What is it?'

'Inside.'

Maleeha has collapsed face down on the sofa in the lounge with her head in her hands. Sally rubs her back with a distant expression. That look is familiar, yet alien. It seems out of place here.

'Come on, we'll go to your room.'

Tim is up the stairs before I can comment. My skin tightens as I ascend behind him.

'What's up, Mr Thorn? I'm not due to see you until Friday.'

'Call me Tim, please.'

'I like to keep things professional.'

'Very wise, Katie.' His smile is cruel and confident. He's broken stronger girls than me. 'I came with the police to pick up Nancy, your friend. They've taken her back to prison to do the other half of her sentence.'

'Why? What did she do?'

He wanders around my room, picking up the odd picture or memento, and then sits on the bed. He reclines and rests his head on my pillow. Due to his height, his shiny shoes hang over the end.

'All those times in prison, Katie. You know she never stood a chance. Seventy percent of people like her have re-offended within a year. We heard from a nightclub in town that four women reported having money stolen. We suspect there were more, but they probably put it down to drunkenness. Clever thief, you see. Took the cash and returned the purses. Nightclubs are dark verminous places.'

'What makes you think it was her?'

'I know you all had an evening out yesterday.'

I say nothing. Sadly, he's right. I've found most low-level thieves habitual. The prison staff call them frequent flyers as they are in and out so often. Sometimes it's the buzz, other times it's an addiction.

'There has been an increase in shoplifting around town of late, too. A mini crime wave we weren't expecting. It must have been too easy for her. A different place where no one knows her. Superdrug took a fair old battering. When I found out, I thought now who's new to the manor? Who could this be?'

Clearly enjoying himself, he sits up, and raises his eyebrows at me.

'What? You think I was part of it?'

'Of course not. If you and Maleeha had been involved, we'd have been dealing with a bloodbath. That's not to say others didn't accuse you. I like you though, Katie. I have high hopes for your future. As for Nancy? She couldn't help herself. We arrived here and found her clothed, unconscious, and lying on the floor. That's breach one of her licence. Breaches two to ten were still in their cellophane wrappers except for some perfume. I expect you all smelled lovely last night.'

He rises from the bed and straightens his tie. 'We'd hate for you to have to finish your life sentence, wouldn't we? You owe me, Katie.'

A knock at the door startles us both. I open it to Sally's concerned face. She looks straight at Thorn.

'You know the rules. The bedrooms are for residents only.'

'I was leaving anyway. Keep your nose clean, Katie. Sally, have the paperwork completed by the weekend. I'll let myself out.'

Sally receives a disarming smile, I get a nod. After he's gone, she closes the door. 'Be careful with him,' she says.

'Do I need to be?'

'I'm not sure. He's a bit slippery for my liking.'

'Has nobody else who stayed here ever said anything about him?'

Her face drops to the empty expression she had earlier. Now, I remember. It's a face that's seen it all before. Time-served prison officers wore those looks as they separated fights and called for assistance after suicides and stabbings. Nothing scares or surprises her. Sally knew Nancy was unlikely to be a success story. Should I be worried about Thorn?

'Well?' I ask.

She remains silent for over a minute before telling the truth.

'One girl. She said he made her touch him in her room. Who knows there might have been more.'

'Why is he still here? Why isn't he in prison?'

'He stated she fabricated it because he'd recalled her. She was a compulsive liar. She'd actually done time for multiple false-accusations of rape. A history like that combined with substance abuse and mental health issues doesn't indicate a reliable witness. They suspended him but nothing came of it. The girl disappeared afterwards. That's when we made the rule on who enters the bedrooms.'

'Well, that's perfect. What's the point to it all? My life is over. Why do you work here, Sally, amongst all this bullshit? I can have the floor pulled away from underneath by him, or you, just like that.' I click my fingers in her face. 'Back to jail. I've served my sentence, yet here I am. It's just more time in a new hole. If I'd known, I wouldn't have bothered.'

'Don't give up, Katie.'

'That's easy for you to say. This is your job, not your life.'

Her eyes drop to the floor, and I wonder if I've overstepped the mark. She pulls the chair from the desk and sits down heavily. I examine her features and see a jowly fifty-year-old woman with little to live for. Her clothes are clean yet shabby. A face free of make-up but covered with sorrow.

'I work here because I, too, saw the end of the line. My son was found in a crack house, stripped and beaten, dirty and dead. I'd only seen him a few weeks beforehand and thought he was fine. Thin, perhaps. The inquest spoke of years of addiction to which I'd been oblivious. I wanted to die. He was the only family I had.'

A shocked gasp escapes from my mouth. I stifle it as she continues.

'When I made that decision, a weight lifted from me and I looked forward to being with him again. Which was a little weird with me not being religious. A friend picked up on the changes and pleaded for me not to do anything rash. When he left that day, he spoke the line that gave me a reason to carry on. Interested?'

'Go on.'

'He asked if my son would want that. His life was over so he couldn't offer the world anything. I lived. Why didn't I help others? Those like him who lost their way. So, here I am. It's hard still, but I hope I'm helping. Days like today are sad but many do make it back. Search inside yourself. There will be something that motivates you. Use it. Perhaps there is a God, and he has a purpose for you. Find the strength within, Katie. I know it's there.'

I lay down for a long time afterwards and considered her words. People read about the fragility of life every day but they think it happens to others. Then it surprises them. Death can't be bribed, and God doesn't play fair. Sally's misfortune is my gain. She wouldn't be here to help without her loss.

It dawns on me that it feels good to have someone in my corner. I want to be happy again. It seems so long since I was. At the moment, pleasant times are poisoned. While Maleeha and I were dancing, Nancy had been robbing those who watched.

I need nice memories with decent people. My history is prison grey, yet there was colour before then. Even though it's been twenty-five years, I'm taken back to the first time I felt like giving up. I heard powerful words that day, too.

16
THE FOURTH MEMORY - AGE EIGHT

I arrived at the children's home on a freezing cold day. I'd only met the lady from social services who took me there once before, and she wasn't interested in talking. She must've been stressed as she smoked a lot of cigarettes out of the car window. My seat was behind hers. If I'd known I would be travelling in a wind tunnel, I would have put on warmer clothes. Although, the shivering was mostly due to worry.

No one told me what to expect, so I stared aghast, and feared a long drive up to a creaking mansion. My nerves were so shot to pieces that when we arrived at a large building on a street corner, I still couldn't relax. In fact, I was close to weeing myself.

An old lady came to greet us after we rang the bell. I stood in the foyer while the driver got my things. Mrs Gill spent those minutes staring at me in silence. She could have been anyone's granny in looks, but there was a fierceness to her which made me extremely nervous.

The house had high ceilings, a wide staircase, and many doors over three floors. It was as cold inside as out. We went through to a big kitchen where the adults talked around a table. The lady —

who I assumed was my new support worker — patted me on the head and said she'd see me later in the week. Then she left.

'Any questions?' asked Mrs Gill.

'Where's the toilet?'

Her weathered face twitched at the side. After she showed me to a small room under the stairs, we sat around the table again.

'Juice?'

'I'm okay, thank you.'

'Hungry?'

'I'm okay, thank you.'

'Lonely?'

Looking down at my clenched hands to disguise my weakness, I considered her question. I was afraid because I was alone. I decided then not to worry about saying the wrong thing. It was time to tell the truth and be damned if it went badly. I failed to understand the world in which I lived.

'Yes, I'm very lonely.'

'There are fifteen other children here, so you will make friends. They're all at school now, but they'll be back soon enough. You'll like it here.'

My set chin displayed my intentions to one as experienced as her.

'You're planning to run away when you get the chance. Fear can do that to you. Don't be afraid of what might be. Sometimes you need to be frightened, but not often, and not here. I should think you've been through a worrying few days, and probably not for the first time either. Do people keep leaving you?'

'Yes.'

'You're a tough little thing.'

A solitary tear ran down my cheek.

'Come with me, Katie.'

She ushered me to the back of the house, unlocked a door, and led me into a big room with a large desk. There were grey filing cabinets along one wall, and a roaring gas fire on the other. The heat was so welcome I gasped.

'Go on child, warm your hands.'

I crouched next to the fire. My blue clawed fingers unfurled and reached out. She closed the door and sat in her high-backed chair.

My memories before that day were mostly just snatches: images, smells and sounds. But the fire reminded me so clearly of that last Christmas morning with Uncle Jack, it cleared my mind. I would remember Mrs Gill's speech for the rest of my life.

'You believe you've lost everything, and no one understands. Everyone feels like that here. I know plenty about loss. I lost my family. I'm not sure there's a minute goes by where I don't think of them. My daughter would be forty now. I could've had grandchildren. Perhaps, someone as pretty as you.'

Why did her words imprint themselves on my soul? Perhaps it was because I was so wired and tuned in that my brain was set to record. Maybe it was only then I considered that others were suffering as well. Her soft voice and the warmth of the fire exhausted me. I knelt on the rug and enjoyed the heat on my face.

'We are your family now. It does get easier, possibly better. We care for each other here. Families argue too, though. We wouldn't be human if we didn't. Don't judge yourself harshly, Katie. Take your time. Find a way to live. Don't hurt yourself, or others. Don't leave us. If it gets too much, remember we're here to help. Go to sleep on things, you can always do something drastic in the morning.'

I shivered, and she rose from her seat. She picked up a blanket and placed it over my hunched shoulders. She stroked my hair as we stared into the flames.

'Life will be better tomorrow.'

I appreciated her words and kindness at the time. I knew I was safe there. As for those words, I kept them with me. They were my mantra, and, for a child, they are usually true. I would need them later when I needed to survive. I also realised the truth of what she said. Don't give people all that you have, because if they take it, you're left with nothing.

In prison, many years later, I would ponder her little phrase about sleeping on things. I decided that there is always hope, and I believe that still. But there will come a time in everyone's life when tomorrow appears hopeless.

17
APRIL

MISSING NANCY

Maleeha and I recovered from Nancy's absence by spending even more time together. I found her history interesting. She was brought up as a modern Muslim. They followed their religion loosely, much the same as most people follow Christianity. Yet, there were lines that couldn't be crossed, and she had run through all of them. Her life had changed more than mine had, and that's not considering the fact her children were growing up without her.

Strangely, we never discussed my case. I'd rebuffed Nancy's probing questions to a certain degree. Eventually in jail, I was able to put it to the back of my mind. It began to feel like it all happened to a stranger whom I once knew. When I hear Maleeha's tale, I could be listening to any of hundreds of women's prison stories I heard over the years.

Her abuse was physical and sexual. That is what you'd expect, but it could have been emotional, financial or psychological. Constantly being put down or ridiculed is a form of torture. Being told you're worthless or kept without money and possessions can be harder to bear than a beating. The relentless nature of it chips away at an individual's self-worth. The inability to change their path, or their children's, causes them to snap and then futures are ruined and lives are lost.

I realised early on in prison that many of the inmates were victims as well as villains. A traumatic upbringing was a common theme. People got into destructive cycles from young ages and lacked the skills and help to break the pattern. It's not an excuse for our behaviour, but perhaps an explanation.

Maleeha always wanted to talk about her children which seemed strange as she hadn't seen them for so long. Someone, a kind relative perhaps, had sporadically sent her pictures. These were her treasured possessions. I would listen because that's all she needed. I often thought it would have been better for her to let go but when I considered that properly, I realised I was wrong. There are things from which you can't move on.

We talked about Nancy. I saw that she had been the most upbeat of us, yet she was the one who'd never had it easy. She'd given up on life some time ago. Maybe she cried herself to sleep at night but I didn't think so. Nancy still had the capacity for fun and she loved to laugh. There would be no changing her casual racism, rude questioning, or her light-fingered ways, but we missed her.

We only need to sign in twice a day at our house now, and once a week we must visit the probation office. Tim Thorn is away on holiday, so we don't even have to see him. It's strange. I've only been free a few months and I'm jaded. In prison you had acquaintances more than friends, but there were always people about and the routine to keep you occupied. Everything on the outside costs money we don't have.

'Can we get a job?' asks Maleeha.

Sally had arrived a few minutes ago for her late shift and was filling in paperwork when we found her in the office. A perceptive look creeps onto her face, though.

'I'm so pleased that you've asked. It's one of the positive signs we hope to see.'

'We're bored.'

'Ah, Katie. How can you be? There's a whole world out there. Go for a walk. The art galleries might be a nice thing to do. Watch people. Laugh at the students who think they know it all and mostly don't.'

The thousands of students trigger a mixed response in me. It's great to see youngsters laughing and enjoying themselves. Most are extremely polite, even the drunken ones. That said, I feel an element of jealousy at their carefree lives. I'm sure they feel pressure from exams and deadlines, but it must be wonderful to have a whole life of possibility and excitement ahead of you.

I wonder if my life could have been different. The prison tutors all thought I had an aptitude for learning. I breezed the tests I revised for. I even have vague recollections of being told I was bright at school. Put some effort in they said, but I could never engage. I existed in a bubble waiting for the next awful thing to happen.

'We want money, Sally,' I add.

'Ah, now you're being honest.'

It's true. I didn't care about clothes and make-up in prison. I wasn't bothered about perfume and stationery, and all the other things people focused on collecting. Why spend cash on a writing pad when the library would give you plain paper for free?

This world is different. It's changed. We saw the other revellers that night at the club and felt separate. It was like we'd gone through a time warp from a previous period. I want to fit in, not stick out. I know I'm being manipulated by advertisers, yet I yearn to be glossy. I need those new running shoes and the latest hair colour.

Maleeha spent all of her savings on a modern phone and fiddles with it for hours. I'm not sure what she's doing, but she looks happy. She drifts off into some virtual space and ignores me — sometimes in the middle of a conversation. I laugh thinking what Mrs Gill in the children's home would have done if you'd absentmindedly stared at your mobile while she spoke to you.

However, I kind of understand. The fact your phone can take videos still sounds like magic, never mind what Facebook, Instagram and Twitter are all about.

There is one part of my life that I have to change immediately: my tattoos. There is a parlour in town with the fattest man I've ever seen working in it. He chats to me like an old friend whenever I pop in and flick through the brochures. Everything is so expensive, though. I tried to flirt with him a little. Not too much, just to see if there was a discount to be had for friendly banter. He laughed his head off, and said, 'Good try.'

'What sort of job do you want then, ladies?' asks Sally.

Obviously, we'd discussed it. Maleeha at least had worked before, but she'd been an administrator in a children's day nursery.

'We'll do anything,' Maleeha says. 'Together if possible. I assume we can't work with children?'

'No, there are rules for people like you.'

There's that phrase again. I didn't like the sound of that at all. 'What rules?'

'You're unable to work with vulnerable people for a start. That includes kids. You both had sentences over four years, so if an employer asks you to disclose any previous convictions then you must, or you're breaking the law.'

'I bet that would be another reason to get recalled to prison,' I say.

'It would.'

'I imagine employers are treading over each other to employ people like us, as you so nicely put it.'

'Calm down, Katie. A lot of companies don't ask as it's not important to what they do. You do have to be aware that with such a big student population here, many jobs are filled by them.'

'That doesn't sound promising,' Maleeha says.

'You'll find there are quite a few roles they don't like and won't do.'

'That sounds even less promising.' I laugh but feel down.

'There is a company we work with that will take anyone we send to them.'

Maleeha and I glance at each other and pull hopeful, cautious faces.

'Doing what?' we ask in unison.

'Putting magazines in envelopes. Minimum wage but they'll pick you up from the bottom of the road at four p.m. and bring you back at ten p.m. Money paid weekly straight into your bank account.'

'We don't have accounts!' we both shout together.

'No problem. We can sort that tomorrow afternoon if you like?'

Later, I return to the kitchen as I can't settle in my room. Maleeha is the same. We keep stealing looks at each other and grinning. Another girl has arrived to replace Nancy. She is about as interested in talking as Firestarter upstairs, but she does sit downstairs to eat with us. Even she picks up on our energy.

'What's new?'

'Sally got us a job,' I say.

'Really? Can everyone have one?'

'She said so, after you've been here a little while.'

It is the first time I've seen her smile. She makes no further comment, and we carry on eating in silence. I can't believe I'll be working and don't care what it is. I think of those students with the excitement of an undecided future and I feel the same way.

18
MY FIRST JOB

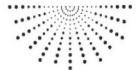

It's two weeks later and we nervously wait at the meeting point. Sally told us to wrap up warm which seemed strange. Regardless, we sweat in our coats under the early April sun. A minibus arrives packed full of foreign-looking folk and we sit at the front in the remaining spots. We wonder why they are empty until we find there are no seatbelts. The way the driver drives, I suspect they've just wiped the previous occupants off the inside of the windscreen.

He speeds to an industrial estate twenty minutes down the road. We are first out. A tall Asian man with thick glasses beckons us over as the rest trudge through a huge open garage door. There are cheap chairs around a horseshoe of tables. The others sit down, many of them flex their fingers. A beeping van makes us step away, and he reverses into the doorway.

'You are Sally's girls?'

We nod.

'Good. You're here for six hours. There's a ten-minute break for a cigarette or whatever after three hours. Visit the toilet before your shift starts, but obviously go if needs be. We have work for six hours and that's what we pay you for. If we have to stay late to get it done, we will do. Any questions?'

We shake our heads. A cool breeze blows through the high-ceilinged building.

'Don't look so worried. You're stuffing letters, how hard can it be? I don't care what you do while you work. Talk, sing, or dance if you want. We usually leave a little early if everyone keeps moving. You'll get a payslip on Friday and your money will be in your account the following week. I'll give you a tax code and a bank form tonight. Return it to me by tomorrow.'

And that was it. We have a job. Us, eleven East Europeans and three Iraqis sit in a chilly warehouse and put magazines in envelopes for six hours. Nearly all listen to music through earpieces connected to their phones. No one cares about us, our history, or my prison tattoos. In fact, I see a few more. There's no slave driving from the bosses. There is no need. These people work fast.

It's mind-numbing, of course. Maleeha talks about her kids. I tell her a little about what happened to my parents. I don't mention my brother, Billy. We eat the packed lunch Sally sent us off with when it reaches our break. We enviously watch other workers sip hot drinks from thermos flasks. An older gentleman notices and, without talking, pours a small amount each into two polystyrene cups. It is good strong coffee.

I point out how much we'll get paid for the shift. £40, more or less. Every time I say the amount, I laugh. When you've been earning £2 per day for sixteen years, it's a fortune. I think that's why the others work in an easy-going, relaxed manner. They're under little pressure and are probably making the same as a doctor back in their own countries.

Maleeha and I discuss what we'd like to buy. There are so many things that, all of a sudden, £40 doesn't seem so much. Then I realise we'll be paid this every day. We will be rich. She wants new clothes. Her other focus is a savings account for her children.

I feel like saying her need is greater than theirs at this point, but it's not a time for negativity and I keep quiet.

Later, she gets onto a story about falling in love when she was at school and only sixteen. It's weird, she says, but even though they only kissed a few times and knew because of their faiths it couldn't go any further, she thought about him when she was inside all the time. I tell her to find him, but she soon returns to the subject of her kids.

It makes me remember the first boy I loved. I was only nine, and we only ever held hands. Yet, I thought of him in the same way Maleeha had. I'm not sure I can describe what we had. Unconditional love is perhaps closest. As the last hour ticks by we slip into the past and silence, and I remember Tommy.

19

THE FIFTH MEMORY - AGE NINE

I had been in the children's home for a few months when I first met Tommy. Mrs Gill told me a boy was coming back to them for the third time, and he would make a good friend. I'd kept to myself since arriving there. Most of the children were older and were uninterested in me. One said there's no point in making friends as they only leave.

I went to a new school, and the attitude was similar. I wasn't lonely as such because I'd built a wall around myself to protect me from getting hurt. I read books and watched television. There was no fun. We lived near a historic home called Thorpe Hall. A teacher told me its spooky history. There was a little wood to hide in. Not the place for a nine-year-old girl to hang around on her own, but I did.

I waited in reception with Mrs Gill for Tommy to arrive. They dropped him off with a huge suitcase that was way too big for him to carry himself. A young man ruffled his hair, said, 'See you, Squirt,' and that was it.

Mrs Gill looked at the large case and then our little arms.

'Welcome back. You'll have to help Tommy with that up to room five.'

Tommy was shorter and skinnier than me. He had an uneven crew cut and a small squint in his left eye. He glanced at his belongings. 'Front or back?'

'Pardon?'

'Which would you like to carry?'

'Oh. Front.'

'Deal.'

It took an hour. The case fell open twice and finally split down the spine. We ended up carrying his clothes up on each half. I almost dropped my end when a door we were passing slammed open, and a girl frowned at us. Tommy piped up, 'Did you order the stew, madam?'

Unpacking his things was depressing. Everyone here turned up with pretty much the same stuff. There was always a child's toy, some unloved clothes, and a few delicately handled worn photographs. Tommy had a small bar of soap from a hotel which for some reason made me want to cry.

'Why did you have to come back, Tommy?'

He shrugged. 'The woman hurt her back a while ago. It didn't get better, so she couldn't keep the place clean. There were two other foster kids there, but they were both nearly eighteen and would be going soon. Last in, first out. You know how it is.'

I didn't. "Woman" also seemed a cold term. 'This is your third time here?'

'Yup.'

'Are you sad?'

He peered at me over his smudged glasses as though he'd never been asked that before.

'A little. It's hard to keep moving. Just as you settle in at school or get used to the others, that's when it happens. Back you come. Although, I reckon the foster carer took me on for the money. She was kind and pleasant, but I felt like a guest at a B and B.'

At my confused face, he explained. 'My mum and I visited a hotel once. A B & B is a small one of those. It's okay here. Mrs

Gill's got time for you if you pretend to cry. There're always kids to play with. There are rules but you have more freedom in a children's home than you do elsewhere. It's not all rosy. The washing-up here is brutal and everyone's too busy nicking each other's stuff. Still, you're not likely to get abused.'

I was unsure what abused meant, but I liked him. I didn't want him thinking I was stupid.

'What's your name?'

'Katie.'

'Well, Katie. What will we do this afternoon?'

'I'm not sure.'

'What would you do if I wasn't here?'

I'd told no one about my special place. I loved the fact I saw nobody down there. I decided to take a risk.

'There is a stately home near here. You can climb through a fence at the end of the cow's field and there's a secret garden.'

'A garden. With flowers?'

'No, it's wild. There's water, I throw stones. We can hide there. It's quiet. It even has a big log for picnics.'

'Pirates?'

'Their boats are still there, but I killed them all.'

'Sounds interesting.'

'And, Tommy, the house is haunted.'

That got his attention. 'Sounds fun. How do we get there?'

'We can walk, but I have a bike.'

'Listen to you! I like you more and more.'

'But I don't know how to ride one.'

'I do, I'll teach you. We're going to have a blast.'

His energy fizzed and I bought into it. We found my bicycle in a dusty corner of the garage. Tommy wobbling around on it made me remember Uncle Jack after he'd been to the office on a Friday night. Weird how electricians had to work on a Friday night. I didn't think Tommy had much to teach me, and sure enough, he fell off with a laugh.

We pushed the bike. Tommy reckoned it'd be safer to learn on grass. At the front door, Mrs Gill asked Tommy and me where we were off to. He stood there in his too long shorts, battered trainers and ill-fitting T-shirt and gave her a serious nod. Then, he reached up and put his arm round my shoulder and winked.

'We're going on an adventure.'

I had my first proper friend.

WE HAD ALMOST twelve months together. It was the best year of my life. He was in the same school as me, just a year ahead. He would search for me at playtime and wait to walk back after school. I wasn't alone anymore. His infectious humour had the teachers laughing as well as the kids. He raised my standing purely by being with me. I began to make friends with others, too.

When school finished, we would race home and he made everything exciting. His bike lessons were abysmal. I didn't think I was cut out for cycling as I struggled to trust people. He persisted and would push me as fast as he could, shouting, 'Pedal, pedal,' while running alongside gasping and chuckling. We bruised and grazed together.

We ran riot around the grounds of Thorpe Hall which we seemed to have to ourselves. Even the cows left in winter. We conkered in autumn and rolled down the grassy slopes in summer. Tommy grew wider and taller overnight, but nothing changed. He still gave me lifts on the crossbar of my small bike.

In the deepest copse there was a lake. Well, it seemed like one to our young eyes. A big old sycamore tree stood beside it with thick branches growing out over the water. We'd sit for hours up there, balancing on branches and giggling over the little fish.

We were always going to make a swing but the lack of a rope made it difficult. Tommy stole bed sheets once and rolled an old tyre down there. He fell in with a mighty splash. That would have been funny enough, but the shallowness of the water got the biggest laugh. We believed it was bottomless, yet it failed to reach his hips.

I'd heard at school that the house was haunted. That added an extra element of spice to the dusk. Once we were near the huge building and Tommy pointed at a bus stop on the main road. There was a woman waiting, dressed in old-fashioned clothing. The bus turned up and didn't stop but, after it left, she was gone. We ran off in a panic. I even sneaked into Tommy's bed that night as I was sure we'd seen a ghost.

If everything's going well, one of the joys of being young is to think things will never change. Tommy was convinced he would stay at the home. Who would want an eleven-year-old boy? Other kids came and left, but we both stayed. I suspect Mrs Gill had some involvement in that. In the end, our fates weren't hers to decide. That is when it all went wrong again.

20
WORK

Through our jobs, we re-joined life. Soon we took our phones and listened to music like the others. There was no dancing while we stuffed those never-ending envelopes, but we did have a laugh. As time passed, we'd sit with strangers and chat to them about their lives. I quickly realised that everyone fights their own battles.

The person who scowled at me a few nights back and left me perturbed had buried her mother a few days before. Another who ignored my polite questions had been in agony with sciatica but had to work as he was the only one in his house with a job. We are all born to suffer.

Reading the news, I had believed the immigrants rushed here to steal our jobs. The truth was different. Many had come from extreme poverty. To provide for their families, they moved countries and cultures and left their loved ones behind. When I asked one of the foremen why he employed nearly all foreigners, he replied that they couldn't get the staff otherwise.

At times, I recalled a young girl in prison taking courses hoping to better herself. There'll be no computing jobs or management roles for me, but I don't regret it. Keeping occupied was the most important thing, and I'll be sorted if I ever need to order food in Spain.

My relationship with Maleeha deepens as the weeks go by. But there's an iceberg coming into view — we can't stay at the premises forever. This morning, Sally has arranged for her friend from the council to come in and see us.

'Okay, girls. This is Yvette from the housing department. We worked together for a while, so I've called in a favour.'

'That's not true. She promised me dinner afterwards,' said Yvette.

They pass a comfortable smile between each other. Maleeha and I do the same. Yvette starts the interview.

'I find it's best to ask what you want, and then we can go from there.'

'We would like a two-bedroom flat together,' says Maleeha.

Sally and Yvette share another look.

'Do you have any money?' asks Yvette.

Maleeha's blank face is the answer. This could take all day, so I interrupt.

'We've only got a few quid. We can't afford a deposit, but we'd like somewhere together. It needs to be safe. A flat would be perfect, but maybe that's a plan for the future. At the moment, we will be fine if we're in the same place. If it has to be a shared house, then we'd prefer a female-only one.'

'Good,' says Yvette after giving me a respectful nod. 'We have to be realistic about things. There's a housing crisis in this country. With immigration running at massive levels, the council housing stock is being taken up like never before. In a nutshell, we aren't building enough houses for the people who need them. Therefore, we have to prioritise. The vulnerable and children come first, and, if I'm honest, that doesn't leave much for anyone else.'

'What does that mean? Are we going to be homeless?'

'Let her finish, Maleeha,' says Sally.

'There is private housing available. However, for those places, you must pay a month's deposit or more, and a month's rent up front. There will be administrative charges too. Cambridge is one of the most expensive cities in the country. Even if you live in the cheaper areas like Arbury, you are looking at £1000 per month rent, so that's £2500 at the start.'

She might as well have said £25,000. I laugh, thinking about our £200 a week from the packing job. I sink into my seat with despair. Maleeha gets angry.

'That's crazy. We can't afford that. I thought you paid housing benefit for those on reduced wages?'

'That's right, we do. But only £600 per month.'

She paused while we got our heads round whether we could afford the shortfall between us. £200 each seemed reasonable.

'You would also have to factor in all the extras such as heating bills and council tax, perhaps another £500 per month. Maybe more if you don't want to eat cheese on toast most nights.'

Maleeha slouched too, almost beaten. 'We're a team. We stick together.'

'What we can offer is £80 a week towards a room in a shared house. Now that includes the bills, so all you'd need to spend money on is clothes and food. Sally let me know you were leaving soon. So I kept an eye out. We have a new landlord who will take benefits clients and is happy for us to be responsible for the deposit. Any damage you do, we pay for. We're trusting you.

'It's a four-bedroom house, single rooms only, of either sex. It isn't in the best part of town, but if you two live there, then you are half the occupants. Hopefully, at least one of the others will be nice, maybe even both. It's a start. Small steps. You can save and move on when you're ready.'

I grin at Yvette. Clever cow. She knocked us down and then built us up. She's right. It is something. We could make it nice. The painters are leaving this evening, and the change in the house is staggering. There's a light, summery feel to the place even on a grey day like today. Mad what a bit of magnolia can do.

'Maybe Tammy upstairs would move in as well?' asks Maleeha.

We still see little of her despite Maleeha's best efforts. Maleeha has taken it on herself to be her champion but has failed so far. God knows what Tammy does all day because she's rarely out. However, as a housemate, she is harmless if you forget her history. Sally reminds us of those issues.

'Unfortunately, due to her offending, she wouldn't be suitable for that sort of property.'

'What sort of property is she suitable for?' I ask.

The best thing about Sally is she doesn't feel the need to hide the truth.

'Very few. Specialist places like this are few and far-between, and you can't stay in them forever.'

'Will the council help her?' I look at Yvette.

'We've dealt with Tammy before. She's had every help. She didn't pay her rent or bills and then went to jail. There's so many people in need, that you can't keep giving people chances.'

I've never thought about it like that before. The papers make it out to be whichever government is in charge's fault, or even the councils. They have a tough job to do.

We all shake hands and send Yvette on her way with our completed application forms. She jokes about the lack of dinner from Sally. Tammy's plight makes me consider my own views on life. I believe I have a chance now. In just a few months, I've found work, a friend, and a place to stay. What could I achieve in years?

However, I will myself not to think of the past. Could I live the rest of my life without thinking about it ever again? I feel the hatred inside of me, for myself, and all the others responsible. There is unfinished business and I don't know if I'll be able to move on until those thoughts are dragged into the light. They are issues for another day. I need to build a base and some happiness before I return to that dark time.

The painter, whose name I've never known, stands behind us as we shut the door. He has paint flecks on his face and looks like a snowman sneezed on him.

'We've finished early, so we're off now,' he says to me.

'Okay, well, you've done a nice job, but I'm not paying you.'

Maleeha laughs but he doesn't. In fact, he looks nervous.

'Look, I wanted to say goodbye. We've enjoyed working here with you lot making us cups of tea and stuff.'

Maleeha nudges me obviously, and his neck flushes red.

'Years ago, I was in a place similar to this. I was younger than you, but it still felt like a big hole to get out of. You can do it. You remind me of my mum, Katie. She put up with loads and came out the other side. When I remember, I think of her strength. You've a whole life to grab, if you want it.'

'Not the smoothest chat up line I ever heard,' giggles Maleeha.

He laughs. 'You're both pretty, but I've got kids now. I know all about how absent parenting screws them up. I'm happy and way too tired to cheat on anyone. My focus is my children having two parents and a solid base in life to spread their wings from. Anyway, I just wanted to say good luck.'

His comments cause us both to stifle sobs. I step forward and hug him. It's fantastic to see he means what he's said. I turn to Maleeha with happy tears and watch her flee to her room. He leaves with similar haste.

Maleeha and I have an important meeting today with a tattoo parlour in town. She's been great and came with me to flick through the brochures. The guy who runs it is covered in some bizarre stuff, but he's half the price of the big man around the corner. He said he was building up his business, hence the low price. I've decided on four, simple, yellow roses on each finger. He said the design needed to be solid to cover up the blue ink.

I can't wait to get it done. I should be grateful that I didn't have love and hate done when I was in prison like some I've seen. Instead, I had four diamonds on the first part of each finger where it joins the hand on one side. The other has clubs on it. Incredible really, as I'd never played cards. I keep my hands in my pockets wherever possible.

On my right bicep, I have a skull and crossbones with the word revenge under them. Again, it's in the same faded blue ink. I like the idea but it's so badly drawn, a three-year-old with a crayon could've done a better job. My left shoulder has a small smudged cross on it. It always makes me laugh when I see UK prison films and they have perfect inks all over their bodies. Reality is different. I also received a week in solitary as they are illegal. It was just as well because the shoulder one got infected and I needed antibiotics. I'm lucky not to have caught worse.

I bound up the stairs and knock on her door. 'Come on, we need to get a move on.'

No answer.

'Maleeha, are you okay? I'm coming in.'

She hasn't locked the door which is a good sign, but she has changed from upset to wild and out of control. She paces backwards and forwards with a moist sheen on her top lip.

'Hey, calm down.' I pull her toward me and hold both her hands to stop them swinging around. 'What's wrong? The painter was just making throw away comments. Ignore them. Let's go get our tattoos and have a laugh.'

'The tattoos are your thing. I can't stand it anymore. When I think I'm progressing, a simple comment drags me back to the start. I miss my children. All this other stuff doesn't seem real. How can it improve for me?'

Maleeha was going to have a dove on her ankle as a sign of her new freedom, and because she wanted to be involved. That wouldn't happen now. I don't know what to say to her. It always feels like I'm trying to fix unsolvable problems. Perhaps a different tack is needed.

'It's time to move on. You can't go back to that life. The past has gone. We must build something new, but that's going to be impossible if we crumble every time we're reminded of what we've lost. Come on, today can be a fresh beginning.'

I didn't expect to persuade her and I don't. She smiles though, and it's unsettling. She reminds me of the women who would wish everyone goodnight on the wing, then return to their cells and self-harm in the most unspeakable ways. There's peace in deciding on a certain path and knowing you aren't going to waver.

'You go, Katie. I'll come next time.'

I know I'm being played, but this is important to me.

'Okay, next time, yeah?'

She closes the door on me which isn't like her. I trot down the stairs. She'll be here when I get back. I'll only be gone a few hours. What's the worst that could happen?

21
TATTOO TIME

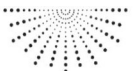

The tattooist gives me a *you're late and I'm hacked off* look. I sit in the seat and it's not dissimilar to going to the dentist's. I don't remember it hurting the first time they inked me on the fingers. Perhaps I was out of it because boy does it sting.

'There's not much fat there, so the needle isn't cushioned. Embrace the discomfort. It's a symbolic moment, pain is part of the experience.'

Easy for him to say. I grit my teeth and try to relax.

'Tattoos fade on your fingers, so you'll need to get them touched up.'

'Yeah, how long?'

'Depends what you do with your hands.' He likes his little joke.

'I'm not a pot washer if that helps.' He doesn't laugh at mine.

'If it starts to look like one on an old sailor, it's time.'

Two hours later, he's done. He wraps loose bandages around both hands and plucks the fifty quid off the table where I'd left it. He gives me a leaflet on aftercare, says he's closing, and ushers me out. It's one of the most addictive things I have ever done. I'm going back in the morning to check out images for my bicep. I can't wait.

Leaving the shop, I want to tell everyone in the street what I've done. They look amazing. I'm dying to uncover them and buy something, so someone has to glance at my fingers to get the money. He told me not to do anything until tomorrow and the first twenty-four hours is the most important stage, so I swagger home.

I rush up to Maleeha's room, but it's locked when I try the handle after not getting a reply. Sally's in the kitchen.

'Did you see Maleeha?'

'She said she had to nip out. What happened to your fingers?'

I can't help laughing and slide off the bandages.

'Wow, very nice. Quite an improvement. Where did you have it done?'

'Tom's Tattoos.'

'Okay. Did you try Shemanskin's on the edge of town?'

'We had a little look, but the price was miles higher.'

'That's because he's miles better.'

'Yeah? You secretly got a bullseye on your backside?'

'Cheeky! We get many girls in here with dodgy blue ink. Jan Shemanski runs it. You should have said. He does a special deal for ex-prisoners. Apparently, it's a thing back in Poland. Freedom Tattoos I think they're called. People still judge tattoos, but it is changing if they're done well. Yours look nice now. Are you having any more?'

Sally is a handy person to know. I show her the smudged mess on my arm.

'Tell him I sent you. He's a decent bloke. Careful though, Jan's a ladies' man, and he'll like you. You may like him too.'

I'm not sure what to take from that, but before I can ask I remember my friend. 'Did Maleeha say where she was going?'

'No. She said she'd be late, but not to worry.'

We only have to sign in first thing in the morning now, so she has a long time to get up to something before anyone misses her. Except me of course, and I've got a bad feeling.

22

JAN SHEMANSKI

I check with the night staff before they leave if Maleeha came home. She didn't. I'd barely slept anyway and would have heard. Where could she have gone, or what could she have done? I should understand more than most about the perils of thinking about things in the dark. For the first time since they released me I felt like taking something to silence my mind. When the possibilities are limitless, there's no peace. I can't even have a shower this morning to wake me up because of keeping the tattoos dry.

I sign myself in at eight o'clock, and still she's not back. It's pointless waiting. I'm excited as well which is a treacherous feeling. I leave my mobile number with the day staff to text me if she turns up. They fret now, too.

I decided during the night to visit the tattoo parlour that Sally recommended: Shemanskins. I have hope about going there, compared to none for Maleeha. We are at the warehouse this afternoon, so I pray she's back for that. That said, missing a "sign in" is important. It may even be too late for her.

Shemanskins has only just opened when I arrive. I'm the only customer and approach the counter.

'Hi, I'm looking for Jan?'

'You've found him.'

I grin. I need to work on my assumptions because I expected a tall eastern-European, covered in tattoos, who spoke with a heavy accent. Instead, I have a shaven-headed black man of my height. He wears only jeans and a T-shirt. The only tattoo I see on him is a full sleeve on his right arm.

'Sally told me to come.'

His smile is confident and cheeky. She was spot on, I am going to like him. We sit and chat. He's lived here for fifteen years and within a few minutes I can tell he is like nobody I've met before. I think the phrase is *relaxed in his own skin*.

He heard about the programmes to help people back into work with unsightly tattoos through other tattooists. Jan doesn't commit to anything now and does it when he's quiet. He and his partner stopped doing them for a while as word got around and his shop was inundated. In my case, he says mine would be easy to cover, and he'd do it for free. If I wanted to get something bigger done, or more complicated, it would make sense to do it at the same time. For that, I'd receive a discount.

We talk about nothing as he makes me a coffee, and then he gestures to some albums and tells me to have a flick through. I find I'm wondering whether his partner is business or sexual, male or female. I'd prefer it to be a work-related one.

'Have a look and take your time. You'll be wearing it forever, so you can't change your mind afterwards. If you want to chat, pop back, or book yourself in. Enjoy your day, and I'll catch up soon.'

His grip is strong, which is understandable. He disappears out the shop rear when a young girl turns up and stands next to the till. I hang around for over an hour. The place has a good vibe. It's reassuring to see so many normal people popping in. I detect the same air of excitement from them.

I haven't received a call or text about Maleeha. I decide to buy some new clothes to distract myself. It's all rather confusing. Some shops are so expensive and others cheap. I purchase a few things from the latter. Sports Direct is reasonable. I want half the stuff in there. I settle for some leggings, a running top and a vice-like bra. Primark is almost giving it away, so I grab enough items to make one decent going-out ensemble.

I whistle walking home. I'd experienced small buzzes finding bargains at the charity shops, but it's even better getting everything brand new.

The house looks quiet when I return. However, the first person I see when I enter is Tim Thorn. He stands in the kitchen with a stern face. Sally, next to him, turns with a sad expression. A life of disappointment has taught me to cope with bad news, so I walk towards them. Sally steps forward.

'Let me explain, Tim.'

'No, I'll tell her. You've made us look unprofessional. It's your responsibility to make us aware when things aren't progressing. Then we can prevent embarrassing events like last night.' His eyes blaze. 'Close the door on the way out, Sally.'

A worried expression crosses her face. Sally touches my arm. 'We'll have a good chat afterwards. Try not to worry. You'll be fine.'

Tim pours himself a glass of water and gulps it down; his professional probation office persona is absent.

'Well, Katie. And then there was one.'

'What's that supposed to mean?'

'First, Nancy back in prison. Now, Maleeha. Nancy will be free soon, but she's had her last chance in a place like this. As for Maleeha. They aren't so forgiving if you've killed someone in the past, are they, Katie?'

'What did she do?'

'A senseless, idiotic thing. They won't let her out for a long time. Minimum eighteen months I would say. You have to be careful with risky people like her.'

His sneering face implies I'm the same. My body courses with wild emotions. I feel dangerous. As if I could snap and do something regrettable myself. He walks towards me and stands in my personal space.

'Two down, one to go. Do you like freedom? You will need to be whiter than white. What are you prepared to do to stay away from prison?'

I'm tired of his leering eyes and suggestive statements.

'What exactly does that mean?'

His jaw bunches before he talks. 'I own you, Katie. A little error and I can erase your future. In fact, there doesn't have to be a mistake. Who are they going to believe? You?'

For anyone who's been inside, the dream about leaving is not having to obey orders. You've yearned to make your own choices even if they are bad ones. In prison, if you're told to get in your cell, you go. Then that door is locked and there's nothing you can do about it. When you're free, nobody should be able to force you to do anything you don't want to.

It's a right we take for granted all our lives until someone takes it away. I hoped to work where I wanted, see who I liked, and travel anywhere I fancied. I thought no one could stop me.

The truth is different. This man controls me. My destiny lies in his clammy hands. It won't be long before he pushes the boundaries. I know what he's after, and if I refuse to let him have his way, it's all over for me. I've seen enough coercion and bribery in my life to be aware the perpetrators often get away with it. But the victim always loses.

He brushes past me as he leaves. It is only a gentle touch, but I am far enough from the doorway to make it completely unnecessary. The message is received.

Sally returns the moment he steps out of the door and pulls

me into a hug. I don't cry. I can't cry. Yet again, someone I trust has let me down. It's just another time that I've been deserted.

'What did she do, Sally?'

'She got the train back to Leeds. They haven't told me the finer details, but she found out where her children lived. They walk to school. She waited until they were almost there and then approached them.'

'Oh my God. Why would she be so stupid?'

She doesn't answer because it's a daft question. Maleeha's children are still her life. She never moved on. It is a testament to the human spirit she lasted this long. Every day became something to be endured. Every attempt at happiness was just a distraction. I wonder if those few moments with her children were worth it. The horror dawns on me straight away.

'The kids didn't recognise her.'

'No. She lost control. Screamed and begged. I'm not sure who called the police, but, as you can imagine, they were there in seconds.'

'Is she in prison already?'

'Not yet. She's in the cells at the police station. It's only a matter of time.'

'Was Thorn correct? Will she be back there for ages?'

Sally pauses, and wonders whether to sugar-coat it for me. She makes the right call.

'Yes, they'll keep her in for evaluation after doing something like that. A year if she's lucky. She killed their father. They will see it as the moment she got out, even though three months have passed and she has made a lot of progress, she did what they expressly told her not to. It's sensible to think that when they release her again, it's likely she'll do exactly the same thing. She could do the rest of her tariff. That's another eight years.'

Poor girl. She would never serve that time. They gave me a life sentence, and tomorrow morning at the police station they will give Maleeha one of death. My friend is gone. Soon to be a further statistic they find at unlock.

'Don't quit too, Katie. The girls wouldn't want you to — even though they aren't here. You'll still be able to go to that house, and there'll be new friends. Trust me.'

What do I care? Yet again, I let someone in and they left me. I won't be making that mistake again. Nevertheless, when I crawl into bed, my thoughts betray me, and I think of Tommy.

23
THE SIXTH MEMORY - AGE TEN

I stared into the pond, unable to take my turn. Tommy scuffed his shoes and looked away. 'What do you mean, you're leaving?' I asked.

'They've found a family who want to foster me.'

The earth tilted on its axis. Denial came first. 'You said no one would want a child as old as you.'

'Mrs Gill told me they lost a boy my age and wanted to help someone similar.'

'Isn't that creepy?'

'I guess.'

I chewed my lip for a minute. We'd put an old bucket at the end of the pond in the secluded spot at Thorpe Hall grounds where we hid. Tommy was taller now and stronger, so he had to throw the stones at the target. I was allowed to skim them in. His handicap made us about even, and therefore we played it all the time.

'I don't want you to go.' Even though I had a strong arm, my latest stone didn't bounce once. The sinking feeling was mutual.

'I don't want to go either. But she said they're rich. They have a huge house and a flash car. They took me to dinner a few weeks ago. It was a posh restaurant. Napkins and everything. They'll take care of my schooling as well, whatever that means.'

'Why didn't you mention any of this?'

'They picked me up from school. I thought nothing would come of it and tried not to worry you.'

'Thanks for thinking of me, but now it's a really big shock.'

'It'll be a nightmare. When they realise I'm not as good as their son, they'll send me back. It's happened before.'

Neither of us were stupid. Tommy was generally a well-behaved boy. They could do a lot worse. His was the chance of a lifetime. The hope we all had.

'I hate to leave you, Katie. I asked if you could come too, but they only wanted one child.'

'Will you be able to visit?'

'I think so. Why wouldn't they let me? You're my best friend.'

I crouched low and, with fury, launched a stone with extreme force. It bounced on the water three times before clanging the dead centre of the metal bucket. There were no high fives all round. We trudged back in silence.

The process must have started after that lunch as Tommy only had one more week. It seemed strange that people were discussing our futures without considering our thoughts. I resolved to be strong and not cry when the car arrived. But Tommy's crumpled face was too much for me, and I sobbed on his shoulder.

I struggled to regain my composure afterwards and shouted at Mrs Gill.

'Why am I left alone? Why do I always get shat on? Everyone else has it easy.'

Despite me saying that, deep down, it wasn't as heart-breaking as before. Tommy had gone to a better place than the others who deserted me. Many of whom had been heading to the cemetery. Mrs Gill loved her lessons though, and my comments wouldn't go unanswered. She took me into her room and gave me one of her mind-juddering talks.

'We're all alone at times. My husband couldn't handle the loss of our only child. He drank for a bit. Hell, we drank together, but that didn't help. The pain in the morning was too cruel to bear. In the end, he just said he had to go. He didn't say where, and I didn't ask. You see, I was pleased. Everything reminded me of our girl, but nothing more than him. His teeth, his nose, even his chuckle — which thankfully I never heard again — she had inherited perfectly. It was only after he disappeared that I began to heal.

'I even made love again. I was much older than you of course. It was different, but still nice. Not great though, like a strong cup of tea and chocolate from the fridge.'

I wondered what was she going on about? My blank face made her explain.

'Sometimes a low point is from where we build. If you hit the bottom, the only way is up, maybe today is where your luck changes. I have good news for you too, you also have a foster home to go to. A couple called Martha and Arthur not far from here are looking for someone special. You'll be able to attend the same school you're at now as well.'

At the time, those words didn't make much sense. But, as with many of Mrs Gill's sermons, I would not forget them. Years later, I would ponder the lesson within them. As for my new placement? I was happy, but not hopeful. Martha and Arthur sounded like a couple who sang country music. The others at the children's home already had their friends, so I was alone again and fine with leaving. I hadn't bothered making connections because I'd only needed Tommy. Nobody would miss me.

Later, I went to ride my bike to distract myself as I couldn't get him out of my mind. It wasn't where I discarded it in the garage. When I checked with one of the staff members, she said she'd put in in the boot of the car with Tommy when he left. They thought it was his.

She expected me to cry when I explained, but I didn't. I wanted him to have that bike, and I hoped he would remember me every time he sat on it. Oh, Tommy. The last words he cried into my neck were that he'd see me again. He never would.

24
MAY

LEAVING THE NEST

Finally, it's time for me to depart from the safety of the hostel. I pile my things up next to the front door. There are more items than I had when I was released, but still not much for it to be everything. Sally takes me to the kitchen for the paperwork. The other girls who'd arrived to replace my friends wished me good luck, but I'd kept my distance from new relationships. Apart from Jan Shemanski.

I chose extensive designs for my arms and, despite what he said about extra costs, he did them for free. I now have a vivid rose covering the random blue cross that was there. The other arm has a large colourful black and red dragon snaking down from shoulder to wrist. The skull and crossbones smudge is gone. I like the spiritual side of an oriental design, and I love the beauty of the flower after what was there before.

He's also shown me further work which he said would suit. I want more, possibly on my back, but my prison ink is covered now, so I'd need to pay for it. The complicated images I desire would take much longer. We'd gone for coffee and there was an obvious mutual attraction. We shared a few kisses. There was no pressure, so it is only a matter of time. He'd offered to give me a lift to my new place and would be here soon.

'These are the forms to sign, Katie,' says Sally. 'You've been a perfect resident here, so keep that up and all will be fine. Maybe let the others have a bit of hot water as well, and you'll be very popular.'

'Thank you. I don't know what I would have done without your help.'

'Listen to me. You are a strong, clever woman. This is part of your journey. Enjoy your life now. Don't be a stranger and forget us.'

'Of course not.'

'I'm always here for advice.'

'I thought Thorn would have been here to ruin things.'

'He's meeting you there with the keys and to explain the commitments you must maintain for him ongoing.'

I dislike the sound of that and can't stop a grimace forming. Sally nods in agreement.

'Be careful of him. I have nothing concrete to tell you, but I'm a great judge of character, and I don't trust him. Never be alone with him.' Her face drops. 'I also see the odd flash of anger, or something similar, in your eyes. Do not let him provoke you, he holds all the power. I'll come with you today.'

'It's all good, Jan's driving me over and is helping me settle in.'

She shakes her head but smiles.

'Do I need to be wary of him as well?'

'There'll be a lesson there too, but it will be a necessary one. You were away for a long time. Even though you're in your thirties now, you haven't experienced modern life, so take things easy, and do nothing rash. Nice people look like your doctor, remember that.'

The doorbell rings and she steals a final hug.

Jan smiles at the door when I open it. I gesture to my belongings with a wink, and he starts placing them in his car. Stepping outside, there's a moment of joy. I'm starting to believe I can do this. Now, I can live.

THE TRAFFIC as always is dreadful. Jan's small vehicle isn't what I expected. I check out the immaculate plastic interior. It even smells clean.

'I had you for a truck driver. What's this?'

'Really? And you say I stereotype people.' He smiles and rests his hand on my leg as we stop at red lights. It's natural to have him touching me. 'This is a Vauxhall Astra. Very nice. Small engine, virtually no emissions. Perfect for those who have to drive but want to protect the environment.'

'Okay, you're the boss.'

He switches on the CD player. *Destiny's Child - Survivor* begins. Many a girl blared that out of her cell of a night. He accelerates into a clear stretch of road and holds my hand. I'm still not sure if I'm a survivor. I do know that I feel great. Cars fly past on the other side ferrying families, couples, young and old, but all normal. That's what I am today, and it is about time.

It's obvious when we enter the rougher area of town. It isn't even gradual. Jan knows the way and brakes outside a reasonably sized house. There's no front garden, so I step out and knock. Tim Thorn opens the door with a grin that fades as he sees Jan dragging my stuff out of the car.

'Your friend can wait here.'

I've prepared for this moment and know what to say. 'No, it's okay. I want him to hear as well so I don't forget what's expected of me.'

He turns and climbs the stairs. Jan shrugs and follows me up. The room is bare but fine. There are no bedcovers which is probably a good thing. On inspection, the mattress and everything else is new. I can cope with bottom of the range.

Thorn hands me an envelope and tells me he'll see me every week on a Thursday. There isn't any more for him to say, so clearly his visit was unnecessary. He drops my keys on the bedside table with a final filthy stare at Jan, who glares right back, and he's gone.

'Who was that asshole?'

'My probation worker. Nice, isn't he?'

'I think he likes you.' He steps towards me. 'As do I.' He gently kisses me. 'We should celebrate.'

'Are you taking me out for a fancy meal?'

'Whatever you like. Not now though, I need to get to work.'

'Do you have ten minutes for me to show my eternal thanks?'

This time the kissing is not soft. His hands are affectionate and efficient, and soon we're standing naked. He kisses my neck and breasts. My skin burns as he ventures lower. He moves behind me and focuses on my shoulders. A strong grip surrounds my waist and his hardness nudges between my legs.

The past descends and my body freezes in an instant. He turns me around.

'Hey, are you okay? We can stop.'

I guessed I would feel strange at this moment. Perhaps, if I don't continue, it will always be a problem. I make my mind up and kiss his mouth.

'You have to look me in the eyes to have your wicked way.' When he offers a querying half-smile, I say, 'The first time anyway.'

With that, I push him backwards onto the bed, grab his wrists and hold them above his head. He is more than ready, and we fit together like a glove. I haven't done it in this position before. It makes me feel powerful to be in control even though his hips match the force of mine.

Greedy hands break free and squeeze my hips. Our rhythm speeds up and his breathing quickens at the same pace. As his expression changes, I recognise the concern on his face. I whisper, 'Do it,' in his ear and thrust harder.

He hangs around for a respectable amount of time afterwards, considering he has to be somewhere.

'That was great, Katie. Perhaps a little quick.'

'Don't be silly. I loved it. And I can't wait for an encore.'

'Tonight?'

'Tomorrow night. I want to settle in first, and I'd hate to ruin the mattress.'

I watch him drive away. I hadn't lied to him, I enjoyed it, but part of me failed to engage with the whole experience. I suppose that is to be expected.

25
MY NEW HOME

I settle into a routine, but I'm not particularly happy. The house is quiet, and the people are nice. They're busy strangers, though, who have enough in their lives without inviting me in. Thorn is all business when I see him. He seemed distracted this morning which saved me from his overlong stares.

I carry on with my packing job but without Maleeha it's boring. Strange how the absence of just one person can completely change your perspective and enjoyment of a place. The others chatter away in their own languages, leaving me with my music.

As the weeks pass, I see less of Jan. He says work is crazy, and he's only able to meet for short lunches or quick visits to my room. We have a lot of sex, in any position he wants, yet I can't orgasm with him. I sense this is a problem for Jan more than me and fake it on the odd occasion. He shrugs off my apologies, but I can tell it affects him.

I wander around the city and see the sights. Jogging every day and joining a cheap gym helps burn time, but still I'm lonely and don't know what to do about it.

The few things I enjoy doing are solitary experiences. I love the first showing at the cinema when the price is low and there's rarely more than a few people in there, so it feels like a private screening. It's nice to be a voyeur of others' exciting lives even if they aren't real. Yesterday's show was a cheesy romance, but it gave me an idea.

There's a deli near where Jan works. Browsing the aisles, it's a struggle to believe how much olives, sourdough bread and Serrano ham cost. I look around to make sure it isn't someone's idea of a joke. The cutlery borrowed from the kitchen and a blanket I saw in a cupboard are already in my bag, so I fork out. The Italian guy is friendly and happy which isn't surprising at these prices.

I'd taken to wearing gloves and sleeves whenever I saw Thorn. He hadn't noticed the changes I'd made previously due to winter coats and long jumpers. I found I didn't want him seeing much of me. I also remember being punished in prison for getting new tattoos. One of the later arrivals at the house had casually commented on them and asked if probation had taken an up-to-date description of me. I realised I didn't want him to be aware of them as if I knew he'd somehow spoil it. I liked having one up on him, too.

Outside Jan's, I duck into a vacant shop doorway and take off the thin leather gloves. I remove my woollen hat too and fluff out my fringe. It's growing now and doesn't look great. A cut and blow dry is needed, but the prices around here are insane. I smile, knowing Jan spends little time looking at my hair.

The sun is out, so I stuff my belongings into a rucksack. As I'm about to move into the light, Jan's little white car pulls up. A tall thin woman steps from it. The door of the shop opens and Jan kisses her on the cheeks, holds her hands, and beams into her eyes.

I clench my jaw to keep my mouth closed. They kiss deeply and the little voice that told me it might be his sister is quietened.

Jan opens the back door of the car, reaches in, and pulls a squirming child into his arms while I shuffle into the shadows.

There's a moment where I feel like beating him with the picnic bag, but the food is too expensive to waste. The rage dwindles, but I've been used again. Deep down, I always knew it was going nowhere so maybe it's better to find this out now.

The vision of happiness continues in view. Do I want to be like that, or is it too late for me? I decide I'm not going to let him completely off the hook and, with a merry whistle, I swagger past catching his eye. I don't say anything — I don't need to. His wife sees his expression before he has time to regain his composure, and I know that will be the last I hear from him.

Sally was right. I have learned a lesson. There are no regrets, though. My heart is wooden and won't bruise so easily. That experience has cost me little, other than the astronomically priced picnic.

As usual, no one is in the house when I get back, so I kick off my shoes and tuck into the food. It isn't bad, tasty even, but definitely not worth £15. When it's gone, I grow bored but pacing the room only serves to increase my edginess. I have already jogged this morning and decide I might as well use the pent-up energy to sort through my belongings.

Throwing the prison clothes away is therapeutic. It reminds me of how far I've come. Most of the items I kept from that time, such as drawings and odd bits of diaries, go straight in the bin. I want to forget that stage of my life. A proper clean start is needed. What's stopping me from making good friends, getting a fun job, or meeting an honest lover?

The answer — probation. I'm stuck here. If I don't sign on each week with Thorn, he'll notify the police, and I'll be picked up and returned to jail. How can I be free if my happiness is in someone else's power? Even though I didn't tell him about Jan, I'm supposed to report any new relationships, and I can't move home or job without telling him. He has the power to order me to be piss-tested at his whim. Once, he even threatened me with an electronic tag.

Strangely, I think I could reach fruition with Jan now I know he's such a massive weasel. I lie back and contemplate masturbating to burn time. Instead, I trot downstairs with my old prison bag and throw it in the general waste as the council empties the bins later today.

I'm halfway to my room when I remember the Ukrainian girl, Rada. I return to the bag and flick through the paperwork, and sure enough, there's the note she gave me. "Polish Porsche, Fengate." What had she said? To come and see her if I needed help with anything?

The kitchen is empty, so I make a cup of coffee and consider her words. I'd love to meet her again. I need support, I know that, but could she provide it? What help could she really give me, other than the comfort of a welcoming face?

All of a sudden, I feel like this is the moment I've been waiting for. I don't have to sign on for a week. I'm not even working tomorrow and could ring in sick anyway. There's a train every hour too. I'm supposed to tell Thorn, but how would he know? There's the risk I could be seen by someone… I glance at the make-up box the prison officers gave me when I left. Camouflage!

Screw it, I'm going. No one can stop me. The surge of independence makes me laugh out loud. I decide it doesn't even matter if I can't find Rada. I'll have a day out, go shopping, be normal. It's not only Peterborough I can visit; what's stopping day trips to London, sightseeing, or even popping to the coast? How many times had I dreamt of walking along a beach next to the waves?

There isn't really any reason Thorn would stop me going to those places. Yet, I decide I won't be asking for his permission. Space opens up in my mind. Journeys with friends, when I get some, maybe even music festivals are within my grasp. No one is going to drop out of the sky and improve my life. I need to do these things for myself.

There's no way I'll sleep now, but I lie in bed anyway and spend the time thinking. Do I want to visit the places I remember from my youth? Some hold good memories, others terrible. Although, after so long, perhaps many of the bad may have been forgotten. I grab the picture of my parents and wonder how I would feel if they were still alive.

Things couldn't possibly have turned out any worse for me, but it's stupid to dwell on the past. That time has gone, and nothing can be changed. Mai, when she tried to teach me in the prison, would tell me to focus on the here and now. Enjoy my breathing and be present. The future is coming whether we like it or not. Prepare for it. I struggled with that advice behind bars. We argued as I would say that I couldn't 'be present' when I had to share a bathroom with forty women.

She would smile. She was both irritating and calming, and, as I see it now, correct in her advice: "Change what you are able. Be nice. Learn and take pleasure in what surrounds you." I remember shouting in response, 'What? A load of paranoid lesbians!'

Maybe we were both right. I may not have ordinary options, but I still have many. I'm in charge now. There are rules, but I can work around them. Nobody will give me a wonderful life. I must decide on what I want and move towards it with grace and, if possible, happiness. "Enjoy your journey," Mai would say. "To choose not to is crazy."

I will try to take her advice as my newfound confidence teeters on the brink of hopefulness. Fond memories of her soft skin and calm voice lull me to sleep. Peterborough will still be there tomorrow. If I'm honest, it's unlikely anyone will care if I visit or not. That said, I recall the last time I returned to a place with hope and that was a big disappointment.

26

THE SEVENTH MEMORY - AGE ELEVEN

The people they sent me to, Martha and Arthur, were an old couple who had been fostering for years. They lived in a pleasant neighbourhood close to my school. I could walk if I wanted, but Martha usually drove me. We had a home-cooked meal most evenings and the odd takeaway for a treat. It should have been perfect.

However, a few days before I left the children's home, Donna, one of the other girls there, knocked on my door. She told me she'd been to that house and the old guy was a pervert. Donna had a reputation for being full of shit, so I assumed she was just winding me up. Nevertheless, I still had a word with Mrs Gill.

She explained that Donna was a troubled girl. Social services placed her with them but she had proven disruptive and chaotic. Martha and Arthur couldn't handle her. She was out all hours, rarely at school, and hung around with older undesirable people. They gave up on her after they found her passed out drunk in the front garden at seven a.m. after a night of worry.

This all rang true. The other boys in the home called her Donna-do-you-wanna due to her willingness to do more-or-less anything with little persuasion. Needless to say, I was cautious. I ended up spending six months with the couple before it was ruined.

The police and social services collected me from school one morning with all the possessions from my bedroom. Next thing, I was in Mrs Gill's office surrounded by adults. Mrs Gill did the talking.

'Katie, you've been brought back to us because serious accusations were made about Arthur. We need to ask you some questions. You must be completely honest with us. Do you understand?'

'Yeah.'

'Did you feel comfortable living with Martha and Arthur?'

I felt uncomfortable in front of four adults, but as far as I knew I had done nothing wrong.

'Yes, pretty much.'

They all glanced at each other.

'Were you comfortable with Arthur in particular?'

'Yes, most of the time. It was weird at the start.'

Again, there were concerned looks.

'Can you be more specific?'

'Well, it was odd to begin with, they're strangers, and I'm in their house. I knew to be polite and stuff, but there wasn't a list of rules like there is here. Donna also told me that Arthur was a pervert before I went. I mentioned that before, remember? So obviously I was a little wary.'

'Did he behave unusually around you?'

'No, to be honest, I didn't see him much when I first arrived. Mostly just mealtimes and the evening, you know, in front of the television. Donna told me he used to watch her in the garden and was often hanging around outside the bathroom when she came out.'

'Was he ever outside the bathroom when you left it?'

'Sure. A couple of times. It's not a big house. I was paranoid to start with. After a while I settled in. They were nice people. Arthur took me to places.'

'What places?'

'Parks, McDonald's, a few restaurants, the museum, even a football match once which was cool. I'd never been to one before.'

'Did he ever take you shopping?'

'No, he never got involved in any of that stuff. My period started when I was there. Martha spoke to me about it and threw the sheets away. It was no bother. The truth is, I'm happy.'

'Arthur never did anything to make you anxious?'

'Nope. Almost the reverse. They're both really gentle. I dropped a dish once. Martha had spent all morning making a massive lasagne, and I offered to help carry it even though she warned me it was heavy. The dish slipped through the oven gloves and smashed on the floor. It was embarrassing, and worrying as I've been belted for less.'

'What did they do?'

'They smiled. Said not to mind and accidents happen. They have a little fat spaniel. His name is Smarty. I called him Farty because he did that a lot. He thought it was Christmas. Never seen him move so fast. Martha laughed her head off. Arthur got his coat and said he was off to the chippy. Like I told you, they're cool.'

This time there were resigned shrugs and sad glances in the room. Mrs Gill gave them a nod, and the rest left us alone.

'Does that mean I can go back now?'

'I'm afraid not, Katie. I'm sorry.'

'But why? He did nothing wrong. That Donna's a liar, you know that.'

'She is, but unfortunately, she filed an official complaint and accused him of touching her.'

'She made it up!'

'That's probably the truth. But we can't send you back. If something ever did happen, I'd never forgive myself.'

'What if I want to go? It's my choice, isn't it?'

'Not under these conditions. Try not to worry. It will be lovely to have you here again, I missed you.'

As my predicament sank in, the emotion I felt was helplessness. It was a familiar sense of falling.

'Come on,' Mrs Gill eventually said. 'I'll show you to your new room. There's a surprise in there for you.'

I wandered behind her, nodding at a few of the usual faces. Luckily, I didn't see Donna because I don't know what I would have done. Then it occurred to me that Tommy might have returned. As we approached the last door on the first floor, I pictured him sitting on my bed grinning. Perhaps, being back wouldn't be too bad after all.

Mrs Gill pushed opened my door and pointed in the corner. Instead of Tommy waiting for me it was my old bike.

'They brought your bicycle back. Tommy said they put it in with his things by mistake.'

'He's here?' I asked with a voice full of hope.

'No, his foster parents dropped it off.'

I would have loved to see him more than anything. 'Will I be able to visit him?'

'No. We find it's best for children to have a fresh start.'

'Can I have his address at least?'

'We can't give that out. It's a child protection issue.'

It all finally got too much and my shoulders heaved with the ensuing sobs. Mrs Gill pulled me into an embrace and stood there swaying with me for the age it took for me to control myself. As she left, I followed her to stand in the doorway, tears still streaming down my face.

She stopped halfway along the corridor. 'We'll find somewhere for you, Katie.'

I shook my head. 'There's no point. It's not fair and I give up.'

She pondered that statement and agreed. 'Life can be cruel.'

With a resigned shrug, she walked out of sight. I gently closed the door to lock the world away. She didn't need to say that. I knew it already.

27
BACK IN THE 'BORO

I step off the train as it arrives in Peterborough. It's overcast but warm. I'd caught the eleven o'clock train so there were few onboard. I chose a fitted white T-shirt, jeans and ankle boots as my new look. When I stared in the mirror at home, I had to stifle a laugh. With my sunglasses on, I looked so different from the pasty girl who arrived at the start of the year.

I catch admiring looks from the odd man. There are glances from both sexes at the tattoo on my arm which snakes down to the one on that hand. This time though, I fit in. I'm just another person with their own individual style. There's nobody checking tickets at the exit, so I throw my coat over my shoulder and stroll to the bus station.

Peterborough has changed. It's the same old cathedral in the background towering over everything, but the people are different. I thought the prison had become multicultural during my stay there, yet it's nothing compared to the different races and accents I see and hear on my short walk.

'Big Issue?'

I freeze. It's a voice from the past. I stride over to a girl, well, a woman now although creature might be more appropriate. She was in the cell next to me for six months a few years into my sentence. I can't remember her actual name, but all the prisoners and most of the staff called her Flakes on account of her dandruff. She said it was due to eczema. It's a harsh condition as her hair was beautiful.

She was a sweet kid. Thick as pig shit and easily exploited but kind and pretty. She got a nasty sentence for looking after her boyfriend's gun. She refused to rat on him. Then, after she was sentenced, he dropped her. She made excuses for him for months until another inmate who knew them both explained he'd moved in with his girlfriend.

She wasn't the same after that. Maybe it was that which broke her because looking at her now, the years have been brutal. It looks like she hasn't washed her hair since I last saw her.

'Go on, I haven't sold one all day.'

I decide to try out my new disguise and remove my sunglasses.

'How much are they?'

'Two and a half quid.'

'What?'

'Just give us some change if you don't want to read it.'

Her dead-eyed expression displays no recognition or emotion. I press a pound coin into her shaking hand.

'Use it wisely, Flakes.'

This time I see the beginnings of a toothless smile.

'Yeah, that's my name.'

She packs her stuff away and leaves to spend that pound before I can ask her if she knows which bus I need to catch. I have to queue at the information desk. Talking makes my cheeks feel stiff with the heavy make-up on them. There isn't a route out to the industrial estate, so I hop on the cinema bus. I don't mind the walk afterwards, but the nerves build the closer I get. Polish Porsche has seen better days. I was expecting a dealership. Instead, it could be the place where Del Boy gets his van fixed.

A stunning teenage girl works on reception. She glances up but carries on typing.

'Can I help you?'

'I'm looking for Rada.'

The smile slips and the fingers stop. She looks me up and down.

'Who wants to know?'

'A friend. She told me to look her up when I was free.'

Her English flows but the accent is heavy. Even so, the emphasis I place on the word *free* breaches the language barrier.

'Wait one minute.'

I expect to see Rada when the door opens. Instead, a thickset bald man enters. There's a fleeting resemblance to the young girl. He, too, checks me over. I do the same to him, glad of my shades. He has a football shirt on, tracksuit bottoms and smokes a cigar. Weird.

'My name is Radic.' He rolls the 'r' and it rhymes with 'itch'. 'Come to my office.'

He turns, and I follow. Despite his outfit, he is a man who's used to people following his orders.

'Take a seat. You won't need your sunglasses in here.' There's only one chair in front of a messy desk, so I plonk myself down and do as he says.

'That's better. The eyes don't lie. What do you want with Rada?'

'She's an old friend. I wanted to catch up.'

'Don't you call her by her first name?'

I open my mouth to say it, but I can't recall what it is. My eyes widen as I realise I never knew it. His face is hard. I may only get one chance at him letting me see her.

'Miss Rada?' I guess.

He drums his podgy fingers on the surface of a thick book, and then he smiles. It's a genuine one that changes his entire demeanour. I instantly warm to him.

'You're Katie.'

I'm taken aback. 'Yes, how did you know?'

'Nice tattoos, but unusual to have them there on each finger. I would guess you've covered something over. There's a guarded aspect to you, too. A cautiousness that people who've been in prison carry with them.'

'Very clever.'

He beams again. 'Not really. It was quite a while ago, but Rada said a girl called Katie from the joint might call for her.'

I laugh. Mischievous sod.

'Is she here?'

'She works at my club. I'm going there for lunch. Come with me, I'll give you a lift.'

Again, I trail after him. We get into an old car. I wonder, should I be worried? Yet, I trust him, which is strange when I'm cautious with nearly everyone else. He glances at me as we roll off the forecourt.

'Seatbelt, please.'

'Is this a Porsche?'

The grin is back. 'Very amusing. This is a Ford. I prefer to keep under the radar.'

'Radar or Rada?'

'She didn't tell me you were funny.'

I can't help checking out all the transformation of the city since I left. I never knew the centre of town well, but I admire the new buildings. High-rise flats and small terraced estates dot the skyline.

'It's changed, eh?' he asks.

'Yeah, the place, the people. I read that Eastern Europeans would come when they joined the EU, there were loads arriving in the prisons. Must have been even more out here.'

'I've been here many years now. Even I can see the effect of high immigration. Strange to hear someone like me saying build more schools, houses and hospitals because places like this one can't cope.'

We pull up outside a basic-looking pub with a creaking sign and whitewashed walls. He parks on double yellow lines. I've never driven but I'm aware you aren't supposed to park on them. I walk behind him into an entrance with a door on the left and right. He chooses the latter and I'm surprised to find us in a cosy, thick-carpeted room with a long wooden bar.

I receive a few interested looks, but when they see my company they nod respectfully, avert their eyes, and continue their quiet conversations. Radic has a quick chat with an older woman behind the bar. He nods towards a table in the corner which I assume is a message for me to sit there and he disappears through a further door at the back of the room. It stays open and I hear pool balls knocking against each other.

The lady delivers a smile and a coffee. I relax. This is what I expected from a pub. Perhaps too much television gave me false ideas. The bars we'd gone to on our nights out had been brightly lit places of glass, or loud warehouses with sticky carpets and too many people.

I don't know what to expect. I'm surprised I came. However, sitting here, I have a feeling that this was meant to be.

28
WE MEET AGAIN

An attractive woman in tight jeans and a billowing white shirt breezes through the door by which Radic left. Cold eyes behind heavy eyeshadow pass over the crowd and me. She turns to leave before glancing my way again. This time, her head cocks to one side.

'Katie?'

'Rada?'

'Wow, look at you, Katie. I'm so happy you came. If Radic hadn't told me you were here, I'd never have recognised you.'

I am stunned by the vision in front of me and need a few seconds to regain my composure. 'I decided to enjoy a day out and thought it would be nice to see you again. Shared problems and all that.'

'You have problem?'

'No. Well, many, don't you? I wasn't expecting it to be like this.'

'Come on, let's get out of here. You hungry?'

I nod, so she takes my hand and guides me through the door. A few of the regulars shout goodbye. She has high-heeled ankle boots on which means I need to look up to see her. She looks nothing like the woman I knew. This lady strides rather than shambles. Her chin is raised as though she is in control. I pull my shoulders back too.

'Do you like souvlaki or moussaka?'

'Who are they?'

That amuses her. 'It's Greek food, although they do sound a bit like the names of prisoners. A little heavy, but very good. I love it.'

'Sounds interesting, and expensive. I don't have much money.'

'I will pay. The restaurant is expensive.' She giggles before continuing. 'At night anyway, but it's quite cheap at lunch.'

I find it hard to stop looking at her. She's happy; bouncing even. It's not far and a man in restaurant clothes greets us warmly.

'You want wine?' she asks.

'It's not often I drink during the day.'

As she smiles in agreement, I notice there are almost-hidden bags under her eyes.

'I don't drink much either. Lots of alcohol makes me unstable. After what happened before when I was out of control, it's not a good experience. Now tell me, Katie. How is life?'

I didn't come all this way to hide, so I let it all go. 'I'm lost. I have no family or strong connections in Cambridge, so I don't belong. There's a job which isn't too bad. It just seems that life is happening next to me, and I'm unable to join in.'

She nods as I talk and replies immediately. 'That is how I felt. I thought subconsciously, if that's the right word, my son would be there when I got out. How crazy is that? However, Radic took me in and let me use a little self-contained flat near the pub. I sat in it and cried. It was Radic who spoke to me about what I was doing. We cannot change the past, only the future.'

'I agree. But all this probation stuff makes me feel like I can't be my own person. I want to pack a bag and wander. You know, just do what I like.'

'I hated them knowing what I was doing. In many ways it was

worse than being inside. Radic suggested I tell them I was going back to the Ukraine. I asked about it legally. They said no problem, but I would need to go through the channels, whatever that means. In the end, I sent them a copy of my one-way airline ticket and my passport.'

'Didn't they stop you leaving?'

'Silly! I sent it after I had flown home. Then, I returned but no more Anna Rada. I am Irina Shevchenko, from Poland. Where I came from was close to the border with Poland anyway. I know enough of the language if anyone asks.'

'And now you're free.'

Her face falls. She visibly pulls herself together. 'I am free from the authorities, but I'll never be free from regret. I will have some fun though. As Radic says, we die soon enough. We may as well have a few laughs on the way.'

'I wish I didn't have to abide by those rules. I'm worried about my probation officer too. He's going to try to make me do something I don't want to, I am sure of it.'

'You're in Cambridge, aren't you? That's funny you say that. I heard a similar story from a girl, Oksana, who works as dancer at the club.'

I was interested and confused. 'There are dancers at that pub?'

'Not in the pub. There is a private member's club above it. That's where I work.'

'Ah, okay. What did she say about him?'

'She said he was evil. Worse than the ones who brought her over here.'

'Could I talk to her?'

'Of course. What time do you need to leave?'

'The last train is the eight-thirty.'

'Sorry, she doesn't start until nine. I could ring her. Actually, you could stay over. I have sofa bed in lounge. Go home tomorrow morning. This evening, we do karaoke.'

'No, I must be back...'

But that's not true. My shift at the warehouse doesn't start until the afternoon. No one knows I'm here. Nobody cares either. I want to talk to this Oksana. What she says might be important. I also think, karaoke aside, tonight will be fun.

29
GOOD TIMES

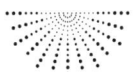

Irina's flat is tiny but comfortable. She insists I sleep in her bed and she will sleep on the sofa. I stop protesting after she takes the sheets off and puts on fresh ones.

The late afternoon sun shines through the window and bathes the lounge in warm light. I wake up in a chair as evening approaches. I've never been good at napping, but I am relaxed here. Maybe it's the distance from Cambridge that's doing it. The anonymity is amazing. Although I suspect the belt-snapping lunch we'd had was the main cause of my snooze. Irina, as I'm now used to calling her, walks in with a towel wrapped around her.

'Sleeping Beauty awakes. Are you hungry?'

I glance down at my still protruding stomach and puff my cheeks out.

'Shower then?'

As always when you sleep in your clothes, my skin is grimy, so I agree. I have nothing to change into, nor any toiletries. I tell her that.

'No problem. I have many things spare. Besides, we are a similar size. You've been in prison, so you can't be fussy.'

I smile at her. She can say that again.

Her shower is powerful. It's like the long ones I took in the approved premises. She's left underwear on the toilet seat; a matching black set. The knickers are full but high-cut at the side. The bra is a size too small and struggles to control their new inhabitants. I don't feel self-conscious. Years of strip-searches removed any such inhibitions. So, I walk into the lounge and do a cheeky pose.

'Wow! The boys are going to go mad for you.'

'Very funny. The bra's too small.'

'Don't be crazy. It is the perfect size.'

She is wearing a small black dress with tights. It's short but the arms are full, so it looks classy. I realise I only have my jeans to wear and return to the toilet to collect them. The steam has cleared and I can see myself in the long mirror. The underwear suits me. My face is bright red from the hot water, but on tiptoes I grin at my profile. I think of Jan and shrug. I've had enough of men for the moment.

Irina holds a blue dress on a hanger in front of me when I enter the lounge. It's a shiny knee-length number. I slip it on and it slides down my body as though it was made for me.

'That really suits you, Katie.'

'It's beautiful. I've worn nothing like this before. Here, you have it. I can wear something else.'

'Don't be silly. The dress was always a bit loose around the chest area for me. I couldn't take it back because I'd stolen it.'

Who knows why things cause people to laugh. That almost has us throwing our underwear away. When we've composed ourselves, Irina guides me into the bedroom. She fetches our wine glasses and tops them up.

'Now, make-up time. When you're putting lots on, there's a fine line between catwalk and circus. You are more Coco the Clown than Coco Chanel. You don't talk much about being young, but I don't think you spent your childhood dressing up.'

She's right. I do not mention my past and I didn't spend it

playing with dolls. I'm not offended either. Maleeha knew how to put her foundation and lipstick on, so we'd get her to do ours. It seemed unimportant at the time, yet now I wish I'd practised. I loved being unidentifiable today, even if I did entertain.

'Will you do mine and show me how?'

'Sure. Look at us having a girlie night. It's fun, yes?'

It is. It reminds me of going out with the girls when we were first released - but this feels less manic. She pulls my hair back into a ponytail and exclaims at its strength. She says she damaged her own locks with dyes ages ago. It's strange to think that, in all those years in jail, not only did my body hide away from the ravages of time, but my hair retained its health as well. Hers is an unnatural shade of red. I don't like it, but I love the idea of a new colour.

She talks about growing up in the Ukraine. Like many youngsters there, she dreamed of a good job and big salaries abroad. They were easy pickings for the players in the criminal world, in particular the traffickers.

She confuses me by talking about concealer, primer and foundation, along with blusher and highlighter. When she gets to mascara and eyeliner, she giggles.

'Is there, perhaps, a werewolf in your family tree?'

'No, why?'

'If it is the full moon tonight, these hairy beasts may wake up and attack us all.'

I glance at my eyebrows and then at hers. There's quite a difference. It had never occurred to me that I would want to trim them.

'What about Cara Delavigne? Hasn't she got bushy ones?'

'Bushy yes, these are like woodland. Maybe a job for another day.' She looks in the mirror and our eyes connect. 'Will you come back again?'

There's no pause. 'Definitely.'

'Cool. I'd love a friend who understands what I've been through. See how you get on with everyone. I won't say any more as the club won't be what you're expecting.'

'Sounds interesting. What exactly does Radic do?'

'He'll be there tonight, you can ask him yourself.'

30
THE CLUB

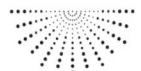

A bouncer dominates the doorway when we arrive. He sports an approachable, sleepy face, but he is absolutely enormous. I don't think I have ever seen anyone so large. There's unlikely to be any trouble with him standing there. We walk through the pub to good-natured whistles and cheers. It's surprisingly busy for a weekday.

The upstairs is not what I expect at all. I've been thinking gentleman's club. Perhaps something like a secluded bar in a nice hotel. Instead, it resembles a strip club with the lights turned on. There's a raised platform in one corner with an aluminium pole in the middle. Even I know what that's for.

Light pop music comes from a sound system on a table next to a small bar. There are six round tables in the centre of the room, three of which have a solitary bloke in one of the seats. There's a booth on each side which makes me think of drug deals from films, and a dance floor in front of the 'stage'. Classy does not spring to mind.

Irina grins at my bewildered expression.

'I said it wouldn't be what you expected.'

'You'd be right.' I chuckle. 'It's like a sinister McDonald's.'

Irina laughs too. 'Hey, it's not a brothel. That's for a pole dancer. We have a girl who is professional. Come on, let's drink some vodka.'

I notice a mirrored wall near to the bar and gasp. I am the swan from The Ugly Duckling. The top of the dress covers my chest but the cut highlights it. My arms are toned and lithe. However, the tattoos do not quite fit with the image, and the blue of the outfit shows my skin to be alabaster white which I suppose it is. I don't mind either fact.

I had to give her the shoes back as they hurt when I walked. She kept saying walk on my tiptoes, but I'd have fallen over if so much as a fly landed on me. The only thing I don't like is my hair. Irina covered it with vast amounts of hairspray, and I have the sensation of wearing a polystyrene helmet. I can taste the stuff. Irina stands next to me.

'We look good, eh?'

'We do.'

'Not bad for two convicts!'

She's right. We are nothing like those girls from prison. My face doesn't have a blemish on it, although my nose looks bigger than I imagined. The mascara lights up my blue eyes so even I'm drawn to them. Irina's legs shimmer and lure above her high heels. I stare at my flats and shrug. They'll do.

'You look beautiful, Katie. Really, you do. A little ghostlike maybe. Is the sun not allowed in Cambridge?'

'Sunbathing is boring.'

'Cheat then. Tan in a bottle is almost as good and much quicker.'

She hands me a drink with a small amount of liquid in the bottom. After chinking hers against mine, she knocks it back. 'Za vas!'

I reciprocate. God knows what it is, but my nipples harden. I cough out a question. 'What does *Za vas* mean?'

'Here's to you.'

Even under the face paint, her affection is obvious.

'Thank you, Irina.'

'No problem.'

'No, honestly. I feel like a different person. I never imagined I could appear this way. What have I done to deserve this? You don't have to be my friend.'

'Why do you say that?'

'I could've been nicer to you in prison. Been friendlier. I just turned myself off.'

'You listen here. We all did what we needed to get through it. You saved me, remember. Don't think about things too much. I saw you were lost, like me. People come along in life and help when you least expect them. That's always been the way. You're fun to be with. I wouldn't have invited you to stay if I wasn't enjoying your company.'

I think back to the day she says I saved her. Everyone knew what was going on in that laundry room, and I did knock on the door. The screws were coming though. It's so long ago now that I can't remember if I would have intervened or not if the staff weren't nearby. Or maybe I was warning the others so they didn't get caught.

'Snap out of it, Katie. We live new lives now.'

I roll my head back and stare at the ceiling. I'm not surprised to see a multi-coloured globe. One of the three men catches my eye, smiles, and waves his glass. I glance at Irina.

'What does he want?'

'He wants you to wee in his cup.'

'What?'

She has me for a second, laughs like a woman with no cares and wanders over to him. She pats him on the back and walks to the bar. I follow.

'Irina, why are we dressed up like this? It seems a little over-the-top for three blokes.'

'We look fabulous to have fun downstairs. It will be quiet here until eleven. Only those who don't want to be seen drink here. Oksana can handle it until then. I am hostess later when she may dance. It is easy job. I get drinks, be nice to people, cool down tempers. Some men like to watch ladies' dancing.'

'It sounds a bit sleazy.'

A man's voice interrupts. 'How dare you?'

I didn't hear Radic approach. I jump so high, I'm pleased I'm still in my clothes. He smiles at my scared face.

'Relax, It's a joke. It is grubby. That's its purpose.'

I sense Irina disappear to give the man his drink.

'And what purpose is that?'

'In my line of work, I need somewhere safe to do business. My acquaintances enjoy being distracted. Here, we can experience a good time, among friends. Watch entertainment while having a conversation.'

'They don't appear to be doing much chatting together?'

Radic shouts out to the men. They rise out of their seats and head towards a booth. I study their craggy faces as they walk past. It's obvious these men experienced tough lives. Pain or sadness has erased their emotions. Violence removed their good looks. In their eyes, there is nothing. I involuntarily shudder as they sit in the booth in silence. Radic's laugh draws my attention back to the conversation.

'Perhaps they are sleepy. Now, tell me. How did you end up in my club?'

'Irina brought me.'

'Yes, but she is employed here. Are you going to work for me?'

'Are you offering me a job?'

He laughs. His eyes twinkle.

'There's something about you, Katie. I'm not sure what. You look stunning tonight, you are fun, but there is an untouchable part of you? I need strong women to manage this place. That's all these men respect. Would you want a role here?'

'I suspect after a few weeks you'd have me swinging around that pole and popping balloons with darts from my arse.'

Irina returns at that moment. The pair of them grin at each other and laugh so hard I can't help joining in. 'The job's yours,' he offers, and they fold up again. Finally, they recover.

'There is work here if you wish. I don't care what you've done in the past. But I want to know, so I understand you.'

'She'll tell us when she's ready,' says Irina.

'Fair enough. There's a card game tonight. Set up the table in the back room for twelve. Oksana will cover that. There shouldn't be too many people up here, so you and Katie should manage fine.'

I try not to react but a smile creeps onto my face.

31
A POISONOUS THORN

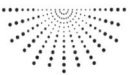

Oksana turns out to be a small girl with spiky black hair and perfect English. She is also dressed to impress. I wonder what they get paid. Would I receive the same? Initially, I wanted the job so much that the money was irrelevant, but now the buzz of the moment has left, it also makes me consider if they have to provide other services. I catch her at the bar.

'Oksana, you had Tim Thorn as your probation worker in Cambridge?'

'Yes, Irina tells me you have the same pleasure.'

'She said you didn't like him.'

'That's an understatement. He was a pervert. I still feel sick now.'

'What did he do?'

She pauses and her jaw bunches before she replies. 'He wasn't too bad to start with, just a bit creepy. Then he made excuses about checking where I lived. He threatened me with revoking my licence unless I sucked his dick.'

'Did you?'

'I didn't understand the rules. I'd never been to prison before. I was involved in an argument in a nightclub. Some crazy cow said

I stamped on her foot. She got right in my face, so I shoved my wine glass in hers. It was an impulsive move.' She takes a few breaths to calm herself. 'The girl was blinded. The police blamed it on me and the jury took her side. They gave me three years. I really struggled inside and couldn't bear going back.'

I touch her arm. What do you say to that? 'Could you have told anyone?'

Her face contorts into a snarl. 'Who would they believe? An eye-removing nobody like me, or one of their own?'

'How did you get away from him? Did you disappear?'

'No. My licence ended. I served 18 months of horror inside, and then 18 worse months under his guidance. I wish someone would fuck him up.'

'Can't Radic help?'

'No. There'd be too much heat. He is a government employee after all. One of Her Majesty's finest. It's almost unbelievable, isn't it? Has he got to you?'

'No.' The thought of returning to him is not appealing. I add the inevitable words. 'Not yet.'

She shrugs, but I watch her drying a glass and it cracking. I realise from her phrases and accent that the reason her English is good is that she is English. What dire stories is she hiding? I'm about to walk off when she turns around.

'I want to forget it all, because it isn't my problem any more. I can't, though.'

'Why not?'

'Because I heard from another girl who's under him at the moment. Literally. And she's only nineteen.'

'Shit. Surely someone can do something.'

'Are you going to do it? Will you be the one to risk your freedom?' Her eyes tighten as vanquished memories threaten to surface. 'Do you know which part I can't shake off?'

I raise my eyebrows.

'The bastard even filmed me doing it.'

32
DANCING

It's much busier in the pub downstairs. Irina gets two drinks from the bar. I notice no money changes hands. Mine smells like pure vodka. I decide to lose it somewhere. I've had enough. Irina, on the other hand, is thirsty. If she's someone who doesn't drink much, then I'd hate to see her on a bad day.

There's an unusual mix of people in the bar from all over Europe. Maybe that's how it is now. No English though. Just a load of other Europeans getting drunk together. The banter doesn't get out of hand. The enormous doorman, whose name I learn is Gregor, is probably the cause of that.

We have a little dance until 10:30 p.m. and then head upstairs. It's been fun. At 11:20 p.m. we hear people leaving outside and a few I recognise come to the club. Radic arrives and most leave for the card game. Oksana carries drinks and snacks for them. Irina and I sit about chatting. We get the odd request for top-ups.

I even have a swing round on the pole which amuses the few who are left. Irina plays a few slow tunes and dances with one of the three men who was there earlier and still remains. I thought they would be in the card room. The guy with a milky eye approaches me. He is heavyset and walks as though he's made of lead. He holds out his hand. Smiling, I go with the flow.

He is super-careful not to be inappropriate. After a minute, he and Irina exchange words. She squeezes his shoulder.

'He says you remind him of his daughter.'

Close up, I can see the damaged eye moves. There are scars around his eye socket. I wonder if they were caused in an accident or by human intervention.

When the song finishes, tears slide from his normal eye. The man who danced with Irina puts his arm around him and guides him to the door. The remainder of the patrons disappeared while we were dancing. Alone, we tidy up and clean. It doesn't take long. Oksana tells us she'll lock up and we head off back to Irina's.

So much for Irina not drinking a lot. I undress her and roll her deadweight into bed with a grunt. She pulls me next to her. For a moment, I assume she wants to have sex with me. Instead, she curls herself into the foetal position and drags my arm over her, so I'm cuddling her. Her breathing settles after a few seconds and she's out. I stay beside her. I force myself to keep awake because I don't want the evening to end. As the sheets warm up, my eyes droop.

What a night. I felt pretty and desirable, and I had a purpose. The people present enjoyed my company. There were certainly shady goings on, so I need to show caution. Could I start again here? I can't see Tim Thorn giving me permission to move away.

Irina mumbles in her sleep. I shush her and stroke the side of her face and she settles back down. I could live with these people. I think I could enjoy life with them. There is hope and friendship, and that's what I need. As always when I consider the future, my mind returns to the past.

I was thirteen years old the last time I had a new beginning. That was a fresh start for me, too. I prayed for a settled, comfortable home and I expected things to improve. Instead, it would lead to murder.

33

THE EIGHTH MEMORY - AGE THIRTEEN

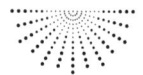

I heard the car crunch through the gravel as the social worker drove away.

The woman came back into the house and beamed at me. 'Now, Katie. What do you think of the place?'

I was overawed. My home would be a huge stone farmhouse on the edge of miles of fields. There were a few houses dotted around, but it felt like the middle of nowhere. My new foster mother couldn't have been more of a cliché if she tried. She was middle-aged, plump, and even sported an apron.

'I love it, Mrs Brown.'

'Call me Erin.'

I smiled. Erin suited her.

'Now, my husband works long hours on the farm, so we don't see him much. However, he likes us all to eat tea together at five every evening. He often returns to work, but Teddy looks forward to family time.'

She grinned at me, and I beamed back. That sounded good to me.

'This is Mr Pebbles. He's a Heinz 57 and ancient, but he enjoys a little walk once a day.'

Mr Pebbles looked about four hundred, in human years. He wagged his tail at me and I knew we'd be friends. At that moment, two boys ran in.

'Woah, you pair. Hold up. Let me introduce you to Katie. And shoes!'

Laughing, they backtracked and returned with socks showing. Both their trousers were covered in mud. Erin opened her mouth, but the lads cut her off by bellowing, 'Football.'

She stood between them and placed an arm around their shoulders. 'This one is Simon.'

'Simple Simon,' the tall one shouted.

'And this cheeky one is Bill,' said Erin.

'Billy the Kid,' said Bill, puffing himself up.

'Billy the Dick,' said Simon.

'Now that's enough. Off upstairs and wash your hands before dinner.'

They both smiled amiably at me as they left. Erin guided me into a kitchen chair and sat opposite.

'They're good lads, Katie. Boisterous and full of life. The way boys should be. But it'll be lovely to have female company around here. Teddy and I couldn't have children, so we fostered those two. It's been five years now, and we're a family. I always wanted a girl though. We'll brighten the place up together.'

She returned to the big cooker and stirred the pot.

'Can I take Mr Pebbles for a walk?'

'Of course. Don't be long. Teddy will be back soon.'

'Okay, where's his lead?'

'I wouldn't worry about that,' she chuckled.

We set off. I've never seen a slower dog. His fringe flopped down to his nose, so I kept checking he hadn't fallen asleep. We only got to the first field, and I think he did just that. A large tractor trundled past on the dirt track. Whoever was in the cab was a big man as he filled it. The sun gleamed off the window, and

I struggled to make out a face. I waved anyway. I caught dark eyes as it swept by. My greeting wasn't returned.

I thought he hadn't seen me. Later, I would know he had. At the time I was excited. I had a new family, and they seemed normal. I looked to the horizon which stretched forever over the flat land and felt a sense of peace. The level-headed me told me not to get carried away. I'd been here before. This felt different though. I gained two brothers that day and believed my life would change for the better.

34
THE PROBATION OFFICE

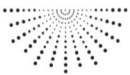

I push the door to the probation office open and tell the receptionist I'm here to see Tim Thorn. The low after the companionship and camaraderie with Irina is fierce. We went for breakfast at a French restaurant when we woke up. She told me we were going to Burger King, which was fine by me. Instead, we had a tablecloth and slippery waiter service. I ate everything, even some kind of spicy sausage thing that repeated on me until the evening.

Irina paid and tried to buy me some clothes when we wandered around the local shopping centre, Queensgate, afterwards. There's definitely more to her post-prison life than I know. Irina did full slap again whereas I settled for a bit of lippy. I had a whopping spot on my chin which I let her cover with some cream. My face must have missed being able to breathe. She said my skin was so clear for my age that even in just lipstick I was attractive.

The packing job was beyond dull that night. A few of the girls I had become semi-friendly with had left, and though I was one of the longest serving, I felt like an outsider. I went to the gym to get some endorphins going but couldn't focus. The glimpse of another life had made mine drab in comparison.

I wait over thirty minutes before Thorn comes out. He takes me into a meeting room and closes the door.

'How are you then, Katie?'

'Good. Just ticking along.'

'Any problems?'

'No.'

'Been anywhere of interest?'

There's an edge to the question which puts me on guard. He can't know but he's suspicious. 'Are you interested in hearing about the park or the museum?'

'I drove past your house a few days ago. I thought I'd stop and see how you're getting on. There was no answer at your door. A redhead told me she hadn't seen you for a while.'

'Did she now? That's not surprising seeing as she's lived there for a month and I've only seen her twice.'

He leans back in his chair and steeples his fingers. It's strange. He doesn't look like a twisted pervert. He's tanned and well-dressed.

'I'm away next week on a training course. You'll have to sign in with another worker, unless you want me to say I'd seen you and everything was great. That way you wouldn't need to come into the office.'

'Sure. That would save me the bus fare.'

'Perfect for both of us. Well, you're making fantastic progress. Hang in there, Katie. There's a long road ahead, but we'll walk it together.'

I DECIDE to visit the approved premises afterwards. I want to see a supportive, honest face. Sally opens the door. Those few months I spent with her when I was at my most vulnerable means she reads me in a split second. We hug for a full minute. I don't cry, I'm more angry than upset. As usual, Sally makes a cup of tea first.

'Tell me?'

For a moment, it's tempting to mention Peterborough. I decide that's not wise. What I'm about to say is probably not clever either.

'I can't stand this anymore.'

'Stand what, Katie?'

'This constant supervision. I think I could cope if it was for a year or even two. But I can't live the rest of my life like this.'

'Has Thorn done anything to upset you?'

'No, it's not that. I don't want to have to tell people where I live, or who I'm seeing. If I quit my job, or get a new one, I want to be able to do it on a whim. Asking for permission for everything isn't living.'

'Katie, everyone feels like that. After a year, you'll only check in once a month. The restrictions will be less. You won't even think about it anymore. We all want what's best for you.'

'What would happen if I disappeared?'

Sally's mother-face disappears. She picks up her empty cup and washes it out in the sink. I've seen her do that often. It's her way of thinking and stopping herself saying the first thing that pops into her head.

'They'll find you. Thorn will make sure of it.'

'Come on, Sally. The only consistent line you or anyone in that goddamn building agree on is that you're insanely short-staffed. You don't have enough people to answer the phone, never mind look for someone who's vanished.'

She pauses before continuing. My heart goes out to her. She has the dilemma of being a friend and an authority.

'What will happen, Sally?'

'They'll issue a warrant for your arrest. They will freeze your bank account and you can't work as your National Insurance number will be tracked.'

'But I won't see my face on billboards or the nightly news?'

'No. They only do that sort of thing for people who are an immediate danger to the public.'

I close my eyes and absorb the information.

'Don't do it, Katie. You have a life sentence. They'll find you. It may take years, but then you'll be straight back to jail. Thorn will sound the alarm immediately. The police will be on the lookout for you even if you aren't on the news. Where can you go? What would you do? What about money? It's madness.'

I stand to leave. I've got a lot to consider.

'They catch over ninety percent in the first week. You're bound to suffer bleak days after what you've been through. It's how you move on that's important.'

'It was just a thought, Sally. Thanks for listening as always.'

'Please think carefully before doing something rash. Come back any time to talk things over. I know what you're going through. I want to help. This conversation never happened okay, whatever you decide to do.'

We hug again. This time it's her that squeezes the hardest. She has the last word as the door closes.

'You'll ruin your life.'

From where I'm standing, I don't have much to lose.

35
A WEEK LATER

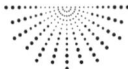

NEW FRIENDS

I returned to Peterborough yesterday. Last night, Irina and I went out clubbing. It's not as student-filled as Cambridge, but I still felt old. I realise I'm more of a pub girl. Irina had a big hangover this morning, so I ran all over the city. I wore my hair tied back, sunglasses and a baseball cap. It was exhilarating. I could have been anyone.

Being a Sunday night, the bar downstairs is quiet. We are sitting in the club upstairs which is packed. Radic is holding court and swanning around chatting to various groups. A wide range of people enjoy themselves although few English. Oksana has called in sick, so Irina, who still looks delicate, is on her own. I offer to help and she gladly accepts.

Radic's wife is here. He introduces us, and she seems nice. I get Sofiya the wrong drink and she laughs it off. I've never worked behind a bar, so I climb a steep learning curve. The lager pump is like a wild spitting beast, and it's winning our feud. These Ukrainians are a thirsty bunch. The big bouncer has come upstairs tonight. He sits on a chair and grins at people.

Irina is eventually sick in a bucket. She covers it well, but afterwards her eyes roll like she's stepped off the Waltzer at the fair. Radic appears and guides her into the bouncer's arms. The next time I look up, they're gone. Radic gets behind the bar and his wife arrives and grabs a tray. It's a new team tonight, and I have a weird, crazy, fun evening.

The Ukrainian singer danced and laughed. Maybe he was a comedian - who knows? Radic stayed all night to help, declining many offers of assistance. He didn't say much to me. At one busy point, he squeezed his wife's arse, and then she slapped his rear so hard he dropped a bottle of wine. They were happy doing something mundane as long as they were together.

I grab the mop at the end of the evening after everyone has gone except Radic and his wife. He shakes a finger at me.

'Leave it. There's a cleaner for downstairs. She will do what's needed.'

Sofiya returns with three coffees from the kitchen. She plonks two down, says 'Goodnight,' and disappears. Radic takes a seat, and I collapse in one next to him.

'You worked very hard tonight.'

'That's what my feet are telling me.'

'We'd have struggled without you.'

'You had plenty of offers. You'd have been fine.'

He airily waves his hand in the air. His eyes narrow and I suspect he is about to be serious.

'Irina told me about your problem with the probation guy. Do you know what you are going to do about it?'

'What can I do? It's the system. I hate it. I'll be a fugitive for the rest of my life if I vanish.'

'So what? Those are society's rules. Choose the conditions you work to. Or accept none at all.'

'What would I do for a job, for money? I can't pay tax.'

'Wow. I've not heard that one before. You can work for me. Only rich people should pay tax. I'll get you a new ID from anywhere you like.'

'How about England or America?'

'America, no. England, maybe. You don't need one of those. Start from scratch. Pretend you are a refugee.'

'Don't they fingerprint asylum seekers?'

'It's not a problem. Look, they have no idea who lives in this country. There are millions of undocumented migrants. I can sort it for you.'

'I just want to be happy.'

'Happy? Pah! Who's happy? Happiness is a dream. Life is up and down. Some people take pills to make them permanently content, but deep down they know they live in a chemical bubble.'

'I'm tempted, but it's such a risk. The operation you're running here seems suspicious, too. I learn quickly but I was away for a long time. My lack of experience makes me naïve.'

'I am party to a few dodgy dealings as you say. Nothing that you'll be involved in. With a new ID, you can go anywhere you like. Work with us for a while then disappear. Look in the mirror. You are changing, like the butterfly. No one from your previous life would recognise you now.'

'I have a question. Those girls I saw circulating near the end tonight, were they prostitutes?'

'Them?' He grins. 'Aren't we all? It's like being taken out for a meal by someone. They pay the bill, afterwards you have sex. Everyone smiles. Sometimes, the lady is not hungry and would just like the money. Then they have sex. Everyone's still happy.'

'Very romantic, Radic.'

'It's true! I like you, Katie. My wife does too. Men downstairs asked after you when you were here last. They wanted to know who you are. I say to them, you have no name. They are not worthy of knowing it. They want you even more now.'

He stands and stretches.

'I'll ring you with you some job details, but there's a condition.'

'Which is?'

'You tell me your past.'

He places money on the table and walks toward the door.

'Do I need to lock up?'

'Gregor will do that. Stay, have a drink and relax. You've earned it.'

At that moment, Gregor returns. He nods to Radic, and then helps himself to a beer at the bar. I get the same sleepy smile he's shown me every time we meet. Radic winks and leaves. A warmth flows through me from head to toe. It's years since that happened. I count five twenties in the note pile and know my decision. My thoughts stray to the farm which was the last place I belonged.

36

THE NINTH MEMORY - AGE FOURTEEN

I loved the farm. Not only that, but I belonged there. My new brothers, Bill and Simon, were exactly what I expected from siblings. They were fun and friendly one minute, cheeky and rude another. We took turns quarrelling but always looked out for each other. If we had sweets, we split them, and if we caused trouble, then we shared the blame.

It wasn't perfect. We had to catch a bus to school due to our isolation. It was a tight-knit community. Everyone knew we were fostered, which seemed to be stigmatised, as though it tainted us. We sat together on those journeys and the boys fought when necessary.

Simon and Bill were a year above me. That meant I knew no one else in my class to start with, and I struggled to make friends. As the months flowed into years, a few girls accepted me and life became easier. Nevertheless, I couldn't wait to get back home after lessons finished.

Teddy, as Erin called her husband, was a quiet man and difficult to judge. He had a solitary, hard job. Perhaps all that time alone changed him, or maybe that's just the way he was. Erin's name for him didn't fit at all, so us kids called him Ted.

For Bill, Simon, and me, the farm became our playground. We hid in barns, haystacks and silos. Ted even let us drive or sit on the tractors and other farm vehicles. Health and safety was standing back from the combine harvester when it rattled past you. Ted loved those boys. Bill, in particular. Despite working long hours, Ted would make time for us kids every Sunday.

Twins lived at the next farm along which was about a mile away, and they joined our gang. They cycled to ours and we'd all pile into the back of the rusty truck Ted drove around the place.

They were an unusual pair. Each had a shock of incredibly thick blond hair that stood up like they'd been electrocuted. Jordan behaved like a typical sparky lad in the same vein as Simon and Bill. Justin, on the other hand, was dim-witted. Ted said he had been dropped at birth. If that was the case it must have been from a great height. He would slip into a trance, stare into the distance for hours on end, and not say a word. It made him continually late and we'd call him Justin Time.

The boys loved fishing, Jordan and Simon in particular. Ted called them Jordan River and Simon Salmon for obvious reasons. When the rest of us got bored with it and ran off to the woods to play, Simon would still stand in the shallows with his eyes hidden from the sun in a low-pulled cap.

The only person who didn't get what she wanted was Erin. I think she hoped I'd call her Mum and plant flowers in the yard. I understood her pleasure at shopping trips and cappuccinos in cafes, but it wasn't me. I would go on the odd occasion to keep her happy. Sometimes, she and Ted would give me the choice. After umming and ahhing, I'd always end up waving to her as we bounced away up the dusty track to the river.

With all four boys older than me, they grew up before I did. I remained a girl in T-shirt and jeans when they started experimenting with alcohol and marijuana. I had the odd taste, but the former made me queasy and the latter induced paranoia. The others weren't that fussed either. Only Bill persevered as though he needed to get used to it.

Bill grew tall and broad, which hinted at raw strength. Only the big muscles were missing at that point. He led, and we followed. Justin Time spent hours staring at him and would slavishly follow. That adoration would've freaked me out but Bill loved being in charge and the attention.

Despite the insecurities I felt at school, I wanted that period to last forever. It was the one time I forgot about Tommy. We discovered a love of nature and exercise, and I learned to swim and would dive in quarries and ponds. We'd try and shoot anything that moved with the twins' air rifle. I'd drop into bed at night and wake up with enthusiasm. I never thought life could be like that.

A few months later, I also received an envelope through the post from Mrs Gill, the warden from the children's home. It was simply titled; A love letter, from Martha and Arthur. I didn't hear about any prosecution against them and can only assume they exposed Donna's lies. I suspect they shouldn't have been writing to me, but Mrs Gill had her own rules.

It read, 'Dear Katie,' and then there were twenty short paragraphs with a dated heading of where we'd been.

'The Park. Sunday 4th April. Katie went on the swing and demanded an ice cream. She had a traffic light lolly but didn't like it and ate Arthur's cone instead. Arthur's tongue turned blue after finishing the lolly.

McDonald's. Saturday 10th April. Katie had a happy meal with Chicken Nuggets. We all laughed when she said, 'Imagine if they made them using real chickens.'

And so on, with three words at the end; 'You were loved.'

I didn't understand it to start with. They wrote of fond times and just normal days out. I still put the envelope under my pillow. As the weeks passed, I read it more often. After two months, I finally got it. They had given me my identity. One role of a family is to remind you of the past. It's how we see where we fitted into the world. If you're always on the move, you lose track of who you are. I knew from that note I was loved without condition, even if only for a short while. It became priceless to me.

37
JUNE

THE JOB OFFER

I received a call a week later from Irina, which was unusual for her as she usually texted. She informed me that Radic wanted a chat. I also got a text from Gregor. We'd had a couple of drinks and a fumble the previous weekend. He didn't push for more. I think he was more tired than I was. Funny how you make judgements. I imagined him to be a meathead. Instead, he told me he's doing an IT course in Huntingdon and his doorman job just pays the bills.

I'm not sure if his posh English left me doubting the truth, or perhaps, like many things in Radic's world, he is a mixture of light and dark. I don't even know how old Gregor is. He said he'd pick me up from the station, so at least he's old enough to drive.

When I step onto the platform in Peterborough, I am a different person. The last time I came home on the train, I saw a girl with a fabulous tattoo on her neck. I asked her where she had it done. That's strange and wonderful to consider. How far have I come when I can approach a stranger and start a conversation which lasts an entire journey?

Maybe things work out for a reason. I found the parlour in Ely. The second design I saw was exactly what I wanted, and they started on it the following day. Now my right leg, from knee to ankle, has a tattoo of a clock in a bed of flowers. I'm unclear as to why that spoke to me. Perhaps it's all that time in the dark. In prison we are grey; the walls, the bars, our lives and our faces. Out here, I want to shine.

I love it. It is armour to face the world. I stride out the entrance of the railway station without a care. A short denim skirt and a vest top are all that's needed with the sunshine. I feel invincible and attractive, and the admiring glances I receive confirm that. I can see Gregor waving in the distance because he is a head taller than everyone else.

There's a gap in the traffic, so I step into the road. I've only got three-inch heels on but even these feel weird. There's so much to remember. Heel first, shoulders back, invisible line, and the one I forget; short steps. I trip into Gregor's arms. Very cool, although he doesn't seem to mind. I'm not sure I'll ever get used to them, but they do wonders for my confidence. Well, when I'm standing still they do.

Gregor opens the back door to a Range Rover. I slide into a luxurious seat and receive a hug from Irina next to me. Radic is in the front passenger seat. He smiles as Gregor gets in. Radic looks the most excited I've seen him.

'I'm taking you for a meal to my favourite restaurant. The food and drink are my treat, whatever you decide, as I have a proposition for you. I hope you're hungry.'

I'm not but it doesn't matter. I expected the offer after the conversation with Irina. His wife had been singing my praises. It's nice to have friends meet me at the station, too. I recall how frightening it was when I first got out and had to walk alone.

I marvel at the opulence of the car and wonder what sort of person could afford such a vehicle. Gregor drives onto the parkway and we soon heading to our destination in Alwalton. Even though I don't fancy a big meal, I like the idea of a glass of chilled white wine and more calamari like we enjoyed at the

Greek place Irina first took me to. I hope I'm not becoming a snob. I should know better with Radic involved.

The site of The Plough jogs a memory loose. It's a chain pub where they cover the food in salt, whack it in the deep-fat fryer, and then pile it high. Definitely no squid. It's cheap, and one of the few places I ate out at as a child. Ted's birthday was the reason for that occasion. Radic is like a kid and hustles us through the door.

I catch up with Irina while the boys attack the salad bar, which I recall is free with all main meals. We sip our Chardonnays in unison and are both pleasantly surprised.

'How's things, Irina?'

'You know, the same. Sometimes I sleep, sometimes I don't. It's lovely to see you again. Are you excited to hear Radic's proposal?'

'Of course.'

She looks tired. I think about what she's been through and can't blame her. The past dislikes being ignored. Her son will haunt her dreams for the rest of her life. I can relate to that.

Radic takes his time. The teenager responsible for keeping the salad cart topped up is run off his feet as Gregor and Radic are relentless. It isn't until they've worked through their main courses of huge rib stacks that Radic remembers the purpose of our visit.

He reclines in his seat like a lion after a particularly tasty gazelle. Gregor goes back for more bread.

'We would like you to come and work for us. We pay good money, cash in hand. Same job as Irina and Oksana. You help keep the club running smoothly from Friday to Monday. Manage your time yourselves. There's a spare room at Oksana's for you to sleep or use Irina's sofa. We will see how you get on and, if you want more hours, that won't be a problem as the bar downstairs is always short-staffed.'

There's no surprise in what he's said. It's fabulous to be offered a job like that. My packing shift doesn't finish until ten on a Friday night though.

'What's the money?'

'£300 per week with bonuses for extra duties.'
'Pole dancing?'
'Staying late.'

It's much more than I get paid for stuffing envelopes. I could earn more money in three nights than I can in five at the draughty warehouse.

'I'll think about it. When would you want me to start?'

'When you like, tomorrow maybe. Oksana has worked all week.' He casts a disapproving eye over at Irina, who nudges her uneaten chicken around the plate.

I'M STAYING at Irina's tonight but she has to work. Gregor said he'll take me out for dinner, but I had enough at lunch. I decide to dress well and have a drink, nothing more. Town has no appeal, so I ask him to drive me to a nice hotel. We settle for The Moat House, which they turned into a Holiday Inn while I was away. It's still quiet which is what I want.

We share a bottle of expensive red wine that he insists on buying. He can't take his eyes off me. I have a green dress on with a slit up the side. It displays my new tattoo. His aren't the only admiring looks. I catch sight of myself in a mirror and have to agree with Irina. Tattoo aside, my legs are as white as lard.

Gregor has little to say for himself. I don't suppose I have, either. I do nothing exciting or different during the week, and he was there when I received my good news. He talks about his course. I keep him chatting with frequent nods and comments, but I'm not listening.

I know I'll take the job. Everyone there did. I'll give my notice on Monday. I won't tell Thorn. He need not know. As long as he gets my signature each week, he shouldn't find out. I will be two people. That shouldn't be difficult. The life in Cambridge, though, is something I want to leave behind.

If I disappear, I'll need to plan. How hard would they look for me? The movies call it living off the grid. That all sounds lovely, but what happens if I have an accident or, heaven-forbid, I get pregnant? I need new ID. I'd prefer an English passport. I don't have the money for that; Irina told me how much they cost. Would Radic help me get one? What would I need to do for his assistance?

I chuckle at Gregor as he finishes his drink. The wine glass looks ridiculous in his meaty paw. There's no sexual spark though. I wonder if prison doused my natural urges. Although I'd been keen on Jan, I didn't seem to be able to relax in his company. There can only be one way to find out.

'Shall we go back to yours?'

'Sorry. I start work in a bit and haven't got time.'

He gives me the same sleepy expression he always does. It's for the best. I'm still not sure what I'm about to get involved in, so I have enough to focus on without romantic entanglements. However, I feel alive in this environment. I worry they play a dangerous game, but I will take a hand.

38
CAMBRIDGE LIBRARY

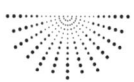

I run two lives now. When I'm in Cambridge, I am a beaten-down ex-convict. I wear no make-up, or perhaps just a touch of lipstick and a brush of eyeliner. My clothes are sporty or practical. You'll find me in jeans and a T-shirt, or maybe jogging gear. The past still haunts me here. I try to keep the memories away, but they know where I sleep and visit at night.

I step from the library and shove the four new books in my backpack. These days, I fill it with bottles of water when I go running. My mind whirs in bed and, unless I'm exhausted, rest is elusive. It's my last shift tonight at the warehouse. I wonder if anyone will say anything. It isn't the sort of place for people gathering around and singing *for she's a jolly good fellow*.

The man with whom I collide is considerably taller than me. The weight on my back causes me to sit down with a bump. We recognise each other at the same time.

'Katie, is that you?'

'Bill?'

'Yeah. Wow, I never expected to meet you again.'

I struggle to breathe, never mind speak. My hands and feet feel numb. He puts his hand under my armpit and lifts me up as though I'm a small child.

'It's good to see you. You look great. It must be seventeen years ago. You've hardly changed.' He steps back and smiles. 'You well?'

My brain recovers from the shock and then my tongue does. 'You what? That's it? That's all you have to say after what happened?'

I stare at him as he shakes his head. The years haven't taken their toll on him. His suit fits nicely, and he still has good hair. His expression is of genuine remorse.

'I'm so sorry, Katie. Please, there's a Costa Coffee over there. Give me five minutes.'

I stumble across the road. The place is almost empty being mid-morning, and I wait in a booth. The time it takes for them to prepare the drinks gives me space to think of the past. I've pushed those memories away so often it's hard to connect completely to them. I struggle to recall how it happened. His placing a beautiful-looking latte in front of me adds to my confusion.

He removes his suit jacket, turns his mobile phone off, and slides it into his inside pocket. His tailored shirt complements his lean body. Wide shoulders remind me of the strong lad he used to be.

'How can you talk to me as though we're old friends? Don't you remember what you did? How you were? Are you aware what happened after you left?'

'Let me explain. Please. We were all messed up by the lives we'd led.'

I sink into my seat and stare at his eyes. Will I see if he's telling the truth? I nod for him to continue.

'It was more a game. Things just got out of hand that day. You recall how I felt about you. Simon wanted you too. There was this huge rivalry between us. I know we should have been nicer to you after Erin died. I can't explain it. We were only eighteen. It was childish. You've heard the phrase; you hurt the ones you love. In a way, we were both happier if nobody had you. Better that than the other person winning. It all went crazy. Anyway, you were fooling around as well.'

Incredibly, it sounded reasonable to that point.

'You're saying I was to blame?'

'No, of course not. I wish none of those things ever happened. I knew I'd done wrong. I used it to motivate myself to lead a good life. I'm a policeman now, with four children. Katie, I will atone for the errors I made when I was young.'

'You're in the police? Not here in Cambridge?'

'I was based in Cambridgeshire, but I moved to Essex a few years back. We have agency meetings like the one today. Each force communicates with others to keep track of the criminals who move around.'

'I thought you went in the merchant navy?'

'I did. They split Simon and me up straight away. It was a lonely life. He enjoyed that aspect, but I didn't. Some of it was brilliant, like being paid to see the world, but it was hard being stuck on the same ship all the time. After five years, I came home and found the police job.'

'Did you go back to the farm?'

'Yes. The twins still lived next door. Their dad had a stroke so I believe they took the business on themselves. I spoke to the dunce, so I got half a story.' He shifts in his seat. 'He told me what happened. It was quite a surprise.'

'Really? That's an understatement, don't you think? I lost my mind. I know it was me that did that terrible thing. But you played a part. Do you have nothing else to say? I was in prison for over sixteen years.'

'I wish I could turn back the clock. It was a long time ago. I work hard for the community now. I take it you live here in Cambridge. Who's your probation officer?'

'Tim Thorn.'

His eyes widen as if that's coincidental news. I realise I don't want him knowing any more. The look on his face matches the sneaky manner he had as a lad.

'Tim and I go way back. Perhaps I'll have a word with him. See if I can get him to cut you some slack. Here's my business card.'

I rise out of my seat and pick it up off the table. I catch him staring down my cleavage.

'I want nothing from you. Keep out of my life. I need a new start and to live on my own terms.'

'That's what we all desire.'

For a moment, a cocky glint in his eyes takes me back to Erin's final days. The boy became a man but nothing's changed.

I slide the embossed card into his half-finished coffee. The emotions return from all that time ago. They're fuzzy still, but anger and rage dominate my thoughts. I flee from the shop before I do something I will regret. A woman at the door scowls as I barge past. I sling my backpack on and sprint up the road. The shock has weakened me and I have to stop. A building beckons and I duck out of sight. I slump against a wall and place my head in my hands.

All these memories. I haven't thought about Erin for years. I loved her unconditionally, but I still couldn't save her.

39
THE TENTH MEMORY - AGE SIXTEEN

Ted stomped into the kitchen as if he wanted to leave footprints in the stone tiles. As you'd expect, Erin's illness had affected him more than the rest of us. His clothes hung on him now. It was as if they'd lost weight in tandem. He looked like he had one foot in his grave, although it was almost time to throw the soil on for Erin.

Life ticked by on the farm. I had just finished my exams and applied to the college for a course in Business Studies. I didn't particularly relish the idea of more studying, but it was a better alternative than getting a job. That said, I was more-or-less a full-time housewife now that Erin was too ill to do any more than sleep.

She'd taken the cancer diagnosis well, if that's the right word. We understood straight away she was in trouble. She had an aggressive type, and the doctor was unsparing with the prognosis. I daydreamed at the appointments, holding her hand, wondering whether I'd want to know. After nine months of chemotherapy and radiotherapy, vomiting and tiredness, Erin said 'enough'. She came home to die.

I'd somehow taken on most of her jobs. It's lucky I didn't have a social life before as I wouldn't have had time for one after. My relationship with Ted was distant at the best of times. Working to exhaustion for him was not coming easy. The fact he seemed ungrateful was pushing me closer to the edge. I realised that he wasn't a happy man, anyway. His surly comments, negative views and general darkness had been obliterated by Erin's sunny demeanour.

I worried what might happen when she left us. Right now, though, I was furious.

'Have you done all that washing?' Ted didn't even glance at me to order me about.

'The ten piles? No, strangely, I haven't. It takes 90 minutes with that level of soiling. Unless you left a time machine for me when you went off to work, then it hasn't been possible.'

'Less of your sarcasm. This kitchen's a mess as well.'

'It's your mess. That is the state you, Bill and Simon left it in this morning. If you cleaned up after yourselves, it wouldn't look like that.'

'That's your job. And why don't you put on some clothes that fit.'

'Why are these all my jobs? I'm not your wife.'

'You stay here for nothing. You need to pull your weight.'

'I am a student, not a skivvy. And I live here, not work here.'

He yanked a seat out from under the table and sat on it with a groan. He removed his head from his hands and after a minute, looked at my face.

'I'm sorry, Katie. I can see you're working hard. We all are. I'm trying to keep on top of things, but the fact my wife is dying is eating me up inside. She's the only woman I've ever loved. I can't bear to be in there.'

He dragged himself to his feet and headed for the door.

'Where are you going now? You need to be with Erin, she's asking for you.'

'I have work to do.'

I chased after him into the yard. 'Work will still be there in a week. She won't.'

He stopped mid-stride. His shoulders curled. A slight twist of his hips made me think he would return, but those shoulders shuddered. Ted leaned back, looked in the sky, and then strode off to the fields.

The day before, the palliative care team informed me Erin had no more than a week left. I wasn't surprised. There was little left of her. I knew plenty about death already, but not up this close. I kept her mouth moist and mopped her brow. Bill and Simon would help lift and move her when I needed to change either her or the bedding. It was usually both at the same time.

If you'd have told me I would be doing something so disgusting before I moved in, I'd have said you were drunk. Yet it had been okay. As I grew into a woman, our relationship changed. The boys' tomfoolery became wearing. Their constant pursuit of alcohol bored me.

Erin had the daughter she always dreamed of for a whole year before her cancer arrived. She was a basic woman who ran a farmhouse. I thought she'd want girlie trips or company to buy clothes. I discovered everything came through mail-order catalogues to save time. Well, the new stuff anyway.

What she wanted was someone to share her life with. When I realised I needed the same thing, we joined together. For those twelve months she had me to pass her recipes on to. I listened as she recalled distant lovers and nutty family members. We giggled as grumpy Ted arrived from the fields and frowned at us testing homemade wine.

Bless her, she tried to teach me to sew and cook. My darned socks looked more like gloves by the time I'd finished. I had more success with baking, although she said my cakes were made by someone with a heavy heart. That heart did become weighed down with affection for her. I found a deep joy in her companionship. We cleaned and aired, washed and ironed. And now, I would be with her when she died.

'Shut up, fool. I got no time for the jibba-jabba. Don't make me mad, Argh!'

I smiled. It was Bill's idea. I wanted to get her a bell so she could call us from her bedroom. He found an electronic keyring that spoke quotes by Mr T from The A Team when you pressed the buttons. Genius. When it sounded, it never failed to bring a smile instead of only worry.

She lay in the middle of the double bed. Ted had insisted that he sleep on the sofa so she could have her rest. I think she understood that he couldn't watch her die. Each day she was a little more tired; there was a little more gone. I often slept next to her. No one should die alone. I'd wake with a jolt and find she had moved her hand to rest against my side during the night.

'Hi, Erin. How are you?'

I received a sleepy smile in exchange. Her eyes followed me to the side of the bed. She'd been less lucid of late. She talked in riddles, mentioning people or things I knew nothing of. Perhaps that's the way the brain copes.

'Get my trainers out. I fancy my chances against that four-minute mile.'

Still joking at the end. I found it odd how the medical staff would discuss her problems in the kitchen, away from her. Did they know the patients didn't want to hear that stuff? I never asked why. Maybe the dying knew, and the advice and guidance was for us.

'Sit down.'

I perched by her side. It was strange how small she'd become. I breathed deeply - death smelled like spring to me. It was a cool breeze through billowing curtains. Floral bedsheets washed again. The gasps as long forgotten memories returned. Smiles when old friends and family said farewell. Or the reassuring tap-tap-tap of raindrops from leaking guttering on blistered window sills beating the drum for the final lament.

'What are you wearing, Katie?'

'I know. I shrank an entire load. I did a colour wash after the sheets and left it on the wrong setting. The boys will castrate themselves if they try to put their underwear on. The only good thing is Ted's shirts might fit.'

Her coughing took my grin away.

'Well, you can't walk around in stuff like that unless you're after a job in a titty bar.' She paused and gathered her breath. 'It's time now. I want to say goodbye properly.'

'I'm so sorry, Erin. You didn't deserve this.'

'Stop that. We all follow a path. I've had a good life. I had it all. A great husband, the kids I needed to make me complete. And then you gave me my dreams. I worry about Ted. Will you stay and look after him when I've gone? Not for too long, of course. You've your own life to lead. Have children, Katie. As soon as you can. A family is everything.'

Bill and Simon arrived at that point. They were about as comfortable with the whole process as Ted was. I wondered what would have happened if I hadn't been around. Who would have done what was needed? Maybe a greater power sent me to help in the same way many years later Irina would help me.

The boys had finished school and Ted got them labourer's jobs on the farm. Bill and I kissed a couple of times when we'd had a few drinks. He was keen to go further, but I made sure that Simon was about. I liked Bill but there was a shade to him of something I didn't like. I couldn't put my finger on it. He was angry when I told him I saw him as a brother and wouldn't do it again.

Not long after, Simon stated he had feelings for me. I explained the same thing to him. Even though we weren't blood-related, that's how I felt. Simon nodded and smiled after our chat. He, at least, understood.

'Come in boys, give your mum a kiss.'

They shuffled in and did their duty.

'Well, you are men now. Look at you.'

It was true. The wiry children were long gone. Manual labour and good food had packed muscle on them without me noticing. Simon reddened as he was examined. Bill remained emotionless. His gaze turned to me and goose bumps popped up on my arms.

I turned to Erin. She'd seen it too.

'I love you, boys. Now get going and I'll see you later.'

Mine and Bill's eyes met as he left the room. His were distant. That should've been a warning. Erin coughed and brought my attention back to her.

'I wish I could be here to help you, Katie. All the men will want you. I'm not being biased. You're so pretty, but distant. A lot has gone on in your life and you've put up barriers. You're unattainable, and people try to take what they can't have. The lads struggle as well. I hope you'll all look out for each other.'

That was the last thing Erin said. She didn't die right then, but she entered a merciful sleep from which she would never wake. Her words made me sad, but not devastated because she was correct. My life had taught me to keep a piece of me hidden. When things went bad, which they always did, the part I held in reserve was protection. It would be that which kept me safe. Dark times were coming, and I would need to be ready.

40
THE SHOCK OF SEEING BILL

I return to my house straight away. My heart pounds and it isn't through exercise. I bump into the landlord as he carries the microwave out of the front door.

'Hi, Katie. They rang me and told me this stopped working. It's pretty old, so I'll bin it and pick up a new one at the weekend.'

I can't think what to say and blink at him.

'Are you okay? You're ever so pale.'

I feign exhaustion. 'Tired. Thank you for sorting that so quick.' He's not convinced but shuffles past with a concerned expression.

'By the way, a bloke in a suit was here asking for you. Handsome chap. He said something about not being able to make your appointment tomorrow afternoon and he'll meet you here instead. There's a note under your door.'

I don't give him a chance to see my face fall, and hammer up the stairs. It can only be Tim Thorn. Sure enough, the note is from him. "Ten o'clock. Be here."

I pace around my bed until I get a cramp in my hips. What to do? I've always known at some point he'd try something on. Tomorrow will be when. I do not even want to think about the possibility of Bill getting in touch with him. Thorn forces my hand by today's demands.

Where can I go? Irina will let me stay and Radic said he would have a place for me. I own too much stuff to take on the train and taxis are expensive. If I'm not here tomorrow when Thorn turns up, he'll be immediately suspicious. I must buy time. Weeks if possible, certainly more than a day. I ring Irina.

'Katie, how are you?'

She sounds as though she had a late night, or perhaps an early morning.

'Irina. My life here has gone rotten if you know what I mean. I'm going to make the move.' Silence. 'Is that okay? I've got nowhere to stay.'

'Yes, sorry. I'm just surprised. No problem. Relax. I'll ring you in five minutes and we'll sort it out.'

'Sure.' I hear a man's voice as the phone line goes dead. It sounds like Gregor. I search my feelings and realise I have none. All I hope is it won't complicate things.

It will be a long five minutes. Mai always told me silence was the answer. Still your mind and let it do its job. Anything was worth trying even though I never managed much in prison. I haven't tried it for years. I think of her and empty my mind of the rest. Images of Bill and Thorn form and dissolve. After a few moments, I surprise myself as a sense of clarity comes over me.

There are only two things of immediate importance. Number one, I need to get away. I don't keep my money in the bank. There's nothing I can't leave behind. And either friends will help me or they won't; that decision is out of my hands. However, should I go before tomorrow? Because number two is Thorn.

He controls my future. Thorn wants to possess me in the way many have tried. People like that don't stop until they get what they want or you control them. Once he realises I'm gone, I'll need to be a ghost. With new make-up I can look totally different. I'll dress so no one would guess from where I came. My striking body-art and dyed hair will be further camouflage. Eventually, I'll be forgotten.

My phone rings and I nearly drop it. The caller has withheld their number.

'Hello.'

'Hi, how are you?' It's Radic. I keep it neutral, I'm not sure why. Surely my phone isn't bugged, although maybe his is?

'Things have changed, and I was hoping to make the move we discussed.'

'No problem. We'll help. I can get someone to collect you.'

Perhaps this mindfulness does work. 'That would be brilliant.'

'Text Irina your address. When do you want the van there?'

'Okay. A car is fine. I don't have much stuff.' I take a deep breath. 'Can you make it tomorrow?'

'What time?'

'In the afternoon…'

41
WAITING FOR THORN

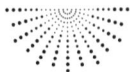

I don't sleep. I can't eat. I do nothing. The peace I found earlier vanishes in a haze of vivid flashbacks. The horror of what happened returns in single pictures. When I finally spoke to a shrink inside, the lady told me I had repressed the memories. She said it's normal to bury horrible experiences. There were still events beyond recall that I vowed I would never acknowledge again.

The morning sun peeks through the curtains and I realise the barriers I put in place in my mind all those years ago were exactly that. They were only a dam against a river. The water boils now and pebbles fall from the structure. It will fail. It's as sure as time.

I don't know how I'll respond. If I'm engulfed, I could lose control. The consequences before were life-altering. Life-ruining in fact. No one knows that more than me.

There's no point packing as I need him to think everything is normal. I dress in my regular clothes, even down to my gloves. When the doorbell rings, I put red lipstick on my otherwise clean face and go to let him in.

It's a mild day, and he loosens his tie. He avoids eye contact and looks beyond me. There's a sheen of sweat on his forehead which today's temperature isn't warm enough to have caused. He's here for something today. That's a fact. I walk up the stairs behind him and notice he hasn't even bothered to bring his briefcase.

He stands in the middle of the room, filling it. 'Well, Katie. What's new?'

'Not much. My life is boring.'

He takes a few steps to the wardrobe and opens it wide. A box with my mementoes on the floor is briefly examined. 'Now that's not true, is it?'

'What do you mean?'

'You've changed, Katie. You're not so meek and mild. I respect that. You look healthy and strong. But you've forgotten where you came from.'

'That's rubbish. I'm aware of what I am.'

'Why do I sense trouble?'

'Perhaps I understand how the world works.'

His eyes narrow as he debates whether he likes that comment. 'Do you regret what you did?' he eventually asks.

'Of course, I could ruin each new day with regret.'

'For young people, regret, although painful to experience, can be a helpful emotion. That pain might cause refocusing and the pursuit of a new path. But do you feel remorse, for that is the higher calling?'

He's right. I had it drummed into me on prison courses. Regret motivates a person to avoid punishment in the future, while remorse leads to avoiding the hurtful actions in the first place. Showing remorse means exposing and revisiting the past to learn from it — something I've been loathed to do. I'm about to reply when I notice the look on his face. He hasn't come to counsel me.

Thorn steps toward me, reaches over my head, and pushes the door shut. 'I ordered you to be honest with me.'

I attempt to remain calm but my core temperature rises a thousand degrees. What can he see? He can't know anything.

'Your job, Katie. You quit your job.'

I decide the best course of action is to keep him talking. The manager must have told him. My brain filters through every reason I can imagine for quitting that job.

'I know.'

'You're supposed to tell me.'

'I was seeing you today.'

'Don't give me that bullshit. Why did you resign? Are you going on a little holiday?'

I insert the confusion I planned into the conversation. 'Actually, I have a friend who said I could stay at his house in Skegness. Is that okay?'

'Is that right? I don't think so. You are mine. I hope you're not going to run.'

'Of course not. Where would I go? And with what? One of the managers was perving on me. The job sucked anyway. An agency on St. Andrew's Street has assembly jobs for more money. They've said I can start next week.'

He considers the answer.

'You'd better not be jerking me around. I believe today is a very good time for us to evaluate our relationship.'

He's so close, I feel his warm breath on my hairline. He puts his finger under my chin and lifts my head so I stare into his dark-brown eyes.

'You are different. That lipstick suits you. You look…' I sense he wants to say pretty but stops himself. 'You know I split up with my girlfriend. This job is stressful, you see. All the lies erode your humanity. It really pisses me off. You've let me down, Katie, and now you need to make amends.'

'I'm not sleeping with you.'

A finger traces my jawline and moves up the side of my face to the top of my head. With his hand flat on my crown, he applies pressure. 'Who said anything about that?'

On my knees again, I steel myself for the task ahead. Ever

since I heard he'd made the other girl do this, I knew that I would be unlikely to escape the same fate. I undo his belt and am unsurprised to find the lack of underwear. The size of his manhood is a shock. Not long but thick and angry. I prise it free and hear him catch his breath.

'Not taking your gloves off?'

'I thought you'd prefer that.'

'Whatever. You girls can be mean with your nails. Get started.'

He's clean but disgusting, if that makes sense. Sadly, I've done worse. I try to empty my mind again, but with my mouth full it's impossible. I decide no one will use me again like this. Rage flushes through my system and an ever more influential part of me says bite it off. What would the authorities do after that? I look up. His face is an unusual mix of anger and ecstasy.

I have no doubt whatsoever from that expression he would kill me if I bit down. Maybe I'm still not doing it right as I'm not convinced he's enjoying it, but then, our gazes meet, and boom! He opens his eyes a few seconds later and they display disgust. He brings his hand back to slap me and I tense. Instead, he pushes me to one side and over.

He reaches down for his trousers and slowly tucks himself in. As he leaves, he grins. 'I'll see you here next week. Same time. Same place. Same thing.'

When the door closes, I spit on the floor.

42
A BOTTLE OF MOUTHWASH LATER

The man who arrives is one of the three quiet men from the club; the guy with the scary eye. He frightens the shit out of the postman. Radic listened to what I'd said and sent a normal car. Tony introduces himself by stating his name. He makes me wait in the room while he carries my things down. When the last item has gone, he looks at me and nods.

'Two minutes. I wait in car.'

After he's left, I peek under the bed and in the wardrobe for the last time, even though I have done it twice already. I leave my keys on the table, adjust the handle so it will lock, and pull the door closed. I wonder who will open it first and how; the landlord with his master when he fails to receive his rent, or Thorn with his boot when he doesn't get an answer?

I step outside and don't look back. There is nothing behind. This place was never home. Tony keeps to the speed limits but we still make good time. I try to chat, but I'm on the side with the ruined eye and find it hard to focus on anything but that. He parks at the rear of the pub at five p.m. and I follow him up to the club. Radic and Irina are waiting. They hug me. I turn to thank Tony, but he's gone.

Radic departs to fetch water after I decline vodka, leaving us girls to chat.

'Radic has a room ready for you. We'll be neighbours.'

'I thought I'd be more unsettled. Somehow, I know it's the right decision.'

'What made your mind up?'

'Two things. My probation guy was as we feared. I can't live under those rules and this is my only way out.'

'No problem. We'll have fun together. Won't we Radic?'

He places cold bottles in front of us and smiles. 'Not too much fun. This club will be busier soon. There are businessmen coming, and I'll need my best girls to run the show.'

I see my reflection in the mirror. I'm washed out. I start from here. The new me will save money, finish her tattoos, take holidays, and live again.

'Blonde hair.'

'What's that, Katie?' asks Irina.

'I'm going to go blonde.'

'Well, okay, I'll do it for you.'

'Umm.'

'Cheeky. I was a trained hairdresser. There are lots of exciting things you don't know about me.'

I sheepishly smile at Radic. 'I will need a new ID. Is that okay? I'll pay you.'

'A foreign one you can have for free. If you want British, then you'll have to contribute. It'll take longer as well. There's no rush. Nobody knows you're here. Begin again now your decision is final. You've made a good call. Screw the courts. You did your time for a mistake as a young girl. It's not fair that it ruins the rest of your life.'

'Thank you. I'm still not sure why you're helping me. It would help if you were honest, even if I may not like it.'

He smiles and then laughs. 'In a way, that is why. You are honest. I need tough women to work in a place like this. I prefer them to be attractive too. The men enjoy more. You can handle yourself. Irina said to help you. That's good enough for me. If I tell the truth, it's because you are also a criminal. You won't be going to the police at a moment of weakness. You know the score.'

Radic doesn't pull his punches. I appreciate that but make a mental note to probe Irina for exactly what he does. My own virtue is not without doubt. Now I experience recollections of my past, I worry how responsible I am for the violent crime I committed. It's a worrying thought as my future heads in a similar direction.

'Wait a minute,' says Irina. 'What was the other thing? You mentioned two reasons why you chose to leave, but you only said one.'

'I bumped into the man who ruined my life. In the street, in broad daylight, if you can believe it. You said I would tell you my story when I was ready. That time has come.'

43
THE ELEVENTH MEMORY - AGE SEVENTEEN

I was seventeen and struggling along with my college course. The atmosphere in the farmhouse had been foul. The loss of his wife ate into Ted so badly that he could see no joy in anything. He refused to eat even if I left a cooked meal out for him. Work was the only thing that distracted him. We would spot him on his tractor in the dusky distance or tinkering in the shed by flashlight with various pieces of farm machinery.

At home, he brewed tea, sat in the posh lounge in one of the armchairs, and smoked. All night. I'd never really been in that room until he ordered me to collect his cups from there. Erin said it was kept nice for visitors, but none ever went in there. Those seats became unfit for visitors as Ted never got changed. By then, I don't think he showered or bathed either.

That evening, we'd had a row as usual. He picked the fact we'd run out of washing-up liquid and went off on one. The days of me arguing back stopped many months before as Ted would build himself up into a frightening rage.

The weird thing was we always did the shopping list together on Friday night. He drove me to the shops and waited in the car every Saturday while I bought the groceries. It was as much his fault as mine.

Sometimes he would say he fancied an ice cream when we arrived. I'd buy a pack of four and we'd eat two each, just like we did years before. It was as though being in the house or around the farm sickened him. But we had to return, and the murderous looks over the slightest misdemeanours resumed.

That night's row had been epic because I'd had enough. The boys were leaving for the Merchant Navy the following day. Simon regularly clashed with Ted and kept out of his way. Bill still worked hard for him, but an exciting world was out there. Incredibly, Ted blamed me for them wanting to see it.

I refused to waste my breath defending myself. I told him that I would also leave soon. He'd shouted "Good" at me and stormed out the house. The problem with that was I had nowhere to go. There were college friends but no one I saw away from there. I'd let myself become isolated at the farm. The boys had given up asking me if I wanted to join them by this point.

It was Simon who found me lying on my bed feeling sorry for myself. He told me that they were having a little party at the barn. Just him, Bill and the twins. A last blast before they left.

'Go on, Katie. It will be a laugh. A few drinks and a fire. Like old times.'

'I don't know. It's freezing tonight.'

'We've got blankets and whisky, and Jordan's nicked five steaks from his dad's freezer. It's our final night, and I'm never coming back here. Bill neither. Come and say goodbye.'

And so, I said yes.

The derelict barn perched on the edge of the land, but the roof was sound. We'd played in it for years. Judging by the number of empty bottles and cans outside when I arrived, they had found new games to enjoy there. The twins turned up and, for a while, we could have been young again. Apart from the alcohol that was.

I rarely drank but, perhaps because of the argument and

feeling lonely, I joined in with enthusiasm. I remember thinking everything was hilarious and wondered why had I stopped hanging about with these guys. They cooked the steaks but nobody ate them. We sat around as it got late and played drinking games. That's when my recollection becomes hazy.

I recall Bill being dared to take his clothes off and doing it. Simon refused, but I didn't. Just my top half. I can't believe I did it. It was so unlike me. The boys roared their approval, and I felt popular. For the first time in my life, I was desired.

I remember the sting of neat spirit as it trickled down my throat and the unfamiliar burn as it hit my stomach. The fire, which was in an old steel wheelbarrow, cast strange shadows. Bill, Simon and Jordan resembled demons from hell as the logs sparked flames into the sky. A moaning Justin struggled to his feet and bounced around in a weird dance. The rest of us laughed.

I can't recall complete details. The next hour has huge parts missing, like someone has taken large, random slices from a big cheesecake. It's as though I zone back in and Bill is kissing me on one side and Simon on the other. I can hear strange noises from Justin while Jordan is cheering.

To my shame, I think I liked it. Simon's tongue was gentle. Bill whispered in my ear. There was heat from naked bodies and warmth from the fire. I laughed and swayed and kissed them back. And then it changed.

Kisses hardened and fingers roamed. What had been soft became hard. There were too many hands. But I didn't stop them.

The next event I recall is being pushed over a stack of huge tractor tyres. They were rough and coarse like the grip that crushed my breasts. My wrists were pulled away from me and my legs spread. I still didn't stop them. Maybe I didn't want to.

There's darkness then for a while. Different voices behind me, different sizes inside of me. I heard laughs as they ridiculed useless Justin, and curses from Simon as he shuddered.

It was then that I spoke. At first, I'm not even sure if I made a sound; just moved my mouth in fear to the rhythmic pounding. A burst of deep warmth had me feeling as if I might explode. Finally, there was someone who was cruel. That's when I found my voice.

There were only two of us then. My hands didn't need holding as I had frozen. I shouted as he smacked my thighs. A bare guttural howl of denial broke from my mouth as a fist clenched my hair. He yanked it towards him and my back arched. And still he went on.

I wondered if my mind left me, as through those flames, I thought I saw Ted watching in the distance. My eyes slammed shut as the pain intensified. When I opened them, who knows how much later, he was gone, and I was alone.

I remained standing next to those tyres. Fluid ran down my legs and my skin burned. Eventually, I kneeled and cried. I raged at the unfairness of life. I sobbed for my worthless self but, deep down, I knew I deserved it.

44
A NEW WAY OF THINKING

Radic and Irina stare at me. It must sound desperate when told like that. For years, I hid those memories away. So much time passed that I couldn't remember exactly why. Now I do. The horror of what happened made me feel like a victim and a fool. What possessed me to make out with more than one boy at a time? Was it the alcohol, or did I have some kind of slut complex that made me want to be treated like that, encourage it even?

The revulsion I experience now when I wonder whether I did enough to stop them is too much to bear. I remember crying out, but did I shout stop? I was a strong girl. Why didn't I struggle? I couldn't even remember who out of the boys had done what. Did they all get involved or was it just Simon and Bill. Did the others watch?

I resolve to re-bury that day. Nothing good can come from living with these thoughts.

Radic is the first to recover. Irina remains dumbstruck.

'What happened after that?'

'Nothing really. I staggered back to the farmhouse. It was dawn and one of those mornings when the fen farmlands are breathtaking. Each slow step along the frost-crusted track towards the weak sun made the previous night's experience seem surreal. I was a stranger in my own body. I think I immediately left the reality of what happened behind in that barn.

'When I got back, the place was empty. Ted would have been at work. The boys weren't due to leave until midday, but the stuff they had packed ready at the door was gone. I didn't know what to do with myself. In the end, I just got on with my jobs. With each passing day the memories fuzzed over or disappeared. Ted looked at me like I was a piece of filth. I knew he had seen us, yet he didn't do anything. Surely if it looked like I was being assaulted he would have done something?'

Irina manages to close her mouth. She stands and pulls me into a warm embrace.

'You poor thing. Those animals. It wasn't your fault. How old were you?'

'Seventeen.'

'You didn't go to the police?'

'No. I didn't think they'd believe me. I couldn't get it clear in my own head. They would ask about the drinking. If I told them I had taken my own top off, they would have laughed me out of the building.'

Radic pours a drink from behind the bar. He downs it in one and then brings me a stiff measure. I decline. 'That's not the answer. Although I don't know what is.'

He has a daughter. I can virtually see him processing how it would make him feel if the tale was about her. 'What happened to these men?'

'Boys. They were boys, really. Simon and Bill disappeared into the Merchant Navy. I never saw them again, and they didn't write. The twins had no reason to come around with the others gone, and I only ever saw them from a distance. Ted never mentioned it. He and I went mad together.'

'What do you mean?' asks Irina.

'We both retreated from the world. He had lost his wife and his beloved children. We were never close. I think I only served to remind him of what he'd lost. As for me, I struggled to get out of bed. My college eventually gave up trying to contact me. Someone came, but I hid in the toilet. Ted couldn't bring himself to throw me out and I couldn't find the strength to leave.

'I spoke little, and he said plenty. As the months ticked by, he would come to blame me for everything. The blame for the boys not staying in touch was a frequent stick with which to beat me. I would sit for hours staring into space. I couldn't keep on top of the housework even though I had nothing else to do.'

Tears burst from my eyes. I was so lonely. My shoulders heave. I'm aware that Radic has been pacing the room. He shouts when he finally speaks.

'If I were you, I would take my revenge. They shouldn't get away with that.'

'But some of it was my fault.'

Irina holds my face in front of hers. 'Stop. What you think is a normal reaction. Many victims feel like that. They are responsible. Who knows what would have happened if you had fought back.'

I push her away. I can't stand for them to see me like this. Make-up stings my eyes.

Irina looks sad.

Radic looks angry.

I scream in disgust, 'I fucking enjoyed it. I had an orgasm.'

Their confused shocked faces give me a chance to recover. I pick up the drink Radic tried to give me and knock it back. The strong chemical taste is heaven sent. I force myself to take even breaths.

'Look. It happened to me. I've repressed that period for a long time but it's coming back now. I couldn't stop it even if I wanted to. Perhaps I'll know what to do when I've dredged up every last moment. In the meantime, please, give me some space and some time. I'm so thankful for your kindness, so don't think I'm not.'

The two of them glance at each other and then nod at me.

'I'm just going for a walk to clear my head. Give me an hour.' I put my coat back on.

Radic walks past and opens the door for me. 'When the time comes,' he says, 'I will help you.'

My instant reaction is to tell him to forget it. However, today there is a new emotion, and that is anger. 'Thank you.'

I take a moment to gather myself and head down the stairs. I stop half way and can hear them talking.

'Wow. I wasn't expecting that,' says Irina.

'No. There's more though.'

'What do you mean?'

'She said she would tell us everything. A gang rape is awful. It's tough to imagine how that would affect a young girl.'

'So?'

'Katie went to prison for sixteen years. You don't get a life sentence for being gang raped. Her story can only get worse.'

45
THE SEASIDE

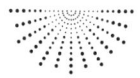

My next appointment with Tim Thorn at the house was two days ago. I smile when I imagine him arriving and me not being in. He must have been furious. My phone then going straight to voicemail would've added to his rage. I'm not sure how easy it is to track phones, so I removed the sim card from mine. Irina and Radic were given the new number. Nobody else needs to know.

Thorn will have been fuming to begin with. When I failed to return his calls, he would've become nervous. I should think another client absconding wouldn't go down well. No doubt confident he could talk himself out of any situation that arose, he'd rather not have to do so. I figured it would take forty-eight hours before he'd consider reporting it.

So, Irina and I planned a trip to the seaside. I informed Radic to keep him in the loop. He told Tony One Eye, as we've been calling him, to drive us here. We sit in the back of the car giggling like teenagers. Tony pulls into the car park behind the fairground at Hunstanton seafront. I decide to get the nasty job out of the way first.

I press the buttons and find I'm looking forward to it. The

implications for him are far-reaching. His life will never be the same. Thorn is a piece of scum. He deserves everything he gets. I'm going to enjoy this. He picks up on the second ring.

'Thorn.'

'It's me.'

'Katie, where the hell are you?'

'Now, now, Tim. There's no need for rudeness.'

'I will be at your house in an hour. You better have a fantastic reason for missing our appointment, or I'll have you rammed back in jail so fast you'll wonder if you ever really left.'

'I don't think so.'

There is a pause. The conceited idiot can hardly comprehend my words. 'What did you say?'

'You've been abusing women for too long. I've met others who've had to endure your urges. How long has this been going on? It must be years. I bet there are hundreds of girls out there who will want to thank me after today.'

'No one believes lying whores like you. They'll say it's sour grapes because I sent you back to prison. I will write such a glowing review that they'll never release you again.'

I give him a few seconds to let him think he's won.

'Katie, you still there? Be in when I arrive and be prepared to do some serious grovelling.'

I smile. I've knelt at his knees for the last time.

'I have a message for you which I'll send now. It might take a few minutes. I won't be able to meet you because I'm at the seaside. Ring me when you've received the email. I'll be having an ice-cream.'

I cut him off, open my email, and send the draft I stored earlier. The signal isn't that strong so I return to the car. He'll need a few moments to process it anyway.

I knock on the driver's window. 'Come on you two. I fancy a Flake 99.'

All the booths on the promenade are shut. A gusting wind blasts the brave souls who venture out there, us included. We find an ice-cream van behind an amusement arcade. I think I mishear her when she charges me £7.50. Thieving cow. It's worth every penny though when I hand one to Tony. His face lights up and he grins such a wide smile that I notice for the first time he's missing one of his front teeth.

We sit on a bench looking out over the caravans and eat our cones like three pensioners on a day trip. I imagined this moment many times when I sweated in my cell. Admittedly, the sun was shining in my dreams. I've just finished the chocolate flake which I saved until last when my phone rings. It's Thorn. I should think a very different one.

'What do you want?'

'This is the final time you speak to me. I'm leaving Cambridge and starting a new life elsewhere. You are going to fabricate your records, or that video will be released to the newspapers. Tell them I'm doing fine, or I'll post images of me giving you a blow job to every single person who works with you.

'You shall become the best probation officer ever, because if I hear any examples of you imposing your sick desires on anyone else, the entire world will know the depraved deviant who blackmailed vulnerable women into providing him with sexual favours.'

'What makes you imagine I won't risk being found out? You'd go back to jail regardless of what happened to me.'

'Because you're not stupid. I researched it. You are guilty of the worst kind of misconduct in public office ever. You'd be lucky to get less than ten years.'

'I can't fabricate records forever. What if I became ill? You have a licence for life. At some point they'll find out and arrest you.'

'You don't get it, do you? I'm gone. Disappeared. I won't exist.

It's better if no one is looking for me, so I'll keep my side of the bargain. Your life, as it was, is finished. Do your job properly or you'll be inside. I bet you can imagine how much we prisoners love bent probation officers. Take care, Mr Thorn. Because I *will* know.'

I end the call, remove the sim from the phone, bend it in half, and drop it below onto the shingle. The other two are waiting on the bench. I see the funfair come into life behind them. It must be open.

'What's the time, Tony?'

'Ten past ten.'

We have all day. I've never been on a rollercoaster.

'I take it by you skipping over here that it went well?' asks Irina

'It did. Now, who wants me to treat them to a ride on the spinning teacups?'

'Me, please.' Irina looks as happy as I feel.

We get on but soon it makes us both feel queasy. We twirl round and round, getting greener by the minute. I shout at the man running it, but he thinks we want to go faster. Irina crawls off at the end, weak with laughter and relief.

We can't encourage Tony onto any of the rides. He shakes his head and holds his heart. When it's time to leave, we walk past the carousel. He stops and stares. I suppose they have them the world over. Everyone was innocent once. Maybe he recalls his own child sitting on the horse in front of him. I wave to the man and pay for us all to go on. Except for us three, the ride is empty. Perhaps that's why we seem to be on it forever.

It isn't the sea breeze which makes water stream from Tony's eyes. I can see his expression without him knowing I'm watching. His thought processes change as his battered face creases. He recalls happy times and is pleased that, even though they are over, he is lucky to own them. His head goes back as he bursts into laughter. I'm sharing a ride with a maniacal goblin who punches the air and releases a whoop. Irina joins in and bellows, 'Go, Tony.'

I stand on my stirrups and roar the words that consume me; 'Freedom!'

Is there a better feeling?

46

A WEEK LATER

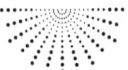

A WOMAN KNOWS

Radic is having a party at his house this evening and has asked me to pop over and help his wife, Sofiya. I thought he wanted me to be some kind of waitress at first. But when he said Tony would pick me up at four in the afternoon, I was confused.

I see a lot of Tony. He talks little. The car ride home from the coast was a silent affair. Irina fell asleep and Tony drove with a half-smile on his face. He's in the club most nights with his two companions. Were the three of them friends from the Ukraine? I asked Radic about them. Unusually, I caught him in a downbeat moment. He frowned and told me that men like them have no friends. They might have acquaintances they drink with but only in silence.

Chilling. I wonder what happened for their lives to be so devoid of emotion. Tony gives me a lift whenever I ask, though. He saves me a fortune on taxis and has a habit of popping up when Irina and I most need him. I guessed he was a heavy for the club at first but there's never any trouble up there.

Tony and I pull up outside Radic's house. It's a big detached building, but still on an estate. I'm not sure what I was expecting. Al Capone's mansion, maybe. I knock on the door and notice Tony remains in the car. I tap on the window which he opens.

'You not coming in?'

'No. Tony waits here.' He winds the window back up so I'm aware it's not up for negotiation.

Sofiya lets me in and kisses me on both cheeks. 'Come in, Katie. We have some cooking to do in the kitchen.'

There are things that need doing but Sofiya does most of them. I think she can do everything without me. She pours me a glass of the wine she drinks, and after a while I forget that I'm being paid to be there. She tells me her daughter is at university now. They moved here five years ago and Sofiya misses her friends. I realise her life feels empty, and she perhaps wanted female company.

'Radic explained your situation. We needed to start a new life too. We had a son who was killed. As you can imagine, it devastated me. My husband only wanted to get even, which he did. That created more problems. It felt like everyone was after him, from the police to gangsters. We came here to protect our daughter most of all.'

'Does your husband do anything illegal?'

Her smile is rueful. 'I don't know. I've spent many years focusing on Karolina. It's obvious he's not just a garage or club owner.'

'Why doesn't Tony come in?'

'Tony has a job to do. Radic was like his little brother when they grew up. The pair of them got into loads of trouble. When I came along all those years ago, we fought for Radic's attention. We quarrelled. I love that word. Anyway, Tony went to prison for a long time and I won. Well, I thought I did. I'm not aware of what Radic is up to, but a while back he called for Tony. I suppose protection would be his purpose.'

'One more question. Is Radic his surname? It makes me laugh that you call him that as well.'

'He has always simply been only that. Now, Katie. Tell me about you.'

I can't help laughing. I realise why I'm there. It was her idea. That's very clever. Radic hasn't prised my history out of me yet. Give the job to a woman, and she'll discover the answers. I don't mind. In fact, I'm ready. Inside, I was able to forget what happened. You have so much time to serve that real life becomes meaningless. Thoughts of outside are pushed away. Then, like anything, the more you practice, the better you get.

I changed recently when I bumped into Bill. The things I buried now work their way to the surface. I am going to have to relive my past if I have any hope of moving on. I *was* wronged, but that doesn't excuse my actions. Did I deserve what I received?

A door slams and Radic walks in carrying a box.

'Afternoon, ladies. Started on the gin yet?'

Sofiya throws a tea towel at him.

'Sit down, Radic. I was about to tell Sofiya about a murder.'

47
THE TWELFTH MEMORY - AGE EIGHTEEN

The night my life changed forever was in the middle of an early summer heatwave. I had dropped out of college over six months before. Even though no one there could have known, I believed they were all aware of what happened. I struggled to maintain eye contact, even with the postman. At home, Ted and I resembled a married couple who couldn't bear to be in the same room as each other but had nowhere else to go.

It was peaceful for once, and I had flopped on the sofa for a rest after a shower. Ted came in early that night. I discovered later he'd found out the farm was being sold. He was going to lose everything. I don't think he cared that I would be homeless too. I sensed him over me and opened my eyes.

'Look at the state of you. Go and put some clothes on. I need to have a word.'

Not expecting anyone, I had worn only knickers and a vest top. I padded out and quickly put on a pair of tracksuit bottoms and a T-shirt. My head was fuzzy, so I brushed my teeth and splashed water on my face. I heard a cupboard slam. He was out of whisky. I can't remember when it appeared on the shopping list. It began as a bottle per week. We were up to three by then.

When he started to fill a flask for work, even three wasn't enough. The strange fact was that he hated the taste. He'd grimace with each sip. It'd make him mean. Some nights, he passed out quickly and snored in the chair which had become his pulpit. Other times he riled me playfully. I could tolerate being called a loser. But as his mood sickened, he'd start on blaming me for everything that had gone wrong since I arrived.

I found it was better to go in the room with him and listen and nod my head when he reached that point. Then he might not shout. It was my fault his wife had died. He blamed me for the boys not keeping in touch. I'd lost him his job that night, too.

Without whisky to medicate him that evening, he stayed awake. I remember watching him as he worked himself up. He hadn't mentioned the night at the barn before. I hoped he hadn't because there was still something left of the man Erin loved. Since she'd gone, it was as if he'd been infected by a parasite which slowly consumed all that was good in him. It must have run out of stuff to eat because this time he didn't hold back.

'The way you were dressed tonight shows what sort of a girl you are.'

I nodded as usual.

'You're a whore. I bet you came from a whore.'

I think I've always had a dark vengeful side. It is the survivor in me. There's a demon in the dark who takes only so much. It's the moment when I fight back. I decided that night to let it free.

'Screw you. Look at what you've become. A cruel monster who bullies an eighteen-year-old girl. You think I'm worthless, but you're beneath me. I am glad we have to leave this place because I can't stand to be in the presence of your rotting soul.'

I'm not sure where I got that last line. It summed him up perfectly. I believe he knew it too, and that's why he said what he did.

'What kind of woman does what you did? One man not

enough for you? What did they pay you, or did you enjoy it so much you did it for free?'

Time was softening my memory of what had happened in the barn, like each day was a fresh bandage enabling me to heal a little bit more. I didn't realise until that day that underneath I remained raw. Wounds like that don't heal. His comments exposed me completely, and that night, he didn't stop.

'Yeah, I saw. I watched for a while.'

I screamed at him. 'Why didn't you stop them?'

Without emotion, he replied. 'You loved it.'

I staggered from the room, his jeers ringing in my ears, and then he bellowed after me.

'We should take you down the docks. We'd make a killing. They always say do something you love and you'll never have to work a day. There's business here, too, seeing as we're not related.'

My memory plays tricks after that. I stumbled as my mind went blank. And then it was as if I became two people; both walking side-by-side. I watched myself grab a knife from the drawer and return to the lounge. There was no reaction, not even shock on either of our faces. Ted didn't move. He didn't even put up a hand to stop me.

They found him in that seat an hour after I rang for an ambulance. I don't know why I didn't ask for the police because medical intervention was futile. Twenty-five stabs had got the job done. I recall the paramedics staring at the body and then looking at me wilting on the sofa. They saw the bloody handprints on the wall and the knife on the table. Together they backed out, and closed the door.

I heard one shouting in his phone for the police, social services and the Coroners Officer. All I remember after is the arrival of many people. And then nothing. They said I went wild and had to be sedated. There were a few strange days with warped dreams in hospital and then they took me to court. I didn't know what to say. What is there to say after doing something like that?

The magistrates sent me to prison to await my trial. And that's where I stayed, for sixteen years.

48
UNFINISHED BUSINESS

There's no shock on their faces, only sadness. I realise Radic knew but wanted to hear my side. Sofiya's expression crumpled in the telling. She strides over and gently holds me with such compassion. After a few seconds, I collapse onto her.

It takes a good ten minutes before I'm ready to untangle myself from her. Smudged make-up covers her face and my top. Radic looks confused.

'How come they sent you down for so long? What is the phrase? Extenuating circumstances? He provoked you.'

'That depends on your point of view. I pleaded guilty to manslaughter, but they made me go to trial for murder. My barrister tried, but I gave him no help. He dredged up my entire childhood. It was hard enough listening to that. He suspected there was something else in the background but I couldn't bring myself to mention it.'

'You didn't tell them about the rape? My God, why not?'

'I didn't want anyone to know. I still felt it was my fault. There was no way I could repeat what happened in front of all those people. I kind of detached myself from the whole experience. The judge called me unfeeling and cold-hearted.'

'Katie, you say whatever it takes to get the best deal.'

'Enough of that,' Sofiya cuts in. 'It still seems harsh for a young girl that's had a terrible upbringing.'

'Without the rape, it was just name-calling. He never hit me. I wasn't in danger. I should have done any number of different things except kill him. The judge described it as a frenzied attack. I had to leave the room and fetch the weapon. You could argue that I've been lucky as he could have given me a minimum term of twenty-five years instead of sixteen.'

'Yes, but if you'd told them what those men did to you, it would have been much less.'

'I know. Manslaughter might have been five years. It's hard to remember now but I recall wanting to be punished. I lost my reason and gave up. I never planned to serve the sentence anyway. It's mind-blowing to realise you're capable of murder. I'd killed someone for no good reason. Do you know what that feels like?'

Radic's impassive face meant I was saying that to the wrong person. Sofiya's sorrow shows she understands.

'There was a final part I had to sort out,' I add. 'But as soon as that was done, it was time to die.'

'You were going to kill yourself?' says a shocked Sofiya.

'Yes. I couldn't live with what I did.'

'What stopped you?' Radic receives a dirty look from Sofiya, but she realises she wants to hear the answer too.

'I came close. I acquired the pills once and flushed them at the last minute. A few weeks after that, I got hold of an officer's porcelain mug. After smashing it, the jagged edge did the trick, but I paused after the first nick. As I said, since I was young I've kept a part of me behind. It's the piece that stops me folding when fate rips the carpet away. I'd been wronged. Somehow, it convinced me I still had a purpose.'

Radic clicks his fingers. 'It is revenge. You must take your revenge.'

'Don't put thoughts in her head, Radic.'

'No, can't you see? It all stems back to the people who did that evil thing to you. If they hadn't done that, you wouldn't have dropped out of school. You could have moved out of home, or at the very least, he wouldn't have been able to call you the things he did which made you snap.'

He's put into words the truth of what's been lurking at the back of my mind.

'What do you think I should do?' I ask his wife.

'Let it go, Katie,' said Sofiya. 'Nothing good can come from it. Start again and build new memories.'

Radic interrupts. 'They ruined your life. As the Chinese saying goes, it's only polite to reciprocate.'

49

LOST HEART

The pretence of helping Sofiya is over. Radic informs Tony outside that he'll drive me home instead, and we get into a smart sports car. Sofiya stands at the front door, waves, and gives Radic a warning look as we leave. He's quiet as he drives. Finally, when we hit the parkway, he says what's on his mind.

'There's something else, isn't there?'

There is something else. It's awful. I swore I would never think about it again and I managed that inside prison. It will kill me to drag the memory from the quietest part of me.

'Yes.'

He doesn't comment further. I'm thankful for that. I want Irina there when I say the words that could destroy me. Radic stops outside the flats and turns off the engine. I place my hand on his and stare out the window. My jaw clenches.

'You better come in.'

We walk up the steps to Irina's and knock. She's just out the shower, and laughs at the fact she's naked behind the door. The smile falls from her face as she sees our's. She steps aside and we enter. Irina pulls on a dressing gown.

'Do you want a drink, Katie?'

'No. I need a clear head.'

Irina hears the account I gave Radic and Sofiya. She isn't surprised as she met me in jail. Radic decides he needs a whisky and Irina joins him. They sit on the sofa, which makes it look full. It would have amused me any other day.

My stomach arrives in my mouth and I wonder if I can do this. I must. I stand in front of them. They regard me with trepidation, and I reveal my deepest secret.

'There is one more memory. I was mopping the floor when they arrived to remove my heart.'

50
THE THIRTEENTH MEMORY - AGE NINETEEN

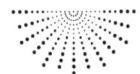

I had desperately tried to keep busy that morning. Anything but think about what was going to occur.

'Katie. They've arrived. Off you go.'

Two officers from the visits hall waited at the gate. My wing officer took the mop off me. She was usually a joker. It was her way of dealing with the madness of prison life. There were no smiles that day. She put her hand on my shoulder.

'Be strong, Katie. I'll be here when you return.'

I nodded. They'd have eyes on me the moment I walked back.

'Don't forget your ID card.'

I rummaged in my pockets. The stress of the situation became evident as I began to panic.

'Calm down. It's around your neck.'

My eyes flittered and my mouth opened to gasp in relief.

'Katie. You must get a hold of yourself. You will remember this meeting for the rest of your life. Try to enjoy it in some way.'

'Thank you.' I wasn't listening but guessed I should say something.

The officers at the gate watched me warily as they let me out. A shout of, 'Good luck,' echoed around the landing. By the faces I saw, it seemed everyone knew my business. Many were interested in how I'd react. The sad expressions and tears of others betrayed similar life-altering experiences. They were the ones who'd help me through the aftermath. I wasn't the first and I wouldn't be the last. Life goes on.

An old con said I'd remember today as if they had etched it along my spine. I might forget at times, but it would always be there until I died. I can still hear the squeak of the officer's shoes on the polished floor. The smell of soggy fish and chips from the kitchens wafting along the main prison corridor could be in the room now.

I fiddled with shirt buttons and ran my fingers through my hair. Anything to stop me focusing on what was about to happen.

I proceeded to the desk and signed in. Senior Officer Blakes, a tall black woman who took no shit whatsoever, managed visits that day. An arm directed me into a cubicle and I received the most thorough pat-down search I'd had since I arrived. She would have felt what I had for breakfast if I hadn't been too nervous to eat anything.

Another prisoner came out of the solicitor booths. She looked defeated. With a gesture to the air, and to no one in particular, she laughed.

'No chance of an appeal. Told me to serve my time.'

She and I had never got on. She received three months when I received my sixteen years and had been sent back again. Career criminals such as her preyed on the new arrivals. She'd tried to bully me. Little did she know I had nothing to lose. You only barge your way into someone's cell once if they have no fear.

Our eyes meet. I didn't expect to see sympathy.

'You can do it, Katie. Good luck.'

Tears stung. I hauled in air.

'The hall is empty now,' Blakes said. 'The final legal has gone, so you have the place to yourself. You have an hour, please use every second.'

They opened the first door and through the glass window of the next I could see the social workers and the prison support staff. Then, as I entered the room, Chloe toddled into view. I staggered a few steps. The weight of my choices instantly became too much for me to bear. I screamed; a strangled sound echoed in the high ceiling. It was me even though it sounded like an animal caught in a trap.

My daughter flinched and ran for the safety of the other adults, falling twice on the way. She either didn't recognise me, or I scared her. My common sense told me she was only eighteen months old, but I engulfed those thoughts in another roar of despair from I know not where. Strong arms dragged me from the room. A firm smack across my face brought me back to life. Blakes loomed large in front of me.

'You only get one more chance at this. If you break down like that again we'll have to take you to the wing. This is the last opportunity for you to see her.'

'I've changed my mind, I can't do it. She's mine.'

I couldn't breathe. My head thrashed from side-to-side. They lowered me to the floor where I wept without restraint. The prison worker who I'd dealt with this matter arrived, and, with help, she gently helped me to a seat.

'We know this is difficult, Katie. You made the right decision. Adoption gives her a hope of a normal childhood. We've found fantastic parents for her. I understand it's hard to say goodbye, but you are in here for another fifteen years. She'll practically be an adult by the time you're released.'

I was aware of all of that. But my senses fused the second I saw her again. I sobbed my answer. 'Send me back to the wings. Take her away.'

I looked up into caring eyes. Surprisingly, Blake crouched to my level. Her tone was soft.

'Once she's gone, that will be it. They won't return tomorrow. There are no re-runs. You have fifty minutes to be a mother. Have some sweets or a cake. Play with the toys and smell her hair. You might think it will be for the final time and she won't remember, but your daughter might come looking for you when she's old enough to ask about her past. You'll need to tell Chloe what happened today.'

I wondered later how she knew what to say. Perhaps I was only a number and her words were just chance. Whatever, they gave me the strength to stand. I stepped to the door and wiped my eyes with a sleeve. I coughed the phlegm from my throat and squared my jaw. 'I'm ready.'

The following hour became my mind's contents for the following year. I don't understand how I managed to be normal. We played and laughed after I coaxed her out of their arms. I'm sure she remembered me. Or at least I told myself that. They allowed me more than an hour, but each passing second chipped another piece off my heart. And then it was time.

Who was that lady who calmly kissed her forehead and cuddled her close? I don't recognise the woman who waved her off with a smile. Yet I understood sniffing that little girl's hair in the hope of storing the scent and moment forever. When Chloe was gone, that person vanished. Only a creature remained. A wretched one that they had to peel from the floor.

I sickened afterwards. When they took her away, they left me with memories and time; neither of which I wanted. Nothing but fifteen years to think about what I'd done. Not eating or sleeping. Professionals talked to me but what could they do? There was no cure. Finally, my sense of survival kicked in. I knew what I had to do. There were few physical mementoes; only a jumper and a couple of photographs. However, the smell in that prison and the looks on others' faces constantly reminded me, and I asked for a transfer. I bagged up those things, and they remained in my cell when I left.

Time doesn't cure all ills, but I did I learn to forget. My refusal to acknowledge that day, and most of the ones before it, got me through that sentence. I couldn't reminisce because it weakened me.

Recently, I have recognised the need to understand my past so I can plan my future. The memory of my daughter was always supposed to be off-limits. I thought that way I could move on. They were the foolish ideas of a terrified, young, exhausted girl. I can't rest until I find answers.

In the end, I survived, but any joy and innocence in me had gone forever.

51
THE TRUTH

I was vaguely aware of Irina's sobs as I told my story. She shakes her head at the end and cries out.

'Why didn't you say anything?'

'It was a way of protecting myself.'

Radic looks dazed. 'The men in the barn…'

'Yes. Not exactly an immaculate conception.'

'How can you joke? How could you let it go?' His face reddens with rage. 'After everything that happened, they forced you to have your child adopted.'

'It was a lifetime ago. I've ignored it for so long now it doesn't feel real. There was nothing I could do about it in prison. It was already too late. And they didn't force me to sign those papers. It was the sensible option. I had no relatives to take over. There weren't any enthusiastic aunts or uncles, no keen grandparents. They could have probably forced the adoption if they wanted, I'm not sure. But I chose to give her a chance that never came my way. She needed a family.'

'You were her family.'

'What good was I? I couldn't provide a shoulder to cry on when things got tough. There wouldn't be a Christmas dinner with all the trimmings. I wanted my daughter to know in her heart that if anything should go wrong, she'd always have a home to go to.'

'I want them to suffer like you did.'

Irina nods at his words.

'To take revenge? At the time, I was too stunned to absorb the enormity of it. I didn't know I was pregnant until it was almost too late to do anything even if I wanted to. By then, I could feel her growing inside me. I don't think Ted connected the two as I didn't show in an obvious way until I was seven months gone. He assumed I'd been sleeping around. I wanted something good to come out of that night even though I knew nothing about babies.'

'You did it all on your own?' Irina finally finds her voice.

'Ted ignored me. The healthcare worker helped me through that time. Incredibly, Ted didn't mention it until I was close to my due date. Then, I came home from a doctor's appointment and it was all there.'

I won't sob for Ted anymore but I still can't stop the tears as they drip off my chin. I stare from one confused face to the other.

'What was all there?' asks Radic.

'A cot. A changing mat. Wipes, nappies, clothes, some toys, a Moses basket. Everything I needed. I asked him why. He said it wasn't the little one's fault. For a while, he thawed. He still worked all hours but he would ask after Chloe and hold her sometimes. That lasted for a couple of months until he slipped back into whatever bottomless place he'd come from. Then he'd be angry, with me for the mess, and with the baby for the noise.'

'A few rights don't make him a good guy,' says Radic.

'Of course not, but that's the point. He wasn't all bad, and he was suffering too. There's good in everyone and in my depression, I killed him. It's the worst crime there is. Whatever you may think. Totally unforgiveable because there's no going back. They're dead, and that's final.'

'Talking of death, someone else you know died too,' says Irina.

'Who's that?'

'Thorn, that perverted probation guy. They found him in his car with a hose connected to the exhaust. Oksana told me. She was pleased about it.' Irina's eyes follow me as I pace the room. 'You weren't involved, were you, Katie?'

I frown. It can only be due to my blackmail. I'm not surprised. Suicide is the coward's way. My cover has gone though, because someone new will take over his cases.

'Did he leave a note?'

'I don't know where Oksana heard it from. She said she was off to celebrate. She wondered if you did it, Katie.' She looks at him. 'Or you, Radic.'

'Katie, sit down. Tell me everything.' Radic's concerned persona vanishes in a flash. There's no point hiding anything now. I have no pride.

'I recorded Thorn forcing me to pleasure him on my mobile phone, then I sent him the video. He would be jailed for abusing his position if anyone found out. I told him to falsify my records, so it looked as though I was still around, or I'd email his bosses. It was supposed to buy me time. I never thought he'd kill himself.'

It's Radic's turn to pace. I can almost see the neurons firing as he searches for a way forward. He claps his hands.

'We stage an accident. A drowning. Someone sees you walk into the sea, someone we know. It can be an anonymous tip-off. We leave things of yours where they'll notice them. Others will wash up. Your clothes shall have your DNA on it, maybe they'll find something with your fingerprints. They won't know for sure, but it will be enough for them to stop looking.'

'Sounds like a plan.' I flop onto the sofa next to Irina. It's hard to believe my life has come to this. I planned to live a peaceful existence when I left jail. Clearly that isn't going to happen. My demons need facing. I blurt out the obvious. 'I must speak to them.'

'Who?' they say together and finally smile.

'The ones who did this to me. I must find out exactly what happened that night. It's important.'

'I'll help you.'

'Thank you, Radic, but I don't want any more violence. There can be no more death on my hands.'

'I think you'll feel differently after you talk to them.'

'Maybe. But I've seen enough lives ruined. I don't think revenge is in my heart. What I need is answers.'

Radic picks up his car keys off the table where he'd thrown them what seems like a long time ago. I watch him lose himself in his own past. He turns to me with a sad grimace.

'Perhaps you're right. Do you know what I realised from before? Revenge is the ultimate pleasure, but you still don't win. Think about it. I'm happy to help in any way, Katie. We'll see you in the club tonight.'

I wave him away with a superficial smile. Bone-weariness prevents me from analysing his words. Those responsible are best approached individually. I'll see Bill last. I reckon he lied to me. About what, I'm not sure. It doesn't matter, because I will do whatever is necessary to uncover the truth.

52
LOVE

I lie face down on the bed after Radic has gone. Irina snuggles me into her bosom. She kisses the top of my head while I search for the dusty images of Chloe that lurk in the furthest corner of my mind. There are so few now. I recall her in the incubator at the hospital. She was thin with such long feet. They fascinated me. Maybe she's a swimmer? I shudder again and resolve not to think like that.

Chloe often slept with one arm out of the cot and a face free of worry. I was jealous. The pictures I keep aren't all happy. The country lanes were rubbish for pram wheels. It sometimes made me scream. I had days when nothing quietened her. We cried ourselves to sleep together.

The years have withdrawn the venom from those thoughts. They hurt but it's more an ache than a fresh cut. My final vision is her tired face waving from a closing prison door. I did the right thing. Will that be the last time I ever see her? I told them I didn't want reminders. She might get in touch when she's eighteen.

A gut-wrenching realisation hits me. I've left the system. Chloe couldn't trace me now even if she wanted to. Perhaps that's for the best. It's unlikely anyone would yearn to meet their murdering mother anyway. Nevertheless, despite all those years of solitude, at this moment, I've never felt more alone.

I unfurl, rest my head next to Irina's and make a strange snuffling sound. She strokes my face. Irina knows she doesn't need to say anything. It's comfort I need. Another sob sneaks out and Irina giggles. I look at her through moist eyes, and hiccup. She laughs again. And kisses me gently.

I've had sex with women before but this is different. In prison, some girls wanted to be rubbed as though I was trying to remove a stubborn stain from a worktop, and they'd moan as if they were giving birth. I wondered if they liked it that way, or just watched porn and thought that's how it was done.

My mind frees itself from worldly concerns. Irina worships, desires and adores me in equal measure. Even the bitter, hard, secret part of me melts under her caresses. The birds quieten, traffic slows, and the clocks stop. Time means nothing, life means nothing. All else ceases to be.

WHEN I WAKE up in her bed afterwards, it's as though I've rested for a year. The clock on the wall makes it less than two hours. Irina is on her side, facing me, fast asleep, and making little bubbles from her mouth. I gently run my hand along her hips and admire her lines.

The concept of whether I'm a lesbian escapes me. I seem to get similar pleasure with a man or a woman, or at least I did until today. Did my fragile state accentuate everything with her? Did our trust in each other magnify our orgasms or were we just relaxed? The sunlight through the curtains highlights her beauty, and I have an urge to do it again.

I know why I slept with women in prison. Adapting to life inside is the key to survival. Many like me had no family. We created our own. If there had been men available, maybe it would've been different, but there was no competition for their attention. Many girls realised they simply found other women attractive, although our affairs aren't to be simply dismissed as reactions to imprisonment.

It was far from being all about sex. We shared emotional comfort and social respect. I knew little of adult relationships because I hadn't had one. Sexual experience had been taken, not given. That said, my upbringing was hard, but it was literally child's play compared to the extreme abuse many of the women I'd met along the way had suffered.

For many of us, it was the first occasion in our lives that we were loved even when they knew our history. Prison, incredibly, was valuable in helping develop a positive self-image. Okay, it was fun and passed the time too. One girl asked me if I was interested because she fancied trying it. For her, the opportunity arose.

That's how it will be in the future. There'll be no gay or straight, bi or whatever. You'll dress how you like, act how you want, be who you are. Then find someone, anyone, that you fancy, and have sex with them. Marry, or don't, raise kids, or go solo. Run your own life, be free.

Irina's eyes ease open.

'You okay?' she asks.

'Better than that.'

I place my finger on her lips and shuffle down the bed. As Radic said, it's only polite to reciprocate.

53
SECRETS

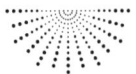

The club is quiet tonight, leaving Irina and me time for small talk. She skips between the tables, collecting glasses and smiling at the guests. How did I end up here in the underworld? I can't help thinking there's been some kind of mistake. This wasn't who I was supposed to be. That said, I do not believe in fate, only luck, and mine's been awful.

'Do you like your life, Irina?'

'It's fine. I have a job and I'm safe. This wasn't what I hoped to be, but I've been in worse situations, so I appreciate it. Why? Aren't you happy?'

'I thought if I started a new life I would be content. The thing is, I don't understand this situation. Radic is clearly up to no good. I'm not sure I want to know what he does to pay the bills which include our wages. Regardless, I feel like a criminal even though I'm not one.'

'You got a life sentence. I've been to prison too. Doesn't that make us criminals?'

'I don't see us as that. You were exploited and made a horrifying mistake. I was abused, and under intense provocation I made a stupid decision when not in my right mind. We didn't set out to rob banks or sell drugs. We're not burglars or thieves.'

'We did the crimes though. All the girls inside had a sob story.'

'That's my point. Most of them were victims too. How many of those women were bad? Desperate is more appropriate. They were drug addicts and shoplifters. There was no one to help them before they went in, and when they got out again, they had even fewer chances.'

'What are you saying?'

'I've ended up here almost without being conscious of it. I crave a normal life with an average job.'

'You want to clean houses? I can't imagine you on a checkout.'

'Why? I'm not proud. I want to do something completely innocent.'

Her smile slides from her face. I wonder if she had plans for me and her. I don't know enough about myself to be of use to anyone else. With a toss of her hair, she lights a cigarette and pulls hard. 'Leave then. You don't have to be here.'

She's right, but I need my new ID. Radic has offered me a Ukrainian passport. Katerina Vaselka. He said the English ones were less suitable under scrutiny. They would look for records of taxation and employment, bank details and a credit file. If I took an immigrant one, I could start from scratch. The fact I didn't speak the language was met with indifference. Who the dead girl was didn't matter.

I realise I don't know these people. I doubt their intentions. Am I being too cautious? Is Irina's first loyalty to me or Radic? Actually, that's obvious.

'I'm just talking out loud. This isn't what I expected.'

Her expressions soften. 'What did you wish for?'

I consider her question. For a long time, I searched for oblivion. Hope hurts those who can't control their lives. I learned that quickly. It's different now because I can do anything. First, I must understand what happened. Bill said Simon remains in

Peterborough. Justin and Jordan could well still be on the farm and I know how to get hold of Bill. I'll start with Simon. He could never hide his feelings. Bill and Jordan were liars. And perhaps poor slow Justin might fess up if Simon doesn't come clean.

I decide not to tell Irina my plans. That may be a mistake but my future isn't with her. I recognise that now. There's an undercurrent here that I don't understand. If I'm not careful, I'll be pulled in. I fell for the nice Uncle Radic approach. I believe he wants to help, but only a fool would think I haven't got something he needs.

Anyway, these decisions aren't urgent. Maybe this is the best I can hope for, so I need to play the game. Irina eyes me up. Am I her opponent or friend, lover or competitor? It's my move next.

'You know what? I think we should have some fun. We've been moping around. What did you dream of inside?' I ask.

'Getting drunk in the sunshine.'

'Apart from that?'

'Getting drunk in the shade.'

'How about football or horseracing?'

'You want to play football and race horses?'

'No, I want to watch them. Let's go. Why not? I went as a child to see a game. Newmarket races is down the road. We'll do both.'

I'm in the swing of things now. We can do this. I need to live. Who knows what the near future will bring. There is danger ahead, of that there is no doubt. 'And a pedalo. We should ride a pedalo!'

'What's a pedalo?'

'A small boat where you pedal instead of rowing. I saw it on an advert and they have them here at Ferry Meadows Lake.'

'Don't you sail a boat? How do you steer one?'

'Who cares, let's find out!'

She reaches over the counter and holds my hand. We look into each other's eyes, both aware that things have changed.

54
JULY

SIMON

Tony agreed to drive me to Milton Ferry. It was the location where Simon loved to fish as a boy. I suspected he'd have to work during the week but fishing was his life. If he was still in the city, then I bet he would use this place.

Tony tended to hang around the bar during the day. He'd drink but slowly. I never saw him drunk. I'd put him in his late forties.

'What's your job, Tony?'

'My work? I drive for Radic. Do odd jobs, not much.'

'A driver? Does it pay handsomely?'

He has a sense of humour beneath the granite features. 'Pay okay. I need little.'

'Did Radic tell you to watch out for me and Irina?'

'If you want a lift, I help.'

He could have been a politician. I hoped for answers today; I might as well start now.

'Do you look out for your daughter?'

The eye twinkle disappears. White hands grip the wheel.

'I send money. No more.'

He says it with finality. My interview technique needs

improvement. I know little of men. Irina told me they like to talk, but she can't have meant Tony.

'Left here.'

He grunts and complies. The track to the bridge and the river is steep, and he takes his time.

'Park up here. I'll walk the rest of the way.'

He gets out at the same time as me.

'Wait here, please, Tony.'

Cold eyes glare back, and then a shrug. 'Where you go?'

'I'm going fishing.'

I continue down the slope and through a gate. The stone bridge is the same as I recall; at least some things don't change. A dog walker passes and wishes me good day. I admire his warm pleated jacket as the sun has vanished. My denim jacket is a poor choice.

The peg, as he called the spot he fished at, is empty. Maybe the overcast weather is no good for bites. I stand at the edge. There was happiness here. I stood in this same spot and laughed. Simon would wade out, despite having no wellies, and cast under the trees on the far bank. He'd stand rigid and watch. We'd sneak up and throw stones at his float and run and hide in the reeds.

I decide to walk further up as I can see a man about two hundred metres away.

'Excuse me.'

He is old. Ancient even, with an air of familiarity in the way he cocks his head to examine me.

'Aye?'

'I was looking for someone. A bloke who fishes here.'

He removes his hat and gives me an unusual look. I dyed my hair blonde yesterday. With tight jeans and sunglasses, I must seem lost.

'Plenty of people fish here.'

I recall the boy and wonder how he'd now appear. I don't think of ethnicity and colour anymore, this old-timer may.

'He's mixed race. Tall and thin.'

He smiles. 'Simon, you mean Simon. I've fished here with him since he was a lad.'

It falls into place. This old fellow was often here back then. I never knew his name. He used to tell us to bugger off for scaring the fish.

'Does he still come here?'

'Aye, most Sundays. He said he'll be here again this week. Who wants to know?'

'A friend.'

He takes his own sunglasses off and grins.

'Get here early, he's usually gone by eleven.'

I leave him fiddling with his rod and walk to the car. Later today, I have an appointment at the tattoo parlour. I drove the owner crazy looking through his designs. In the end, he created one. It defines me; a large image of a female angel and a fiery demon, locked in a lovers' embrace, to cover my back. The hunt for that is over while the search for the truth is just beginning.

Tony pretends to be sleeping in the driver's seat. I watch his chest rise and note it's going too fast. He opens an eye. I give him a grin.

'Do you have plans on Sunday?'

55
SUNDAY

THE CATCH

It was a late one at the club and I've only had snatched sleep. Tony hung around until the early hours as well. He insisted it was no trouble to pick me up and is outside my place as agreed at seven a.m. We're greeted by a bright morning without any breeze. A good day for fishing. Tony says nothing on the drive. No change there, although I detect a focus that isn't always present.

Only one other car is parked up when we arrive. It's a battered truck with a tarpaulin loosely pulled across the cargo box. I hop out and sneak a look underneath. There's an umbrella and a few bait boxes. Anyone could own the vehicle, yet my gut says it's Simon's. Tony distracts me by getting out.

'Shall I come with you?'

'No, it's fine. Wait here like last time.'

Again, he's unhappy with that idea. 'Do you have a weapon?'

That's very perceptive of him. I haven't said what I'm doing, yet he's aware that it might be dangerous.

'I won't need one. I'm only going to talk to him. Stay in the car. I shouldn't be long. He may not even be here.'

I stride down the slope. I wear my running gear with my

newly blonde hair in a tied-up ponytail pulled through the back of a baseball cap. All this and wraparound sunglasses would make identifying me impossible. Have I dressed this way for anonymity? Or due to the fact I could need to run or fight?

I considered taking a knife, but that seemed extreme. Simon wasn't the violent one. The view of the river from the top of the small stone bridge is marvellous. The water resembles a millpond. I jog to the other side and trot along the bank. Up ahead, the section where he used to fish is empty. Simon was a creature of habit so that's disappointing. I decide to stretch my legs for a while. Tony can wait.

I pass a big shrub and Simon stands up with his rod. My steps tail off. I'm surprised by my stunned reaction. It's been a long time but Simon's journey must have been an arduous one. A scraggly beard and beaten up fishing hat can't hide the lines on a weathered face. He hasn't noticed me. I step down onto the gravel and stones next to the edge of the stream and stifle a laugh. Then I recall my serious business.

He has the biggest pair of waders on and doesn't hear me as the water runs much faster than I thought. He sloshes into the river. It's deeper than I imagined and he's soon up to his waist. He stops and, with a flick of his wrist, plops his float on the far side under the overhanging branches of a leaning tree.

A flicker of anger has me on my tiptoes. Nothing has changed for him. Well, I'm about to ruin his day.

'Simon!'

He turns around and immediately looks shifty.

'Who's asking?'

'It's Katie.'

He remains a statue. All I can hear is the drone of the cars on the motorway beyond us and the trickle of water at my feet.

'I don't know a Katie.'

I take my cap and sunglasses off but he knows who I am. Did

the old man tell him someone was looking for him, or, perhaps, he's always been waiting for a tap on the shoulder.

'You are Simon Salmon, aren't you?'

A barely imperceptible nod of his head confirms his identity. I realise that even though I imagined what he might do, I hadn't expected him to remain silently in the middle of the river. There's no rush, and he's not going anywhere. After half a minute, he pipes up.

'What do you want?'

To think, until that night we were friends. If I find better evidence of his guilt than this behaviour, I'll be surprised.

'I need to talk about what you did to me.' Unbelievably, he looks behind him. I'm sure he would flee if the river wasn't too deep for him to cross. 'Feeling guilty, Simon?'

He opens his mouth, then closes it. He visibly wanes.

'I'm so sorry, Katie. We shouldn't have done what we did. I always liked you. But I had to have you one time before we went away. You were only interested in Bill. You kissed me once, and I hoped we'd be together. You just ignored me afterwards. It sent me crazy.'

'That's not an apology. You raped me, all of you did.'

He can't hold my stare yet shakes his head. 'It wasn't like that. You seemed up for it.'

'I seemed up for it? You ruined my life. Do you know what happened to me?'

'It wrecked my life too. I felt so guilty. I had nightmares afterwards. But what could I do by then? It was too late. We had jobs to go to. Bill said to forget that night. I tried. It still haunts me. I've been married three times now. I can't maintain a normal relationship. It messed my head up.'

I struggle to believe what I'm hearing. He is sorry, but only for himself.

'Why didn't you stay and see if I was okay? You left me on my own.'

'We weren't thinking straight. We'd had stacks to drink and all the drugs sent us mad.'

'Drugs, what drugs?'

'Ecstasy. We took loads. We put some in the drinks…'

Our faces fall in realisation at the same time. He shouldn't have told me that. It explains so much, and it changes everything. My free-loving behaviour was out-of-character. No wonder I struggled to understand my actions. Not only did they fuck me, but they drugged me first. My blood boils with fury. My chest rises with each massive gulp of air. If I'd known the truth all those years ago, I wouldn't have despised myself.

I've come for information, but I can't get the words out. If I could touch him, I would pull the skin from his face with my nails. I pick his spare rod up and throw it at him like a spear. His seat follows, and then everything on the bank flies in. He backs up out of reach as a reel glances his shoulder. I grab a stone and it whistles past his ear making him flinch in shock. He is up to his chest and using his arms to stay upright.

Another big stone fits in my fingers as though it has been waiting since its creation for this sole purpose. Smooth, heavy, thick and flat, but almost perfectly round. Subconsciously, the way Tommy and I used to compete with each other, I crouch and fling it spinning towards him. It bucks on a slight wave and skims up at fantastic speed. Simon turns his head at the last moment and, with a sinister crack, the solid stone strikes him on the temple.

There's no drama or shout. He simply sinks beneath the surface. A ripple of his coat and maybe his head catches my eye a few metres downstream. Then nothing. He's gone. Self-preservation kicks in, and I search for witnesses. A man on the bridge stares straight at me. I gasp in relief as Tony waves and heads towards the car. It's time for me to leave, too.

Tony has reversed from our space and has the engine running with my door open. He accelerates up the hill. What have I done? I didn't want to kill again. It was an accident. I just wanted to lash out and scare him, but sweat runs down my sides and back. The healing tattoo there itches, and I resist the urge to rub myself against the seat like a cat. I consider the image; an angel and a demon. Which one am I?

56
HUNTINGDON RACES

I have had a strange week. My thoughts kept returning to Simon. There's been nothing in the local paper. Perhaps he survived and pulled himself out of the water further down the river. It doesn't seem likely. If he's dead, then I've killed again. That should disturb me but when I consider the reasons for losing my temper, notably the fact they drugged me, I'm pleased I did it. I am still furious now.

Today we are off to the races. Irina begged that we get dressed up. I think she expects Royal Ascot but we're going to Huntingdon. I'm not sure what to expect, apart from a lack of royalty, but I haven't popped her bubble because at least she's come out of another funny spell.

She was away for a few days visiting a friend. Oksana covered for her in the club. Despite her heavy make-up, Irina still looks tired. Strange that her trips are for a couple of days midweek but never at the weekend. She was vague and shifty when I probed further. Sounds like a married guy. Suspiciously, Tony was absent too.

Irina asked Tony to drive us. The train would have been fun, but Irina insisted on a pair of lethal heels that could double as a weapon. Walking in them is near impossible. Tony has been in our shadow of late but it's more Irina that he circles. I don't think they're having an affair as he is as business-like with her as he is with me. He insists on staying with the car when we arrive.

We stagger in with Irina clinging to my arm for stability. I cling to her as I see other racegoers in jeans and parkas, but I notice men in suits and hats, and a lady in a wedding dress. The tannoy announces the first race is off in fifteen minutes.

'Look, Irina. Horses.'

'You say it in the same way as someone pointing out a dragon. I have seen these mythical beasts in front of us before, you know.'

A man leaves the fence and I glide to the front. Irina curses behind me. I glance back and note she should keep away from the grass in those shoes. The horses draw my attention. They are magnificent huge creatures, prancing around with bucking heads. Have I ever been this close to them? I don't think so. The farm was arable so the only animals were chickens. Even the surrounding ones rarely had anything more than sheep. What kind of childhood is one where you haven't ridden a horse? Someone nudges me. It's Irina, six inches shorter.

'I brought trainers too. I'm clever, don't you know. Let's get pissed.'

She strides towards an open bar leaving me behind. She appears odd with a short, figure-hugging, yellow dress and a pair of Nikes underneath. I catch her up and watch her wince as she hands over a note for two bowls of wine. She takes a big gulp and snickers like one of the horses I've been admiring.

We find a spot in the stands which looks out over the racecourse. It's not as busy as I thought it would be. I guess most people are at work. Everyone's friendly enough. I spot two sharply dressed Asian lads checking us out. My fake fur jacket isn't as effective as the real thing. The wind curls around the grandstand and I catch Irina trying to sink into her similar coat.

The announcer talks more. I can hear it clearer from where I'm standing. I sense the hustle of people about me. The race starts and many flood from the buildings and make their way to the fence to watch. I hear a big ooh after a comment about a faller. I can't see any horses.

Following the direction where others are staring, I pick up a group of about ten on the far side of the circular course. They bob up in the air and down again. Soon they approach the finishing post. The jockeys aren't trying very hard. It's all an anti-climax. There are a few shouts from the crowd. Then they jump the big fence in front of the stand. Cheers go up, cries too.

A jockey falls off a horse at the back and scrambles to his feet. He finds his whip and thrashes the turf with it. The rest are out of sight around a bend. I don't think I've seen anything so real and exciting before. My heart dances in my chest. I pick the horses up as they come into view. Another rider goes down but this time the horse falls with him. More moans from the crowd. More excitement from the commentator.

They head to the finish line. They ride hard. Whips crack through the air while the commentator shouts the drama. The crowd hollers. I jump to my feet and join in. The grey horse beats a brown one. Three more brown ones arrive at intervals. I look at Irina, who is staring at me as if I've appeared by magic.

'Bloody hell. That was brilliant.' My eyes feel like saucers.

'What were you cheering for?'

'It's thrilling. I got caught up in it all.'

'I was going to say we should have a bet on the next one. I'm not so sure now because you might wet yourself. Another drink?'

'Too right. My round. Now, how do you put a bet on?'

'Ask them.'

I stare at the men next to flickering boards who are handing money back and forth. The two Asian men are in view. I pass Irina a twenty.

'You get the drinks. I'll explore.'

They watch me approach and my nerves flutter. I give them my best smile. Risks must be taken if I want to try new things.

'You two boys got job interviews later?'

Their amused faces mean it's game on.

THREE HOURS FLY BY. I rip up my final losing ticket and throw the pieces in the air. I give Tariq a sleepy grin. What a brilliant afternoon. I'm skint and pissed. Tariq and his friend, Aziz, have been the perfect gentlemen. Tariq loves the racing too and goes all the time. They showed us around, explained things, bought drinks, and generally spoilt us.

Tariq laughed his head off at my enthusiasm. He said that's what he was like when he first went. He had the only winner. I'm looking forward to picking one of those. They're parked in a different car park to us, so we say our goodbyes at the exit. Aziz shakes Irina's hand and laughs. She's wobbling around again even though she still has her trainers on.

Tariq hands me a piece of paper. There's an email address and a phone number on it. How sweet. He must have done it at the bar. He leans in, steals a kiss on my cheek, puts his arm over his friend's shoulder and off they go.

Tony waves through the car window when we come into view. He helps me roll Irina into the back seat. I climb in the front but close my eyes after a few miles. It's unlikely Tony will chat anyway but I want to re-run the day. It was so exciting, such fun, dramatic, but most of all, it felt normal. We joined the world in living life. There was flirting and drinks and nothing bad happened. Quite the reverse, even.

How many people spend their lives slumped by their television when they can be bothered to get out of bed? I missed out on my youth. I've a lot of catching up to do. I think about the note in my bag. Is that how it feels to be chatted up by a stranger? I liked it. But I doubt I'll ring him. A tinge of foreboding arrives to shadow my silver cloud. I have three more men to visit. Who knows how this will all end?

57
THE TWINS

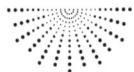

I decide to tell Tony what happened to me as we drive to see Jordan and Justin. I assume they still live in the same farmhouse. He absorbs the information with little emotion, only looking at me when I reveal they put drugs in the alcohol without telling me. I don't paint my role up, or theirs down. It's a torrid tale however you rearrange it. We arrive in silence.

I tell him to park up the road from the house, even though I don't have a plan.

'These are the twins that were there that night?'

'If they're still here. It's been a long time.'

'Two men. They live with each other?'

'Justin is probably best-described as slow-witted. He wasn't a big drinker or lover of drugs. I'm struggling to remember his role. He used to hang around more than anything else. Never saying much and doing less. Even Jordan ignored him. I suspect they grew up together and his parents told him to look after his brother. Maybe he did that automatically. Justin was a prime target for bullies. Jordan could be vicious though, so if people picked on his brother, it tended not to be for long.'

'Take this.'

He removes an implement from the arm rest. The black decorated handle draws my eyes up to a silver push button. He pushes it and a four-inch blade fires out. He reverses the action and the blade springs back out of view. It's beautiful and deadly.

I open the door and step out. When I bob my head down to check his expression, he again reaches to give me the knife.

'Not today, Tony. There's been enough killing.'

The sun beats down. I'm decked out in the same outfit as when I met Simon, and might be someone out for a run along the country lanes. Their driveway up towards the house looks the same. The old, rusting trough next to the gate remains. My skin prickles with familiarity after all this time.

The farmhouse hasn't changed either; perhaps there's a relatively new coat of paint on the woodwork. A doorbell indicates modernisation. The barn has a shiny combine harvester in it, although the tractor alongside could be the one we played on years ago.

I press the button. My body tenses. I recall Mai's breathing techniques. In through the nose, fill the lower lung, then the upper, exhale through pursed lips. I still gulp when the door opens. A pretty woman of about thirty who's also wearing big sunglasses stares impassively at me.

'Yes.'

'I'm looking for Jordan and Justin. Are they about?'

'Justin doesn't live here. Not for five years. Jordan's away for a few days at a neighbour's farm.' She pauses. 'What's he done now, or not done?'

I feel sorry for this woman but don't know why. I take my sunglasses off.

'We knew each other a long time ago. We were friends, I suppose. I wanted to catch up. Nostalgia for old times.'

She removes her glasses. The fading bruises are a road sign to me after prison life. It's a struggle for her to maintain eye contact.

'Justin had a car accident, even though he'd been banned from driving years before. I never knew him when he was young but he was a committed alcoholic by that point. We kept a bed for him but wouldn't see him for days. Jordan regularly found him asleep in ditches. He drove into a farm wall. He's in the care home at Albany Walk. I used to visit, but he isn't there. They wheel him out each day and he sits in front of the television and stares at it. They feed him by tube. He always was a daft bugger. I think the impact knocked the last bit of sense out of him.'

'That's sad to hear.'

'There're many nasty accidents on farms. Anyway, he was a waste of space. He caused a lot of problems for Jordan and me. He was supposed to help out, but we never saw him. Jordan struggles to run the place. It's hard for him.'

Two chubby little girls bang on the kitchen window and stick their tongue out at me.

'Your kids are cute.'

'They aren't ours. We couldn't have kids. My fault.'

There it was again. Her blaming herself and making excuses for him. After a pause she steps back inside. 'Who shall I say called?'

'Is your husband a good man?'

Her face hardens but it's to stop her from crying. She composes herself and then looks directly at me. 'No, he is not.'

'Then don't tell him I'm coming.'

58

JUSTIN

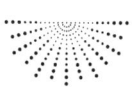

When she closes the door, I sprint up the driveway. Sure enough, I catch Tony trying to make it to the car unnoticed. Perhaps he's being protective. There's no time like the present, so I tell Tony to drive me to Albany Way. We accelerate past the house on the edge of the fields, where I used to live.

'Stop!' Tony slams on the brakes.

I give him a rueful look. 'Sorry, I meant pull over.' He checks the mirror and bumps up onto the kerb. 'I'll just be a minute. Stay here.'

The concreted area in front of the house is empty. The storage buildings on the left are closed up. There are no vehicles in sight. It feels unused. Curtains are pulled upstairs. I didn't come here for nothing, so I walk over and look through the dirty window. The distinct lack of kitchen equipment confirms the place isn't lived in. The lounge blinds are almost closed. Through the cracks, I observe a bare room. I release the breath I'm holding.

It's been well over seventeen years since that day. Fleeting memories make themselves known as I circle the house. Unsurprisingly, they are mostly bad but not all dire. I can clearly see the boys arguing and Bill throwing a stone at a ducking Jordan; it missed and crashed through the dining-room window. The jutting paving slab, which knocked Justin off his bike and ripped his leg open, remains. I recall the look on Ted's face as he came out of the door and saw me driving his tractor in the yard with excited lads hollering in the trailer behind.

At the back of the house, I shield my eyes and glare up the north field at the barn. I won't go there today. A car crawling on an uneven surface attracts my hearing. When I poke my head around the building, it's only Tony parking up. He doesn't listen too well. Never mind. Justin is next.

TONY DOESN'T OFFER me a weapon for the care home. I stride through the reception doors and smile at an immaculately dressed elderly lady next to a desk.

'I'm here to visit Justin Jameson.'

'Hello. I'm being picked up soon.'

'Pardon?'

'My husband's arriving any minute now.'

A head rises from behind the desk. A young girl with an open face smiles. 'Mavis likes to wait here for her husband, don't you?' Mavis beams back, then turns to the window, her eyes straining to see through the glass.

'Have you been before?' the receptionist asks.

'No, I've not seen him for a long time. Someone told me he was here, and I said I'd visit.'

'No problem. He rarely receives guests, so he'll be pleased. Sign in here.'

I thought of a pseudonym beforehand. Dee Montgomery at your service. Maybe only the first six letters. I had a story prepared for my lack of ID but she doesn't ask. She glances at my name.

'Anne, please show Dee to the day room.'

An oriental lady with a stern handshake guides me though some double doors. She stops before another set.

'Have you seen Justin recently?'

'Not for many years. How is he?'

'Physically, he is reasonably okay. He has a scar on his face and he can't walk or go to the bathroom on his own. He doesn't talk either, but some days he'll feed himself. Takes him forever but if we chop it up, he'll eat pretty much anything. A tube remains in for when he won't.'

'What does he do all day?'

'I was here when he arrived. He does nothing. He lives in a daydream. He cries out at night sometimes but don't we all? I couldn't tell you if he's happy, but he isn't suffering. Are you ready?'

I follow her in and recognise him straight away. Maybe it's a big wheelchair, but he looks tiny. He has a dopey look as he drools at the television. There are others in the room but they are ancient and fast asleep. Anne takes off the brake and pushes Justin next to an armchair in the corner.

'Would you like a cup of tea?'

'That's very kind, but I can't stay long.'

I receive an understanding smile, which makes me feel rotten. A gaping shirt reveals a tube protruding from his chest. The edge of a nappy rises out of loose trousers. This wasn't what I expected. Pity and sadness remove any fears. I liked Justin. He was harmless and damn near invisible. I doubt he would have got involved without encouragement.

'Justin, can you hear me?'

He looks into the distance in the same way as he did when he was staring at the television. The scar she barely mentioned is huge and his skull isn't the right shape. There's nothing I could do to him that hasn't been done already. I take his hand.

'Why did you do it, Justin? We were friends. It ruined my life. I had a child, Justin. It might have been yours.'

I detect pressure on my hand. Is it registering on some level? I keep talking.

'The baby had a shock of blonde hair. The same colour as you and your brother. And that small kink you have on the top of both of your ears? She had that, too.'

Again, I receive a definite squeeze. Anne walks in and sees me holding his hand. 'That's it, Dee. Just talk to him.'

'He squeezed my hand.'

'It's involuntary, I should think. He'll find it reassuring and comforting though, so keep it up.'

I shift my chair around when she's gone until we face each other.

'Her name was Chloe. I had to give her away. She'd be nearly eighteen now.'

There is no change in expression at that news. There's nothing else to say. His grip is loose and I remove my hand. Standing there, I struggle for words. He focuses through me.

'Goodbye, Justin.'

Big fat teardrops form in both eyes and roll down his cheeks. That's the best apology so far.

'I forgive you.'

I turn and leave.

When I sign out, I catch the receptionist's eye. Gesturing to the expectant Mavis who is quietly wringing her hands, I whisper, 'Isn't her husband here yet?'

She winks and murmurs back, 'No, he's been dead for thirty years.'

59
FOOTBALL MATCH

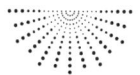

We walk through town, past the courts, and then over the bridge. I spot an old barge moored up, which has been converted into a pub and restaurant. Maybe we can go there afterwards. I steal a peek at Irina and suspect that's unlikely. She is hanging. It was a quiet Friday night and I don't remember her drinking that much. However, fear cloaks her and she didn't want to come.

The swarm of people reminds me of a mass movement at HMP Peterborough. There was a certain camaraderie as you walked with hundreds of your fellow inmates to your place of work. It's the same here. Instead of prison tracksuits, there are matching shirts and scarves. I wish I'd bought both when I came in the week to buy our tickets.

As we approach the ground, I am transported back to the only other time here with Arthur. Martha and Arthur were responsible for many fond memories. Who knows where my life would have led if I'd stayed with them? I allow myself to scan the crowds to see if I can spot him. A smile sneaks on my face. Silly girl. He'd be in his seventies now.

I notice other women proudly wearing Peterborough United's colours. Irina and I have jeans and boots on but still full slap. It's my titanium shield and my disguise. I doubt anyone I know will be here, but I keep my shades on. It was bright enough out of the ground for that not to be weird but the roof blocks the sun in the stand. I'll remove them at kick-off. Irina has found the biggest pair I've ever seen and has pulled the furry hood up on her parka. It'll be like watching the game with a giant panda.

There are many different types of people here. Men in expensive outfits and women who could be famous mix with those in old and crumpled coats and trousers. There are all colours and creeds, and I am no one. Irina follows behind me, through the gates, like a child. We link arms as we go up the concrete gangway and my eyes widen at the vast green pitch. The music blares from speakers above and causes Irina to shrink away from it.

'Come on, grumpy. Row H 26 and 27.'

For some reason, I've been paranoid I'd find someone sitting in our seats but they're empty. The match is a local derby, and the place fills up fast. The cheer for the players when they arrive on the pitch is deafening. The opposition leads two-nil as half-time approaches. Who cares, it's nice to see goals. I remember Arthur's trick of buying drinks a few minutes before the whistle to avoid the queue.

Irina needs a magic elixir, not a coffee, to turn her afternoon around. While we wait for the game to restart, I ask her what's been on my mind for a while.

'Why do you drink so much?'

'What do you mean?'

'You drink to get drunk. I watch guys doing it all the time but you're the only woman I've seen.'

'You noticed?'

'Of course. Is it to do with your past?'

She takes her oversized shades off and stares at me through rheumy eyes.

'It's often the only way I can relax and forget things. It isn't because of my daughter. I'm stressed and it relaxes me.'

'What have you got to be anxious about? We've cushy jobs for good money. Accommodation thrown in. We don't answer to anyone. And we have each other.'

Her eyes search mine.

'It's not just you who has problems. Life rains on us all, Katie.'

Her words shock me. Have I become self-centred and can't see that everyone has struggles? Do I really know what's going on in Irina's head? She's ready to say something when the speakers above blare and everyone rises to their feet.

'Oh God, I'm dying,' she says.

'You what?!'

'No, not that. My hangover's killing me. How much longer does this fun last?'

'If you're not enjoying it, go home. I'll catch you later. I don't mind staying on my own.'

It's a surprise when she pops her glasses back on, squeezes my hand, and shuffles past the clapping supporters and out of sight. The referee's whistle distracts me, and I focus on the game.

THE MATCH ENDS in a two-all draw. I worried beforehand that the big crowd would unsettle me. It hasn't. I'll nip to the stadium shop afterwards and buy a scarf. The throng stream out of the ground. I don't want to get involved in the crush as they feed into the tunnel, so I sit in my seat and people watch.

A familiar man walks by and averts his eyes as ours meet. I know him, and the way his shocked face turns around means he knows me. My brain whirrs. Should I worry? He sneaks a final look and then is gone out of sight. I curse as I replace my shades.

I'm the last to leave. All I think about is trying to identify that man. I bump through the turnstiles and decide the scarf can wait. I want to be at home. Filtering through the crowd with my head down, I glance up and he's in front of me.

'Katie? Is that really you?'

It can't be. I peer at his wavy hair, his familiar blue eyes, and not least his lethargic grin. Tears stream down our faces. I cry because he was right. We would meet again. I step forward and hug Tommy.

60
CHARTERS

What do you say after more than twenty years? Tommy solves the problem.

'Shall we have a beer?'

'Good idea,' I reply. 'How about that boat place?'

'Charters? Okay, I haven't been in there for ages.'

We don't talk the short distance there as we walk with the remainder of the crowd through the traffic light system. We both smile at each other. The steps to the riverside are steep and slippery.

'Careful,' he says. 'I've had a few nasties on these over the years. What do you want to drink?'

'Any kind of cider will be fine.'

A ramp leads us onto the boat and we walk down some gloomy stairs. The place is heaving, as you'd expect on match day. Tommy is no stranger to a bar and navigates his way to the front. He's grown into his looks. His clothes fit well but they have a hint of age about them. They certainly aren't designer.

A couple get out of two seats around a small table. I quickly sit before they're taken. I watch Tommy count change out when the barman gives him the price. He returns at a strange angle and I realise the floor isn't level. There's a good buzz in here though, and it smells as if beer has seeped into the wooden floorboards over many years. He puts a pint in front of me and the table violently rocks toward me. His glass goes on the other side and it bangs back. We laugh at the same time and we're friends again.

After some general chat about the football, I ask him the obvious question.

'What happened to you?'

He's ready for me and I can tell everything will come out.

'The couple I lived with adopted me in the end. They were lovely. Still are. I went to a good school, but I wasn't as bright as their son had been. They never said I disappointed them, but it was always at the back of my mind. I'd missed so much schooling that I could never catch up. Further education was not an option.'

He takes a huge gulp with enthusiasm, and I note he's no stranger to beer.

'I got in with a wild crowd. Nothing too serious, but drink and drugs. My adoptive parents moved away to Lincoln. They asked me to come, and I did. They helped me find a job with British Gas. I just had no focus. HR sacked me for persistent lateness. That annoyed my father, and I left. Living with like-minded lads was a poor idea. I slipped back into my old ways.'

'How are you doing now?

'I won't lie to you. Things were rough for a long time. Did you get the sense you don't belong anywhere? I kept on moving around, taking jobs, losing them. Finally, I got my act together about five years ago. I went and saw my parents and told them everything. They were wary to begin with but then saw how serious I was. I moved back to Peterborough, away from bad influences and started again. There is always building work here. I've been doing it ever since.'

'Sounds like you're doing fine. Any children?'

Immediately, I can see he has a dilemma on his hands. There's something he doesn't want to tell me, or he is embarrassed by it.

Tommy was always good at talking his way out of things. He stands up. I think he's about to leave, but instead takes his coat off. He needn't say anymore as I notice his arms. He has the same blue tattoos I did.

'I was arrested for drink driving. Again. They sent me down to teach me a lesson. I did four months here in Peterborough's nick.'

'Is that where those tattoos came from?'

He idly looks at them and his eyes sharpen as he realises not everyone knows what prison markings look like. 'No, I got these in Lincoln's jail after being caught with stolen property. I did learn, eventually, and I'm squeaky clean now. I've been in the same two-bed flat for four years and had my job on the diggers for three.'

The only thing that means anything to me is that he's being honest. He didn't need to tell me any of that. I take a big sip of cider and slip off my own coat. Tommy admires the dragon on my arm.

'As for kids,' he adds. 'I never wanted any. After all the bullshit we went through, I figured I didn't want to bring any more children into this world. What's your tale?'

Where do I start? How do I explain what happened, what became of me, and worst of all, what I did? I always trusted Tommy. He's taken a chance by telling me the truth when he could have glossed over the past.

'Same again? You'll need another drink for this.'

He will hear everything.

61
ATTRACTION

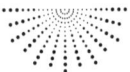

His face displays the emotions you'd expect when you hear a history like mine. If indeed there has been one similar. Shock, anger, disgust, revulsion, and a touch of fear. Strangely, it's the last emotion I find the worst to see.

I decide not to mention my recent visits to Simon and Justin. I update him from the day he left and finish at the football match. He accepts why I slipped my licence. He agreed they can be worse than the sentence itself. I tell him about the probation officer killing himself and bumping into Bill Ivy. I reveal my fears that Bill's now a policeman and knew Tim Thorn. He understands my worries and the severity of the situation I'm in. I even explain I've got myself tangled up with criminals but I'm not involved.

He recovers fast. Kids from care do. There is little that would shock him or me to the core. Which is sad for both of us.

'There's not much chance of them finding you here. I'm unsure why I recognised you. You're so different. Wasn't your hair brown not blonde. The clothes and make-up…'

'Yes?'

'You look pretty, but, powerful I guess.'

'Pretty?'

'Bugger off. Do you fancy another drink?'

'Very smooth.' I'm enjoying his discomfort. There's still that same spark, perhaps even a little more. Our stories make us quite a pair. 'I've got work, unfortunately.'

'What are you going to do about all that?'

'I'll keep you posted. I have a couple of tasks I need to see through.'

'Sounds ominous.'

'It is a bit.'

'Look, I said I have my own place. You can stay any time. No funny business, no judgement. Just an old friend to a new one. I also reckon you might not get recalled if they find you. Talk about extenuating circumstances. They'd want to cover it up as well.'

'That's good to know, thank you.'

'What did you say the name of the policeman was again?'

'Bill, Bill Ivy.'

'I've heard that before. It sounds funny when you say it fast. Let's exchange numbers, I'll see if I remember.'

'Nice! You are a smooth operator. You'll have my bra size if I don't get out of here quick.'

To his credit, he manages to stop himself looking down. I stand and retrieve my phone, and we swap numbers. He also gives me the address of his flat. Outside, we hug once more.

'I'll catch up with you soon,' I say.

'I hope so.'

We begin to walk off in opposite directions when he shouts my name.

'Be careful with that Bill Ivy. I still don't remember, but I've a feeling he's very bad news.'

62
JORDAN'S FARM

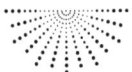

I decide not to tell Tony where I'm going today. Apart from him being an unknown quantity, I want no one else involved. Jordan's wife said he'd only be away a few days, so he should be back now after a week.

Oksana sometimes cycles to work so I borrow her bike. She joked that I should look after it as it was the only thing she has that makes her feel alive. The farm is a five-mile ride. It's a good bike and I fly along. I regret not taking the helmet as the trucks hammer past within inches. I stop, release my ponytail, and swing my head. If I die, I may as well do it with a breeze in my hair. I'm glad of my sunglasses because although the sun is weak at this time of the morning, it's still in my eyes.

I put real effort in for the final stretch and see what Oksana means because I'm soaring. I've forgotten how to be carefree. Ironically, I'm cycling to the area where I last rode a bike. I turn a corner and the wind is now in my face. Muscles burn in new places. I remember how invigorating running was when I first got out. Getting fit will be a priority when this is over. Cycling might be the way to do it.

I've arrived and am contemplating my approach when a car

pulls out of the driveway. I duck behind a tree and watch his wife drive away. The farmyard looks empty. I prop Oksana's bike against a wall. Jordan's land stretches out to the rear of his house. I scan the horizon for movement. There's nothing nearby. I take the water from my backpack and sip as I enjoy the cool air on my sweaty skin.

His farm leads all the way to a big wood. He could be in one of the far fields. I return the bottle and my coat into the pack, sling it on, and cycle down the lane between thick wheat. The huge skies and flat landscape for miles were the things I most loved about being out here in the fens. Everyone was lonely out here. I'm not sure what to expect from Jordan. He wasn't much of a talker on the subjects that interested him.

I see a cloud of dust ahead. A tractor dragging a plough turns over the soil in the middle of a field. It stops and a blond-haired man climbs out and walks in front of the vehicle. His gait and crouch as he examines the ground are familiar. It's him all right. He glances up when I cycle into view. Jordan still looks identical to his twin. They've even aged in the same way. Hard manual work has kept him whippet thin.

Time hasn't taught him any manners. He ignores me and heads back to the tractor. He fetches a spade from the cab and returns to the same spot. I rest the bike on the floor and trudge through the muddy ground. He stands when I arrive and holds the spade like a weapon. I watch him as he judges me with curiosity. I guess he wouldn't see many women out here.

'You lost?'

'No. I've found who I'm looking for.'

'Yeah, and who's that?'

'You, Jordan. Do you recognise your old friend?'

He takes off his sunglasses and hat. There's no flicker of recognition as he analyses me once more. Cruel eyes linger on my tattooed arm and then my chest.

'Nope. Should I?'

'It's Katie.'

'Don't know no Katie.'

His squint betrays him as he covers his eyes and head again. He picks up the spade and digs around the edge of a big stone that the plough must have churned up.

'I'm here for answers.'

Jordan carries on digging and I wait. After a minute, he rests on the handle.

'It was you, wasn't it?'

'Me what?'

'I got a call this morning from the care home. Justin died in his sleep last night. They think his heart gave out. The woman on the phone asked if I'd contact the nice lady who came to visit him recently. I obviously had no clues to who that was until now.' An ugly sneer crosses his face. 'Looks like you killed him. Have you come to do the same to me?'

'I want to know why you did it.'

'We were drunk. All of us, you included.'

'We were high too, weren't we?'

He bites a finger as he considers his response. 'That was Bill's idea, not mine. What's the problem? We had a good time, didn't we?'

'Are you mad? Don't you remember?'

'Not really. We'd been drinking for hours. It's all a blur. I thought it was strange when Bill called around early the next morning. He said to say what happened was consensual. They were his words. I didn't even know what that meant. Are you saying we raped you?'

'Yes, I am.'

He pauses again. 'That was a long time ago, why don't you forget about it? We can't change anything now. Justin's dead. It'd be your word against Bill's and mine.'

I flinch at his lack of interest. If he notices, he doesn't comment.

'What about my baby?'

'What about it?'

'You must have known I had a baby.'

'We assumed you'd been whoring around, so it could have been anyone's. I know you murdered Ted, too. He always was a dick.'

'One of you was the father.'

He lets out a chuckle. 'Well, it wasn't Justin. He failed to rise to the occasion. Don't think he wanted to anyway. Bill kept shaking him against you while Simon held your arms over the tyre. Was pretty funny.'

'I thought you couldn't remember anything?'

'Look. Why don't you piss off? I don't care what happened back then.'

'It was your baby, Jordan.'

'Yeah. Nice one. Had to be mine, didn't it?'

'Her hair was blonde, she looked like you. That little crimp at the top of your ear, she had that too. The others were dark skinned. It can only have been yours or Justin's. I hadn't slept with anyone else.'

He rams the spade into the earth with venom but doesn't comment.

'You became a father. How does that make you feel?'

'It's too late for me to give a shit. Why didn't you tell us back then? I can't do anything now. She must be nearly eighteen. You here for maintenance, that it? No problem. Look, I'm so rich that I dig stones out of fields by hand.'

'I wanted somebody to care. Nobody was interested. It was only on the day I gave her up that she had grown into her features and I saw who she resembled. Chloe was a beautiful baby.'

'Yeah, well I never knew her. If you've had your say, be on your way. I'm busy.'

'What kind of person are you?'

His nostrils flare and his lips purse. He steps towards me.

'You're the murderer. It'd be in your interest to get off my land. People go missing out here.'

Unbelievable. He dismisses me so easily. I watch as he checks around the rock and tries to lever it out. There's no rage this time, not even anger. Later, I won't be able to blame my actions on emotion. I know what I'm about to do.

My fists clench with purpose. No one talks to me like that anymore. I am done with being ignored. I open my bag and pull out my gloves. I put them on and, when his back is turned, stride to the tractor and haul myself up into the cab. The key's in the ignition. I dip the clutch and turn it on. Jordan turns around with a puzzled face. It's not until I rev the engine that he knows to be afraid.

I punch it into gear and move forward. The transmission roars due to my lack of familiarity, but who cares as long as it doesn't stall. This old tractor is little different from the type we rode as kids. It has a windscreen, that's all, and through it, I see Jordan scramble away. He makes ten metres and stops. If anyone knows you can't outrun a tractor on a muddy field, it's him.

Jordan stands and faces me. He holds out his arms as if to say, 'Come on, is that the best you can do?' I'm close now and we stare into each other's eyes. There's a new expression on his face. It might even be regret.

He makes a small cry. I imagine a vision of the back of the tractor, dripping with blood. Ripped clothing and a work boot with a foot still inside but no attached leg hang from the blades, and Jordan's mangled body is left pressed into the mud. I lift my foot from the pedal and steer away from him. Soon enough to avoid Jordan, but not the obstacle he was trying to clear.

He was right about the stone, which causes a huge clanging sound when it hits the metal of the equipment as I drive over it; a loud bang follows. The engine judders beneath me and cuts out, bringing the vehicle to a stop. I jump from the cab and turn to the rear. The smell of burning oil and diesel fills the air.

I've felt like this before. That time, I walked into a kitchen and fetched a knife. I step lightly towards Jordan and he sinks to his knees. Radic's advice sits fresh in my mind. Revenge would have been a great pleasure, but it wouldn't have changed the past. My future would also have been darker because I'd have been as bad as them.

His words are barely audible. 'Thank you.'

'We all deserve a second chance, Jordan. You have a wife waiting for you and a life still to be lived. Look after her and yourself, and seize this opportunity.'

I doubt he'll tell anyone and I hope he changes. As I cycle away, I think of his partner. Will she be happy now or sad? Have I lightened her burden or added to it? We women are a strange bunch. We carry too much, even if it breaks us. His wife was a smart lady though, and she was spot on. Farms are dangerous places.

63

FOUR DAYS LATER

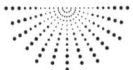

IRINA'S END

I've come to the club at lunchtime because I can't find Irina. She's been away all week but told me she'd be back this morning. We're off to Ferry Meadows to use the pedalos. Or we are if I can locate her. Maybe she's hiding. She reckons it's impossible to look glam on a plastic boat.

I walk through the pub which is deserted despite opening in a few minutes. I jog up the stairs on weak legs. Oksana opens the door as I push it, and I fall into her. Her red bloodshot eyes widen at the sight of me.

'Hi, Oksana. Are you okay?'
'No. Have you heard about Irina?'
'What happened?'
'She's been arrested.'

It's a real kick to the stomach. My mind searches for explanations. I pray for it to be a mistake. 'Why? What for?'

'They picked her up at Birmingham airport. She was coming back from Spain. Poor Irina.'

'Why? I don't get it. What's she done?'

Oksana looks worried as well as upset. She tries to brush past.

I grab an arm and spin her around. I've had enough of being lied to. 'Tell me. Now.'

'We haven't got all the details. The person she was with made it through but saw her being taken away. They surrounded her. They knew.'

My stomach heaves as I catch up with events.

'Drugs! She's been caught bringing drugs into the country?'

'Shh, Katie. You didn't hear that from me. Look, we understood the risks involved.'

And then it becomes clear. In many ways, my life's been sheltered. However, in others, I have been at the coal face of the hardest mine on earth. I've known murderers and rapists, con artists and swindlers, thieves and burglars, fools and liars, the innocent and the guilty. I have met them all, and there are mules.

Mules are those who carry drugs across borders for organised crime. They are usually vulnerable and poor. Many are drug addicts. They take the risk while the owner of the merchandise makes a massive profit if the products get through. If the authorities catch the mule, they go to prison. Penalties are harsh.

I squeeze Oksana's arm harder. She's scared. 'Why would Irina do that?'

No answer, no eye contact. Pain won't break her loyalty. Not to him.

'Do you do it too?'

'Yes.' It's a sad resigned whisper.

'Where is he?' She tries to pull away, but I yank her back. 'His office?'

She nods and then slips from my grip. At the exit, Oksana pauses as though she has something to say. She shakes her head and hammers down the steps. The door bangs at the bottom. Why won't these women talk?

Radic's office is open. Sitting on the other side of the desk, he massages his temples. He gestures for me to sit in the seat opposite. Mind games or politeness? Who cares? I've obeyed him for the last time.

'I'll stand, thank you.'

'Fair enough. How can I help you?'

'Very funny. You know why I'm here.'

'Ah, yes. Irina. Terrible for everyone.'

'I think you'll find it's mostly terrible for her. How could you use her in that way?'

A sheen of sweat on his bald head shines under the light.

'It was her choice. I explained the job, and she chose to accept.'

'You shit. You've been using thieves and junkies. They stopped making good choices long ago. You used them purely for money, and they risked everything while you swan around here pretending to be nice.'

He rises and leans on the table. His voice is hard. I've never seen him like this. He rules by fear.

'They knew the dangers. Besides, the amount wasn't much. She'll receive four years at most, out in two.'

'Only two years? That's virtually nothing. You can send her some crayons and a colouring pack so she doesn't kill herself. You aren't so bright either. Irina has three years left on her licence. Drug smuggling, unsurprisingly, is a breach. She will likely get four years added to her three years. She'll never survive that. You've killed her.'

Radic swells with anger at being spoken to in this way. I suspect it's been a long while since someone back-chatted him. Have I overstepped the mark? But he needs to be aware of the consequences of his actions. Radic slumps back in his seat. There is genuine remorse and feeling there. That still doesn't absolve him of his guilt, and I'm not finished.

'And what about me?'

'What about you?'

'You gave me an easy job for good money. A nice place to live for free. I even have my own driver.'

'I never asked you to do anything.'

'Not yet.' I scream at him. 'You were grooming me.'

My bellowing has caught someone's attention. Footsteps echo on the dance-floor. It's my shadow who says nothing. Instead, he waits at the door and looks at Radic. I turn my fury on Tony.

'You knew too, didn't you? Of course you did. You were protecting his investment. And after our chats, did you come back here and report it to your boss like a good little soldier?'

Tony shrugs.

The sheen of sweat on Radic's head is now a trickle of water. He's not scared, only guilty. At least he doesn't deny it.

'You want me to say sorry?'

'It's too late for that. If you are, don't do it again. I'm out of here. I'll be out of your flat by Sunday night. Get your henchman here to drop my new ID and my pay there before then.'

I turn and walk away. Tony stands in the way of the door. We both look back at Radic.

'I always liked you, Katie. No hard feelings. How can I make it up to you?'

I want nothing off him, and then I realise I do.

'Pack up and box Irina's possessions. Deliver money and clothes into the prison. Visit her. If you can't do it yourself, send someone else. Tell her she has a job and a place to live when she gets out. Whenever that is. Let her know all of her things wait for her. And that, next time, you'll keep her safe.'

Radic's smile fades. I hope it's a dawning realisation of what he's become. Being forced to look in the mirror and see the harsh truth of what you really are, can make you or bury you. There is good in him, but he needs to change. I wonder if, like many of us, he is too far down the road to turn back.

'You got it. I'll do my best.'

'One last question. Does your wife realise you do this?'

He laughs. It's unconvincing. 'We all have private business. Don't we, Katie?'

I nod back at him. Touché. We are similar in a way. That statement means we are tied in life. I trust him with my secrets and he will let me leave with his.

'Goodbye, young lady. Perhaps we'll meet again.'

'I don't plan to go far. Our paths may cross again.'

At the door, Tony opens it for me.

'Not going to wish me luck, Tony?'

'You do not need it. You're a strong woman. I admire you very much.'

He's sad, and so am I. Tony's lined face and weathered skin have been a source of comfort. I realise I'll miss them both. Regardless, the play is ending and I'm almost ready for the last scene. I shake his hand and ask for a final favour.

'Tony, when you drop my new ID off, leave that knife at the same time.'

64
PACKING

I own more things now than ever, but it's still not much. I bought a big rucksack this morning and a smaller one that you can place on the front. Visiting backpackers wear them as they walk around Cathedral Square. I glance over at my new passport. The knife rests on top. Dare I use either?

I thought I wanted to find a quiet job and be normal. Live a simple life with no drama. I now believe that won't be enough. I only have a bra and pants on, and I catch myself in the mirror. My finished back tattoo looks incredible. I accepted my need for them, yet I know I won't get more. They are not just a disguise because the image is me. Both sides. Are the demon and angel fighting or making love? Who wins, or is it the balance between good and evil? When my wings unfurl and spread, will they be feathery white or leathery black?

I have two calls to make.

'Hello?'

'Hi, Tommy. It's Katie.'

'Hey, I'm pleased you called. How are you?'

'Fine. Look, I wondered if I could crash at yours for a few days.

It won't be for long. I've money saved, I just need to get my head together in a quiet spot.'

Tommy replies in an instant. I am so glad there wasn't a nasty pause. 'Of course. When do you want to come?'

'Tomorrow okay?'

'No problem. What time?'

'Will you meet me somewhere first at midday? I'll have my things with me.'

'Very mysterious. I like it. Where?'

'A place where only we know. Do you remember?'

Again, no break in thinking. 'I'll be there, assuming it's not a housing estate by now.'

'And Tommy. If I don't come, then don't worry. I'm fine, but I'll be gone. Forget about me. Live your life.'

This time there is a few seconds of silence.

'What do you mean by that?'

'Nothing much, just trust me, please.'

'We'll catch up tomorrow, Katie.'

The second call will be shorter. I wonder if he'll pick up. Shady people in power like him have few fears, and he answers straight away.

'Yes.'

'Bill, it's me.'

'Ah, Katie. I was wondering where you'd got to.'

I knew it. There was no chance he would let me be.

'I want to meet. I have most of the truth, but I need the rest. When I know what happened, I'll understand who I was. That's the only way I have a future.'

'Where and when?'

'The old barn. Eight o'clock tonight.'

There's a long pause. I almost hear his mind whirring down the phone.

'Agreed. But we both come alone.'

'See you later,' I say with a breeziness I don't feel.

Events are in motion, and I have one last thing to do. I need to go into town to buy some rope.

65
THE BARN

It's a dark night. Heavy rain lashes my face and vehicles splash puddles over my leggings. I wish I was wearing more substantial clothes. Luckily, Oksana's bike has lights, or I'd have to walk. There's no pleasure in the ride this time. My heart is burdened with a sense of doom. I must hear the truth from Bill even if it's terrible. The knife in my coat pocket is reassuring. I hope he will come alone, but I can't believe his intentions are noble.

I'm soaked through when I arrive at our old house. The lights are off and the drive is empty. The track is muddy and unfit for cycling, so I hop off and walk. At two hundred metres away, I notice the barn is lit up in the gloom. It's a flickering light which means there's a fire.

Sure enough, when I get to the entrance and push the remains of the door open, I'm greeted by a large oil canister blazing unnaturally and the stench of petrol. Of Bill, no sign. My coat is sodden. I am lucky it's not a cold night, or I'd develop pneumonia. After some hunting in the dark and shadowy edges, I find a rusty picnic chair. I wrap my coat around it and place them close to the heat.

The flames are calmer. Big pieces of wood in the canister give off a more natural blaze. The accelerant used has burned off. Bill did this. He must have been watching when I arrived. But where is he now? I'll warm up first and worry about that when necessary. It will be a horrendous cycle home without dry clothes.

Twenty minutes later, I've turned my coat over to toast the other side and my hands are back to their normal temperature. I still don't have company. I start when my phone rings. I'm expecting Bill's number to show but Tommy's name flashes up. I contemplate whether to reject the call. I must answer because it might be important.

'Hi, Tommy. What's up?'

'Hiya. Look, sorry for ringing, but I got hold of my mate who knew Bill Ivy. I decided I'd better ring you. It's what I thought. There were rumours about him faking evidence. Things went missing from crime scenes. That sort of thing. My pal reckons two girls, admittedly prostitutes, said he raped them. Other women vanished. He's bad, Katie, as dirty as they come.'

'Ok, Tommy. I'll talk to you tomorrow. Thanks for ringing, you may have saved my life.'

I jump again when Bill's voice echoes from above me. I forgot the loft in the far corner.

'Who's Tommy?'

'Just a friend.'

'Someone I need to get to know?'

'No. He's had enough bad luck.'

Bill slowly walks down the steps. He's a brave man because it was unsafe up there twenty years ago. He stands on the opposite side of the fire and seems enormous. A padded jacket magnifies his size, and I feel minuscule in comparison.

'What did he say to you?'

'None of your business. Personal stuff.'

'Can't have been good news. You were relaxed before you spoke to him.'

'We're here to discuss the past not the present.'

'Right you are. Ask your questions.'

'Do you regret what you did that night?'

'Of course. It was a bit of fun that got out of hand. I wish it never happened for all of our sakes.'

'Too much drink?'

'Yes, we did enjoy doing stupid things.'

His tone is cautious and phrases are chosen with care. I detect him edging around the canister getting closer to me.

'Like drugs?'

That stops him in his tracks. 'The others told you about that.'

'Correct. They said it was your idea.'

'Well, they would, wouldn't they? Who'd want to admit to that?'

'I don't hear an apology or see any genuine remorse.'

He leers through the flames. His chuckle is cold. His words are ice. 'There's no apology because there's no regret. Get over yourself. It was a laugh, nothing more.'

'I think you planned the whole thing.'

'You do? We could ask the others if that's true. Oh no, that won't be possible. It appears they're dead or scared shitless. Shortly after receiving a visit from you.' He grins wide at my shocked face. 'Yes. An old fisherman recalled an attractive woman looking for Simon. He heard he had a lucky escape from a cracked skull.

'Anne from the care home told me someone with a blonde ponytail was there before Justin died. Jordan admitted the truth after some gentle persuasion. Said you almost killed him although he strangely told me to leave you alone. He will need to be silenced. His wife was a nice girl, I must pop back and see them both some time.'

'You piece of filth.'

'That's not all. Even your probation worker came to a nasty end. Let's not forget Ted either. Did the prison train you up to be the next Grim Reaper? You're awfully good at it. Or did you lie in your cell and plan your revenge?'

'I had to give up my baby.'

'Oh, I heard about that when I returned. Did it look like me?'

'It was Jordan's.'

'That's a shame.'

'Surely, your three kids are enough?'

'True. Quite true.'

He moves again and is close now. I smell his aftershave.

'Although you said before you had four kids.'

The anger on his face seals my fate.

'Three children, four. Who's counting? It's easy to lose a kid here or there. Of course, you understand that.'

The bastard. I'll have one chance with Tony's gift. Bill is taller and stronger than I am. If I fail, he'll kill me. I recall Jordan's warning about people going missing out here. Desperation adds strength and speed to my lunge. The flick-knife is out of my pocket in a blur.

He doesn't move. His eyes drop to the movement. The blade strikes out, and I plunge it under his ribs and towards his heart.

The juddering stop of its progress almost causes me to lose my grip. It's as though I've tried to stab a book. His hand comes from behind him brandishing a short baton. A twist has it extended and bearing down on my wrist. All I can do is slacken my arm. The pain is immense and the knife clatters away.

I stagger back, numb to the shoulder.

'For dark nights such as this, I wear special clothes. My favourite is a stab vest.' He walks towards me, twirling the baton. 'I was up in the loft to check you came alone. Watching you brought feelings to the surface that I'd long forgotten. I wasn't sure what I was going to do until I saw your face after that phone call. What did he say to you?'

'That you are a rapist of women. The worst kind of man alive. You disgust me. You will rot in hell, and I planned to send you there.'

'Nice speech, but it doesn't matter. You were right. It's time to close the circle. I always worried you'd tell someone. Soon, there'll only be one person left who was here that evening, and I won't talk.'

His arm shoots out and grabs me by the throat. I try to knee him in the groin but he is too far away. His strength is overbearing.

'How about a quickie, for old time's sake?'

He pushes me over the tyres, just like before. There's nobody to hold my arms this time, but he's so powerful, it's unnecessary. I hear his belt release and, while a hand crushes my neck, he yanks up my T-shirt so my back is exposed.

'I enjoy seeing what I'm doing.'

Those words; "I enjoy seeing what I'm doing." That night resurrects itself from my memory in a flash. I recall them all in glorious detail as they took their turn. There's Jordan's face, full of laughter. Simon's expression was eager love. Justin's red eyes and flowing tears, followed by Bill's bare-teethed snarl of violent lust.

He chuckles. 'Great tattoo.'

I feel hardness searching for entry.

His breath behind me is ragged, just as it was that day. Jordan, Simon and Justin were finished in seconds. Bill took his time. He was the one who slapped me.

He yanks my pants down to my knees and pushes them to the floor with his foot, as he did back then. He kicks my feet apart. I recall the women in the prison saying it was better to relax and not fight. You couldn't win, and that way it hurt less. I heed their advice as he begins.

Then, for the second time in my life, I'm raped in a rotting barn with firelight and four men. The years collapse. Yet, the men are not the same youths of the past. The sound of a heavy gun being loaded causes Bill's body to tense. Apart from the hard part, and that slips out of me. He releases my shoulders. I turn and am greeted by the sight of Tony and his two quiet friends from the club. One has a large shotgun levelled at us.

I know men such as these because I entered their world. Not evil, but uncaring. Life, and their experience of it, has removed their emotions. They have no part in how they survive. As a police officer, Bill will have met their type before. He comprehends there will be no mercy or pity. Doomed, he looks at me. I step to the side, twist, and ram the heel of my hand, just like Mai taught me, under his chin and knock him off his feet.

The men are on him. In a few seconds, he kneels with his arms held behind his back. Tony stands next to him and grabs his hair. He holds his head so Bill's desperate eyes search mine.

'We will take care of him for you,' Tony says. 'Unless you wish to watch?'

I shake my head. 'And the body?'

Tony replies without feeling. 'No body.'

I pull my clothes up with a sniff. I recover my now dry coat and put it on. A guttural voice barks orders and duct tape unwinds. With no backward glance, I stagger from the barn. The rain has stopped, and the moon is out. Seconds pass as I collect my thoughts. Do rapists ever deserve forgiveness?

I walk down the track, and a bird swoops overhead. Its screams shatter the silence. I look above to recognise its sorrow but, other than a white plastic bag caught by the wind, the sky is empty. Another pained screech is heard, and it's human, and I know I have to return.

Bill is taped into the rusty chair. Tony towers over him, wielding a bloody saw. Those beside him acknowledge my presence. These are grim men. Men who drink alone. Laughter has left their lives. They do what they're told without question. They are fit for little else.

I wander over and reclaim my knife from the floor. My thumb touches the razor-sharp blade. I show it to Bill's wide eyes. He squeezes them shut. I step towards Tony and hand him the weapon.

Bill's eyes open and there's a flicker of hope. How has my life come to a scene like this? I open my mouth to say, 'Let him go,' but don't. He would have killed me tonight and others in the future.

'Goodbye, Tony. You'll never see me again. Burn the barn.'

I stare at Bill's beseeching expression, but even now I can see rage and vengeance in the creases of his face. I'd never be free of this devil.

'Goodbye, Bill.'

66
SUNDAY MIDDAY

TOMMY

Tommy chooses to walk to meet Katie. The blue sky is patched with huge, billowing, white clouds. He has much to ponder in the fresh air. The past few years have been better for him, but the previous ten before that were a blur of petty crime and substance abuse. Prison was inevitable, and he considers himself lucky. Most of those he hung around with back then are inside on long stretches or have returned to dust.

Tommy is bright enough to understand that his upbringing led to his lack of self-esteem. You don't need to be a genius to realise many who struggle in life feel abandoned. Tommy sometimes wanted to know who his real mum and dad were but never followed it through. There wouldn't be gold at the end of that search. Betraying his adoptive parents wasn't high on his list of priorities, either.

Stepping over the stile to enter Thorpe Hall grounds, he recognises the big building in the distance. This is the first time he's been back since he left. With twenty minutes to spare, he wanders up to the trees where they used to play. The sycamores and horse chestnuts are smaller than in his dreams.

Even the mansion no longer resembles the haunted house of his youth — Katie and Tommy's youth.

Why didn't he look for her before? Was it guilt after he'd left it so long? A half-hearted web search failed to reveal her whereabouts when he once checked. That wasn't surprising after the sentence she received. The internet was in its infancy when she was sent down.

It was hard to think of her killing someone. However, Katie always possessed a core of strength. There'd be a tilt of her chin to let you know you'd gone far enough. She would only take so much.

Sleep had been elusive since he'd seen her again. Thoughts of anything but Katie had been rare, especially after he heard the news about the corrupt policeman. Even though they'd only had two drinks together over a few hours, she still had the same effect on him. He didn't want to leave her. He'd forgive her one act of madness seventeen years ago.

Beneath that heavy make-up and dyed hair, under that toned body and shocking tattoos, she remained his little friend, and the only person who made him stop thinking. With her, life just happened. Nothing scared him except the chance of them being separated.

He glances down at a squelch and curls his lip. It seems they still keep cows in the field. Big ones, by the looks of it. He scuffs his way downhill to the small wood on the edge of where they hid. The one which shielded them from prying eyes.

A splash of rain raises his scowl to the now dark-grey clouds. He regrets wearing shorts and a T-shirt. When he enters the cover of the wood, the trees are thicker than he recalls. The barbed wire fence, a few metres in, looks more lethal, but his job keeps him fit and he vaults over it. Branches and memories tear at him as he slips down the bank.

Tommy follows the stream. He's keen to see her. He often thinks of his childhood and she appears in most of his happy recollections. Katie, the serious girl with caramel hair. A squall of rain ruffles the canopy above and a sense of foreboding settles upon him. The leaves whisper that he is too late. When the trees clear, a wall of nettles faces him. They've been pushed through and resettled as some are broken. He rues his choice of clothing for the second time.

A nearby big stick will do; he'll scythe his way through. Their tree is beyond the undergrowth. He notices the rope hanging down from a thick branch. With his hearing straining, he ceases swinging his arms. The creaking sound indicates displeasure at holding a heavy load. It swings as though it's a dead weight. Tommy throws the wood in front of him and charges through the stinging barrier.

There she is. Silent, beautiful, staring. He laughs, well, it's more a cry, when he sees a second rope dangling next to the other one. She finally got the swing she wanted. Katie waves and slides along the thick branch she's using as a seat. She wobbles. She won't be getting him on that thing.

67
THE FUTURE

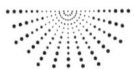

Tommy breaks through the nettles like a mad person. I can't help laughing when I see he wore shorts. I wave and my stomach flips as I nearly fall. Building this swing today finished off my youth. We always wanted one. I'm not sure Screwfix was open back then, but surely it wouldn't have been too hard to get our hands on some rope.

Tommy kind of collapses and laughs at the same time. It's as though he's relieved. That's how I feel. He walks along the side of the lake towards me and it's as if the final piece of missing jigsaw has turned up and slides into place.

'Going to give me a push?'

The rope slips off on one side and dumps me on the grass. We grin at each other.

'We could always skim stones,' he says.

'I've probably done that for the last time,' I say, with a rueful thought.

'Why did you want to meet here?'

'I wanted to reconnect with the time when we were friends and I was happy. I don't want to live looking backwards, so I came to say goodbye to all this in a positive way. The last few weeks revealed a lot about my life and who I am. Some of it good, much bad. Today is a new beginning.'

Tommy absentmindedly scratches his knees. 'Sure, Katie. No problem.'

I knew he would say that, even though after two decades he should be a stranger to me. We are both relaxed as we stare across the pond. In a way, I know nothing of Tommy the man, yet I have a feeling it will be a pleasure finding out. That can't happen yet. Not in the normal manner, anyway.

I hope I can leave it all behind now. People have died again, but it was the only way that justice would be served. I will heed Sofiya's advice and forgive those who wronged me, but I will also forgive myself. I hope I am fixed now, and I'm no longer a danger.

There was a point to my discovering the truth; an inner need. I lost the best years of my life in a concrete box, but I served my time knowing that I wasn't all bad. I should never have done what I did but as with all things in life, nothing is black or white.

Nothing can bring my little girl back, those years have gone, but there is Tommy. My Tommy. I won't ever let him go again if he'll wait. Maybe now there is a chance for me to salvage something from this wreck of a life.

'Tommy, I'm going to hand myself in.'

'What? Why? I thought you had a new ID and everything sorted?'

'I thought I couldn't live under those rules, but Thorn made it unbearable. Living a life looking over my shoulder would be worse. I'll show them that video and pray that you were right about them not wanting the publicity. Surely, they'll see I couldn't stay under those conditions. I'll have to go back inside for a while but I'll cope if you visit and write.'

'I understand and of course I will. That's probably the right thing to do.'

'It's the only thing to do. When I'm out I want to find out about my parents and brother. I know nothing of them. It's not right that they're forgotten. At the moment, I don't even know the day they died. Researching that will be a whole lot easier if I can say they are family. Most importantly though, my daughter will be eighteen soon. If she wants to meet me, she has to be able to find me. I couldn't put her through that. A life of regret is no life. Even though she was so young, for some reason I'm sure she'll remember. The thought of seeing her again will provide me with the strength to carry on. I'll build a life and be a person she can be proud of. I'll make new memories.'

'Do you have to go to the police station immediately?'

'I suppose not.'

'Let's go to the coast for the weekend. Stay in a nice hotel and have a glimpse of what life will be like when you're free again. It'll give you something nice to think on and remind you that you can be happy again.'

'I am content, Tommy, and that's enough for the moment.'

Despite what's ahead of me, I sense a releasing of my spirit. I must learn to take risks and trust people. To do otherwise isn't living. I was wronged and I have done wrong, but that's in the past now.

Bright light breaks through the clouds and filters through the branches above. I remember Irina's words as Tommy places his arm over my shoulder. Life does rain on us all but, if you hang in there, the sun will return.

The End.

ABOUT THE AUTHOR

I worked at HMP Peterborough for four years. It's the only prison in the UK that houses men and women. There's a big wall between them, of course, or it'd be a popular place to serve a sentence.

I found the difference between the two places immense. At nearly six-foot-tall and fifteen stone, I never feared for my safety on the female side as I sometimes did on the male wings. That said, you were more likely to be assaulted by a female prisoner, but it might be from nails or a bite. The men seemed more intent on beating each other up as opposed to the staff. However, when the men did fight, it was often with a weapon.

The staff joked that the men were bad and the women mad. As with most clichés, there's an element of truth. The male prisoners were like big kids that hadn't yet grown up. Some were pensioners and never would. Master criminals were scarce. Most of them resided behind those walls due to stupidity, greed or violence.

The female inmates, on the other hand, blurred the line between victim and villain. Some argue that most women's offending is driven by unmet mental health needs. Domestic abuse and coercion are significant factors. In the UK, we lock up few women — only five percent of the prison estate. That's less than 4000 females at any one time. They have to do something illegal many times or a dreadful act once to be sent down.

Most of those women are mothers. A typical inmate will have been raised in a broken home. Their own life may mirror that.

The children she leaves behind could have a father who is absent or useless. Or worse.

If we send Mum to jail, even for a few months, who looks after those children? What will happen to the house? A mother with substance issues or a shoplifting habit will nearly always still be caring for her kids. It may be a chaotic place but could the state provide a better one? A mother is irreplaceable. Even when the authorities take the children away for their security, they still want to go home.

If the family unit falls apart, then the ripple effect can last generations. A safe home is everything, however much money you have. 95% of children are forced to leave their home when mum is sent to prison. Those kids experience shame, anger and confusion through no fault of their own.

The lifers are different. If you commit that most shocking of crimes, then you must bid farewell to your young. They'll grow up and you'll barely be involved. Those children will be adults and strangers when you're released. That aspect of prison life fascinated and horrified me.

I'm an author and a househusband. I hope I'm better at the former as I'm poor at the latter. However, I do get to spend a lot of time with the kids — more than my wife does. Yet, I know without a moment's hesitation that if we split up and they were given the choice, they would go with her. For me, that's sad and uplifting. Perhaps that's the way it's meant to be. I don't believe there is a closer bond than the one between a mother and her child. So, imagine how you would feel if, like Katie, you had to say goodbye to your children because of something you did. What would it do to your state of mind?

How would you survive?

facebook.com/RossGreenwoodAuthor

ALSO BY ROSS GREENWOOD

This book is a prequel to The Dark Lives series. All of the books are standalone but some of the characters cross over. If you were intrigued by Radic in this book, you can meet him again five years down the line in The Boy Inside.

If you've enjoyed Shadows of Regret, you'll love the first in that series - Fifty Years of Fear.

www.rossgreenwoodauthor.com

Thank you for reading, please leave a review.

Printed in Great Britain
by Amazon